THE HEARTS THAT HOLD

THE HEARTS
THAT HOLD

Linda Sole

This first world edition published in Great Britain 2000 by
SEVERN HOUSE PUBLISHERS LTD of
9–15 High Street, Sutton, Surrey SM1 1DF.
This first world edition published in the USA 2001 by
SEVERN HOUSE PUBLISHERS INC of
595 Madison Avenue, New York, N.Y. 10022.

British Library Cataloguing in Publication Data

Sole, Linda
    The hearts that hold
    1. World War, 1939-1945 - Great Britain - Fiction
    I. Title
    823.9'14 [F]

    ISBN 0-7278-5629-4

Typeset by Palimpsest Book Production Ltd.,
Polmont, Stirlingshire, Scotland.
Printed and bound in Great Britain by
MPG Books Ltd., Bodmin, Cornwall.

Part One

One

I heard the clatter of noisy feet down the stairs and went out into the hall to investigate just as James and Lizzy arrived, their nurse following close behind. It was a glorious summer day, sunlight filtering through the stained glass of the front door, sending a shower of rainbow colours across the pale carpet.

"I'm sorry, Mrs Reece," Sarah Miller apologised, the sparkle of laughter in her eyes. "They're excited because of the school concert. I hope they didn't disturb you?"

"I haven't really started to work yet," I said, kissing and hugging my son and Lizzy with equal warmth. It didn't matter to me that Lizzy was the daughter of my friend Sheila. During the years she had lived with us, she had become as dear to me as my own child. "But I must start in a moment. Sol and I have a lot to get through this morning."

"You are coming to the concert this afternoon?" James demanded, a hint of mutiny in his expressive, dark-chocolate eyes as he struggled free of my embrace. Although charming and very lovable, my son had a forceful personality and was fond of having his own way. "You promised, Mum. I've told everyone you're definitely coming this time."

"I promise faithfully," I said. "I'll be there at half-past two."

"James is singing all on his own," Lizzy said, her large, soulful eyes solemn and awed. James was Lizzy's hero, and I believed she loved him more than anyone else in the world. "Don't you think he's ever so brave, Emmie?"

"Yes, darling. Very brave and very clever."

I looked at my son with pride. He was eight years old now,

3

a sturdy, healthy boy with the promise of startlingly good looks when he was older. His slightly curling hair was more black than brown, and his cheeks were tinged with rose, but there was a stubborn jut to his chin.

I believed he would break hearts one day – and that was hardly surprising. His father had been both charming and handsome when we first met. I had thought him very like one of the film stars I had admired so much in those days. I had been very young and immature then. James did not look particularly like Paul Greenslade, but sometimes there was an expression or a frown that reminded me of my first lover.

James was an active, energetic child. However, his school had discovered a talent none of us had ever dreamed he possessed. He had the most beautiful, clear soprano voice, and produced the kind of pure sound that brought tears to the eyes. He looked so innocent when he sang in the school choir – like a beautiful angel. That look was very misleading. My son was more devil than angel!

Both he and Lizzy were forever into some kind of mischief, and I was never sure who was the instigator of their naughty escapades. The two were forever whispering into each other's ears and giggling at their own secrets, which the grown-ups were seldom allowed to share. James appeared to be the leader, but Lizzy was never far behind.

Although in no way related, they looked as though they might be brother and sister, for Lizzy's colouring was much like my son's, though her hair had developed rich highlights as she grew older. She was a beautiful child, her smiles full of a naughty but wistful charm that meant she almost always gained her own way with even less effort than my son exerted. She too would break hearts when she was older!

"Off you go, you two," I said, giving them a little push towards the door. "I'm sure it's all going to be lovely. After the concert, we'll go out to tea."

I smiled as the children and Sarah left the house together. Sarah was genuinely fond of them both. They tried her patience sorely, but she was a helpful, good-humoured woman, well able to manage them, and I never needed to worry when she was with them.

She was much kinder than their previous nanny, who I had dismissed after an incident which had caused Lizzy to fall down the nursery stairs and break her arm. Fortunately, no lasting damage had been done, but I still felt guilty that I had been too busy to notice that Nanny had been ill-treating Lizzy.

I returned to the front parlour after the children and Sarah had gone. It was an elegant, spacious room decorated in shades of green and gold, but the hangings had faded over the years and some of the upholstery needed recovering. I had been reluctant to do anything, however, because it had been Margaret's favourite room, and even though she had been dead for nearly three years now I did not want to make changes. I knew Sol felt the same way about his late wife's parlour. We had both loved her very much, and we still missed her: changing her room would seem like a betrayal of her memory.

Sol was poring over the papers and some sketches of Dior's New Look we'd had specially brought over from Paris. It was an exciting design that was already creating waves in the press. After the plain and skimpy Utility fashions we had all been forced to wear during the war, the softer, fuller look seemed like a miracle.

Even after some of the clothing restrictions had been lifted in 1944 the Utility garments had still clung on. The quality was reliable, and anything not covered by the label usually needed extra coupons, so that not everyone could afford the luxury of choosing such items.

We had hoped that when the war finally ended, we would see the abolition of rationing, but in some instances it seemed almost worse now than during the war. Many people were becoming very angry with the Government for not getting the country back on an even keel before this. In Paris some of the fashion houses had continued to function right through the war, and the French designers had clearly decided that the women of Europe had had enough of austerity fashions. Even in America, where a certain amount of rationing was still in force, things were much better than here.

"Children get off all right?" Sol asked, glancing up as I sat opposite him. "It's James's concert this afternoon, isn't it? I should like to come, but I shan't have the time."

"That's a pity," I said. "It would have been nice if you could have come too, Sol."

Sol and I were partners in a wholesale clothing business we ran from the Portobello Road, but we were also close friends. He and his wife had taken me into their home and their hearts when I first came to London, and despite Margaret's death, and everything else that had happened during the war years, I was still living in his home.

"What do you think of this New Look, then?" Sol asked. "Everyone seems to be going mad over it – but what is your honest opinion?"

"I like it," I said, picking up a sheaf of papers. "Let me study it for a while."

The new fashion was certainly very different and very attractive. Dior was just one of the French designers making news at the moment, but his New Look was grabbing the headlines.

Fashion was changing quickly this year. I rather liked the designs of Claire McCardell, who had created what was known as the "American Look" during the war and who was now as much admired as some of the Paris designers. She had been the first to use denim for dresses, a fashion which I thought rather exciting, but which hadn't as yet really caught on here.

My friend Jane Melcher had sent me some of the designs that Claire McCardell had presented for Townley, the New York ready-to-wear manufacturer, after she returned to America at the end of 1944. Jane and I kept in touch regularly, and I got most of my information on the American ready-to wear market from my friend. Her letters, together with pictures from magazines and a few samples, had given me a lot of ideas we could use in the showroom. Our own range was now much more substantial than it had been even before the war.

This had helped me a great deal in setting up my small chain of retail dress shops, because the profit I was able to make on direct purchases from our own workshop was quite substantial. I was becoming a woman of some property. Besides the three separate businesses in my home town, March, I had three small shops in London now – which I had bought outright – and recently I had begun to make plans to expand by taking on a concession in a large department store.

"I suppose we shall have to try and copy it," Sol said. I had been silent for longer than he thought necessary. "Are you going to stock it in your shops, Emma?"

"Not this expensive version," I said. "But something more affordable, I expect. Annie said she had a woman in the other day asking when we would have it in."

Annie was Sheila's cousin, and I had put her in charge of one of the shops recently. Now that her children were older, she could work more hours, and I knew I could trust her.

Sol nodded. He had helped with the finance of the London shops initially, though when my share of the money that he had invested abroad before the war came through, I was able to repay him. I had received a cheque for thirty-five thousand dollars, more money than I had ever expected to earn in my life.

And that was due to Jack, of course. *Jack . . . oh, Jack, my darling . . . Where are you today? Are you thinking of me? I think of you every day, every night of my life.*

I was still in love with Jack Harvey – the wealthy American who had been my lover during the war – though it was years since I had seen or spoken to him.

I had kept his letters and gifts, and I still sometimes took them out of the bedside cabinet where they were stored. I had grown accustomed to the sense of loss I'd felt when I'd sent Jack away, however, and it no longer hurt in quite the same way. I missed him, but I could think of him now without pain, or at least only a very little.

Jack had sent the money my investment had earned direct to Sol, because we had quarrelled bitterly when I refused to abandon my invalid husband, Jonathan Reece, and go to America with Jack. Such terrible, cruel things had been said, things that I regretted, but that was all behind me now. I had thrown myself into my work – and into helping Jon begin a new life.

"You look very thoughtful, Emma." Sol looked at me over the top of his gold-rimmed reading glasses. "Still thinking about your answer – or are you miles away?"

"I was just thinking of Jon . . . wondering how he was getting on. He sounded a bit down when he rang last night."

"You worry too much, my dear."

He was right, of course, but I couldn't help it.

Jon had been severely injured during the war, and for a time we had believed him killed in action. From the first moment I'd heard that he had been found alive, but badly wounded, I had been determined to bring him home as soon as he was able to leave hospital.

Although Jon had spent several periods of a few weeks at a time with me in London during the last two years, he was back in hospital again at the moment for a further operation. His recovery had taken much longer than anyone had ever expected, because Jon had been very ill on two separate occasions, and the long process of restoring some sort of normality to his poor, burned face had been postponed to give him time to rebuild his strength. However, his stay in the hospital should be short this time, and then he would be home for good, all the months of pain he had endured behind him.

So far Jon had seemed content to spend the time he was allowed out of hospital at Sol's house in London. He had once spoken to me of a wish to go and live in France, but had not mentioned the idea again. I had not pushed the idea. It suited me to live in town, because of my partnership with Sol – something that had gone from strength to strength since Margaret's death.

The death of Sol's wife, who had been my dearest friend, had brought Sol and me even closer together. It would have been hard to define our relationship to a stranger. We could have been father and daughter, but there was something different about the bond that held us – we were more like twins, though we had no blood ties and were far apart in age and appearance. We suited each other, our ideas about work and fashion complemented each other's, and we thought alike in many ways. Both of us liked to work for work's sake. We enjoyed success, shared the same jokes, the same triumphs and disappointments.

After the war, we had decided that we would expand our workshops. We now had two more besides the one Sol had owned before I came to work for him, and managing them took all Sol's time and energy. I had also offered him a partnership in the shops, but he had thought about it and then declined.

"I'll leave that part of it to you, Emma," he had told me. "It's best if I stick to this end, but I want you to be a part of the expansion of the workshops. I need you, your energy and drive. You've got more ideas than me about what's needed these days."

It was the perfect combination of our talents. Sol had so much experience in the trade, but I had youth and enthusiasm – and a hunger for success.

I was better off than I had ever been in my life. Money was no longer a problem, but I wanted more than that. I was searching for something, though I could not explain even to myself what I wanted. To the outsider, I would appear to have everything: a husband who loved me, children to love and care for, and a comfortable life. Yet there was a need in me, a restlessness . . . perhaps simply a wish to find my own way in life, not to rely too much emotionally on others, because I did not wish to be hurt again.

Sol was looking at me, an anxious expression in his eyes. I knew I was fortunate in having him as my friend. Without his help and encouragement I would never have come this far.

Solomon Gould was a well-respected name in the clothing trade, and he could cost a new dress in his head within seconds. I could do it, but I needed a pencil and paper, and

Sol could usually beat me both in terms of speed and price. He knew every way there was of saving an inch of material. He'd had enough practice during the war, when we were only allowed a certain amount of cloth for each garment.

Things were much better now, and our businesses were flourishing. The only real problem we'd had recently was finding the time to accomplish all we had to do. That was the reason why my son was so anxious about his school concert. I had let him down the last time.

I was determined to be there this afternoon, but first Sol and I had to plan our strategy for the New Look.

"Don't you worry about me," I said and smiled. "I'm just dreaming – and I do have an answer for you. I was just thinking about the way things are – but I'm ready now."

"Fire away then, Emma! What's the verdict?"

"It's romantic," I said to Sol as I flicked through the photographs and sketches, applying my mind to my work at last. "Really feminine. Look at those soft shoulders, the narrow waists and lovely full skirts – way below the calf. I would love to be able to reproduce it exactly, but we shall have to modify it, of course." I looked at him. "How soon do you think we could get our version into production?"

"Within a few hours if we dare. The Government isn't going to like it, Emma. I know they eased the restrictions on our use of cloth, but they won't be pleased if all the manufacturers bring this style in."

"If we don't, everyone else will. The Government will have to give way this time. Women have had enough of being told what they can or can't wear. Besides, I think we can reproduce the look and still stay within the limits. A costume like the one I've picked out would cost about fourteen coupons and sell at a price our competitors would find hard to match."

We had started to manufacture costumes this last year, though the showroom was still best known for its dresses.

"What I was thinking—" I made a quick sketch of a dress I had in mind. "If we did a nipped-in waist with a skirt that reaches to mid-calf . . . it would be sort of midway between the short skirts everyone is so fed up with, and the new length. I believe a cotton version would sell retail for about three pounds nineteen shillings, and probably require six clothing coupons."

Sol did a rapid calculation in his head. "Seven coupons, and we could sell a rayon version for thirty-five shillings in the showroom."

We looked at each other and smiled. There was always a spirit of competition between us on price. Whatever I suggested, Sol would find a way of undercutting me.

"Emma . . ." I glanced up as Pam came to the door of the sitting room. She looked at me apologetically. "I'm sorry to trouble you – but these flowers arrived for you. I thought you might like to see them before I put them in water."

Pam was one of my closest friends these days. She was some years older than me, a quiet, pleasant woman who had come to live with us after her husband was killed during the war. I relied on her for so much. She lived as a part of the family, and did anything that needed doing, usually without being asked. I knew she helped Mrs Rowan with the house quite a lot, saving the housekeeper all kinds of small tasks, and she was always there to lend a hand with the children or act as an unofficial secretary for me.

She was carrying a large and very beautiful bouquet of lilies and roses. They had clearly come from an expensive store and were slightly ostentatious.

"There's a card here," she said, offering the flowers for me to smell their perfume.

"Thank you." I took the card and looked at the message. The flowers were to thank me for my help in making up an order, which had apparently been successfully received, and had come from one of the regular customers at the showroom. He owned a large department store in London, and was a wealthy man. He had been showing a lot of interest in me recently, though he was well aware that I was married. "Put them in water if you will, Pam. I'll write a thank-you note to Philip later."

"Don't put him off, Emma," Sol said with a grin as Pam

carried the flowers away with her. "Philip Matthews is one of our best customers. His order gives us a lot of prestige in the trade. We don't want to lose him."

"I don't know why he keeps sending flowers," I said and sighed. "That's the third time this year. He must know I'm married. I've spoken to him about Jon many times."

"You're far too attractive," Sol said, a hint of amusement in his voice. He had aged a little since Margaret's death, but although almost fifty now was still very attractive himself, with smoky grey eyes and wiry hair that had gone a kind of rusty colour with grey streaks at the temples. It made him look worldly, a man of experience, and he turned heads wherever he went. "You can't blame a man like Matthews for trying in the circumstances. You don't look or sound married, Emma."

I said nothing, but in my heart I acknowledged the truth of what Sol was saying. My marriage had been in name only for a long time. Jon and I had slept in the same bed on a few occasions, but there had been nothing but kisses and a loving embrace between us. As far as I knew, Jon still believed that his inability to be a proper husband to me was temporary and would change once we were living together as man and wife.

I knew it was unlikely. His doctor had made it clear to me from the start that the severe injuries Jon had received in the sabotage attack in which he had been involved, which had gone wrong, had damaged him. There was always the chance that his body might mend itself, but it was only a chance.

In a way we had both been damaged, for during the war I had been concerned that I had not conceived my lover's child and visited a specialist. I had been told it was not impossible that I would have another baby one day, but because of some internal scarring after the premature birth of my son, it was unlikely.

That had caused me some grief, because at the time I had believed Jon was dead, and I had been planning to marry Jack Harvey at the end of the war. It was, however, something I had learned to live with and made little difference to me these days. Jon could never give me a child, and there was no one else in my life now.

It was not for want of offers. Philip Matthews was not the only man who had shown an interest in me these past few years. Most of the customers at the showroom, where I still worked from time to time, knew that my husband was an invalid. I had been asked out to dinner or to the theatre on many occasions, and some men, like Philip, took every excuse to send me flowers or small gifts.

I had refused them all with a smile and a small joke. It was not that I disliked Philip. He was a good-looking man with fair hair and soft blue eyes, and his manner was always gentle. Had I been a widow, I suppose I might have been tempted to accept some of the invitations I received, though there was only one man I would ever truly want.

"What do you think of this costume?" Sol asked. "It's not so very different from one we already make – except for the length of the skirt."

"The jacket has longer cuffs, which give it that extra style," I said. "But you are right. It is almost the same."

We exchanged smiles. Of all my friends, Sol was the one I always went to when I was in trouble. He knew my secrets, my hopes and fears – even those I tried to keep private. My past was an open book to him.

Sol knew there had been four men in my life: Paul Greenslade, my son's father; Dick Gillows, my first husband; Jack Harvey, and Jon – but Jack was the one who had given me the greatest happiness.

Sometimes, when I was alone at night, and my body ached for his touch, I almost regretted my decision not to go with him to America. When I saw Jon again, however, the tenderness I felt for him came flooding back, and I knew I could never have been happy if I had deserted him when he needed me so desperately.

Jon was a dear friend. I had known him long before I met Jack. He had been there when I needed him, when I was tied to Dick Gillows, a man I could never love, and utterly miserable. He had given me not only money but hope, hope that I would one day escape to a better life. I would always be grateful to him for his gentleness and kindness, and in my own way I loved him very much.

I shuffled my papers and sighed, wondering why I could not settle to my work.

"Something wrong, Emma?" Sol asked, sensing my restless mood.

I shook my head, unable to explain why I was haunted by thoughts of the past that morning.

Jon's face looked much better now than it had when I first saw him in the hospital. He had been injured while working with the resistance movement in France during the war. He would always bear the scars of his wounds, of course, but his mother was able to look at him now without going into hysterics – which she had on that terrible afternoon she first saw the burns.

I was fetching him home at the weekend, and if all went well he would not have to go back to the hospital that had been home to him for so many months. He would be free at last to live a normal life, or as normal as was possible for Jon.

He was conscious of the scars, of course, even though they were so much better than they had been at the start, but he was aware that people still stared when they saw him in the street. It was something he had accepted for my sake, because he loved me and he wanted to try living in the way that we had before he was injured. We had been to the theatre once during one of his visits home, and to the pictures on other occasions, but I knew he preferred to stay home and listen to the wireless in the evenings.

He was always happiest sitting quietly in his own room with a book or walking in the countryside. Sometimes I took him away for the weekend, and that was when he felt most relaxed, away from people and noise. I knew that eventually I might have to consider buying a house in the country.

It would present no problems as far as money was concerned. Jon had a small income of his own, which would have supported us had we needed it, and I was earning many times what he received. I supposed, now my businesses were running so smoothly, that I need not work, but without my work I would have had too much time to think.

"You're far away, Emma," Sol said, recalling me to the task in hand after I had been silent for some minutes. "Still thinking about Jon? About fetching him home?"

"Yes." I smiled at him. He could usually read my thoughts. "I was thinking things might have to change soon, Sol. I may have to buy a house in the country."

He nodded, his expression serious. "Make sure it has a good mainline station near by, Emma. You'll want somewhere not too far away so that you can pop up to town when you like."

"Yes." I had known Sol would understand me. "I wouldn't want to be too far away . . ."

I had been turning the pages of my newspaper idly. Suddenly, a face from the past was staring up at me. I read part of the accompanying article aloud.

"Mrs Sheila Jansen, wife of the popular American jazz singer Todd Jansen, was seen having tea at the Ritz yesterday. She is in the country to visit old friends and make arrangements for her husband's concert tour next month."

Sol looked at me as I finished reading. He knew what was in my mind. "You're afraid she might try to take Lizzy from us?" I nodded, staring at him in apprehension. He reached forward and patted my hand. "Don't worry about it, Emma. If she had wanted the girl, she would have been in contact with us before this."

"I hope you're right, Sol. James and Lizzy are inseparable. I don't know what they would do if they were parted."

"I can't see Sheila wanting to take her." Sol frowned as he saw my distress. "Her husband doesn't know she had a child, does he?"

"He didn't know," I said, swallowing hard. My throat was dry and I was really upset. "But supposing she comes here? Supposing she does want her daughter back?"

"Then we'll fight her," Sol said. "You still have the letter she sent when she gave Lizzy to you?"

15

"Yes . . . but I can't do that, Sol. I love Lizzy, but she *is* Sheila's daughter. She gave her up because she had a chance of a new life with Todd. You can see that things have gone well for her – she looks marvellous. She's wearing the New Look, and not a copy either. She must have bought that in Paris. Jane told me that Todd was doing well, but I hadn't realised he was as successful as all that – though I know he's a good singer."

"All the more reason for her to hang on to what she's got with him," Sol said. "If she comes, it will probably be just to see Lizzy. Believe me, Emma. That woman is as selfish as they come. There is no way she would risk her comfortable lifestyle for Lizzy's sake."

Sol had never liked Sheila, and perhaps he had good reason. We had always been friends, though she had been jealous of my success for a while after her own attempt at shopkeeping had failed at the start of the war. From the way she looked in the photograph, she had no need to be jealous of me now. Todd was obviously giving her everything she had ever hoped for.

All I could do was pray that she didn't want Lizzy back.

Two

"**Y**ou made it in time, then," Sarah Miller whispered as I took the seat next to her in the school assembly hall a few minutes after the concert had begun. "I'm so glad."

"Me too. I wouldn't have missed this for the world."

"Doesn't he look wonderful?" Sarah whispered as James made his way to the front of the stage.

"Yes. Wonderful." I was so proud of my son.

My eyes filled with tears as I listened to James singing the beautiful hymn. Where had his talent come from? No one in my father's family – that I knew of – had a decent singing voice, nor anyone in my mother's. Perhaps he had inherited it from Paul?

Thinking of Paul renewed my fears about Sheila's intentions. There had been a time towards the end of the war when I had feared that Paul would try to take James from me, though my fears had proved groundless. It would have been difficult for him, because James's name had been changed to Reece when I agreed to marry Jon. My husband had been a lawyer before the war, and changing James's name was one of the first of many things he had done to protect us.

Neither of us had wanted James to bear the name of my first husband, because Dick Gillows had been a self-confessed murderer. Nor had we wanted James to have his true father's name.

I was not certain what James thought of Jon. When he first visited us after the war, on a rare break from the hospital, I had introduced him as my husband, explaining privately to James that he had been away fighting for a long time.

James had protested that he wanted his "Daddy" back,

17

but I had told him that was impossible. Jack Harvey had been like a father to James during the war, but now he had returned to America and we had to stay here. Whether or not James had vaguely remembered Jon from before the war was impossible to say. Just how much could a child of a year or so remember?

He had never spoken of Jon as his Daddy, but to my relief James had accepted my husband when he came to the house. He had not screamed or made a fuss when he saw Jon's face, merely taking the mutilations in his stride. He had never been affectionate towards Jon, however, but treated him with the same kind of politeness he would show a stranger.

His school had taught him that. As a small child he had often screamed and kicked up a fuss to gain his own way, and I was not sure he had ever forgiven me for sending Jack away. He never spoke of that night in late 1944, when he'd crept down from his nursery to hear us quarrelling, but I knew he had not forgotten the man he had called Daddy.

James had long outgrown the pedal car Jack had once bought him as a Christmas gift, but he refused to be parted from it. I sometimes wondered if he remembered the promise Jack had made him to return just for his sake one day.

I thought the enforced parting from the man he adored might be one of the main reasons behind his attitude towards me, which became rather disagreeable at times. James loved me as I loved him, but there were moments when I felt that perhaps he did not quite trust me.

I tried hard to show him that I loved him more than anyone, but I was not always able to give him as much of my time as he needed. Lizzy never seemed to resent it when I had to work, though of course as much as I loved her she was not my own child. She remembered another life – a life that had been much less pleasant – and she was always grateful for whatever I gave her.

But I was allowing my mind to drift from my son's performance. Sarah and I both clapped enthusiastically as James finished his song and went back to stand with the other performers.

"He was so nervous," Sarah whispered. "But he pretended not to be."

I wiped the tears from my eyes as the applause for James's singing reverberated round the hall. He looked such a little angel. No one would believe that this was the same child who had recently put a frog in Mrs Rowan's bed.

She had made such a fuss! I had had to punish both Lizzy – who insisted she was the culprit until James owned up – and my son, by cancelling a trip to the pictures for them both. It had been a Laurel and Hardy film, which they had both been looking forward to seeing. I had regretted having to discipline them, but it had had to be done. However, I was going to give them a special treat this afternoon, and perhaps we would go to the cinema another day, during their summer holidays.

The concert was to celebrate the end of term, and most of the children who could sing were performing. Sarah touched my arm. "It's Lizzy's turn now. She looks so pretty – but very nervous."

A woman behind made a shushing noise and Sarah pulled a face, subsiding into silence. Lizzy was singing in the chorus. Her voice was not remarkable, but her enthusiasm made up for what she lacked in tunefulness.

I had chosen this particular school because it accepted both girls and boys, but the time was coming when Lizzy and James would have to go to separate schools. I did not look forward to the day I had to part them.

What was I going to do if Sheila wanted her daughter back?

Sol and my mother had both warned me that this might happen one day. I had dismissed their fears at the time, but now I was beginning to worry. Lizzy had become so dear to me that I would miss her terribly – but not as much as my son would. He would be devastated, and so would Lizzy.

The concert was over now. I got up and moved to join the other parents who were claiming their children. Mr Smithson, the children's headteacher, came up to me, his face wreathed in smiles.

19

"You must be very proud of James, Mrs Reece."

"Yes, I am. Very proud."

"I am so glad you could come this time. You missed the last concert, and that was such a shame."

"Unfortunately, I was working."

He nodded, but I caught the disapproval in his eyes. Obviously he did not approve of mothers who worked, not now that it was no longer our patriotic duty, though it had been very different during the war of course. Jon's mother held much the same opinion. Dorothy was always hinting that she thought I ought to give up work now and devote myself full time to looking after my husband and the children, but that was something I was not prepared to do, despite my devotion to them.

Lizzy and James ran towards me.

"Did you see me, Mum?"

"Emmie – wasn't James good?"

"Yes, darlings. I saw you both and you were both wonderful."

"Lizzy was scared but I wasn't," James boasted.

"Can we have ice cream, Emmie?"

"Yes, I should think so, darling."

I nodded to Mr Smithson and took the children by the hand. Their chattering was relentless throughout the car journey, and showed no signs of abating during tea, which we had at Lyons, because they preferred it to a hotel where they felt they had to be quiet.

We had rolls of vanilla ice cream, little cream cakes, tea for Sarah and me, and fizzy orangeade for the children. It was a happy occasion, and I indulged their liveliness, even though I noticed one or two matrons giving me a rather jaundiced look.

Well-brought-up children were not supposed to be quite as noisy as my two, but I didn't see why they shouldn't enjoy themselves. Perhaps they were spoiled, but I loved them both so much that I did not like to curb their natural excitement – though I stopped James when he started flicking the paper from his ice cream across the table at Lizzy.

"That's enough of that, James," I said. "It's time we went home now."

They protested that they wanted to go to the park, but I did not give in. The wind was cool that afternoon, and Lizzy was prone to chills if we were not careful. Besides, I had some work to do. I had given up the afternoon to attend the concert, but I would have to make up for it by working on my figures that evening.

"Mum, can we go to the seaside this summer?" James asked as I opened the car door for them to pile in. "Pam said her sister would have us for a week – but I would like to stay in a hotel this time, or somewhere different. Like the place we went with Jack that year."

My heart stood still. He had not mentioned Jack for so long that I had almost believed he had forgotten him. Yet in my heart I knew he would never do that – any more than I could.

"We might go to a hotel somewhere," I replied, carefully keeping my voice level. "But we can't go there, darling. Not to the Cottage. It belongs to Jack."

"He would lend it to us if you asked," James said, pulling a face. That hint of mutiny was in his eyes again. He would never truly forgive me for sending Jack away. "I know he would. If you wrote to him in America and asked."

"I don't know his address," I said. "Besides, there are lots of other nice places we could stay."

"But I liked it *there*."

"Well, we'll see," I said, hoping to change the subject. "I'm not sure Jack still lets people stay there. He might have sold it."

It was unlikely that Jack had sold the Cottage. It was a lovely old house that had been in his family for generations. I did not know if he ever visited it these days – or if he even came to England.

I had heard nothing from him since the night we had quarrelled.

I was still thinking about Jack and the few days we had

spent at his cottage in Sussex as I parked the car, then ushered the children into the house.

Mrs Rowan came out into the hall, her face wearing its disapproving look.

"You have a visitor, madam. I asked her to wait in the parlour."

"Thank you, Mrs Rowan. Did she leave her name?"

"Mrs Jansen," the housekeeper said. "I think she's American."

My heart caught with fright as I told the children to go upstairs. Sheila had come, just as I had expected after reading the newspaper article that morning.

I went into the sitting room. Sheila was standing by the window, looking out at the street. I knew she must have seen us come in. She turned to me and smiled, and I saw she was wearing a very smart costume, similar to the one she had been wearing in the photograph. Her shoes were made of the finest leather, and her hat was both smart and attractive. Her hair looked lighter, as though she had had it rinsed to an ash blonde, but it had been done professionally and did not look cheap or tarty. She was wearing a large diamond ring as well as her wedding band, and looked very comfortable with her new status.

"Hello, Emma," she said. "Are you pleased to see me?"

"That depends on why you've come," I replied. "Lizzy is very happy here with us, Sheila. I wouldn't be very pleased if you wanted to take her away from us."

Sheila laughed. She looked attractive and well, much more like the girl who had come into my father's shop to buy her favourite toffee pieces than she had when I'd last seen her, but with a confidence she had never had in those days.

"Good grief, no," she said. "Todd has no idea Lizzy exists. I just wanted to make sure she was OK, that's all. I couldn't possibly have her with me. Todd doesn't want children; it would interfere with his career. We travel all the time, Emma. We shall be here for several weeks while Todd is performing in London, and down in Bournemouth. He's starring in a seaside show." Her eyes met mine. "You did know he's a famous singer these days, didn't you?"

"Yes, I had heard it from Jane Melcher, but I didn't realise how successful he was until I saw your photograph in the paper this morning." I was relaxed now, my fears receding. "Have you got time to see Lizzy? She and James have been singing in their school concert. I took them to tea afterwards. If I'd known you were calling, I would have come straight home."

"I didn't mind waiting," Sheila said. "I've got nothing much to do for a few days. Todd is still in Paris. He will be here next Tuesday. I came on ahead to make sure of hotel bookings and things." She hesitated, then went on, "I wondered if I could take Lizzy away for a couple of days, Emma. You and James could come too, if you like."

"They don't finish school until Friday, and I have to fetch Jon home from hospital on Sunday." I saw the flicker of disappointment in her eyes and made a swift decision. "I could send a note to their school, I suppose. We could go tomorrow morning and come back on Saturday afternoon, if you like. It would only be two days . . ."

"Bless you," Sheila said. "I wouldn't blame you if you thought I was a rotten mother and refused to let me near Lizzy . . . but I have missed her."

"I understand, Sheila. It was your chance and you took it. Besides, I've loved having Lizzy with us. She's like a daughter to me – though of course I know she isn't mine."

"You haven't had any more children?"

"No, I haven't." I kept my smile in place. It wasn't so very hard, even though there was a secret hurt deep inside me. "Not yet. Things have been difficult, with Jon in hospital on and off."

"It must have been a shock for you when you heard he was still alive," Sheila said, then blushed as my brows rose. "I met Jane Melcher at a charity concert in New York once. She told me about Jon, and the sacrifice you'd made."

"It wasn't a sacrifice, Sheila. I love Jon. He is a wonderful man."

Sheila nodded. "Well, Jane seemed to think you were some kind of saint." She shrugged her shoulders. "Have you seen my cousin Annie recently? I went back to her old house, but someone said she'd moved ages ago."

"Yes, I know. She and her family live in a prefab. Her eldest daughter works for me, and the younger ones are going to start when they leave school. Annie manages one of the shops for me now. She could only do a few hours to begin with, but now she works a full day."

"Can you give me her address?"

"Yes, of course. I'm sure she would like to see you."

"I'm not too sure about that. The last time I saw her she said she was finished with me for good – but perhaps she will think differently now. Anyway, you and me can talk to our hearts' content these next two days." Sheila grinned at me. "Where shall we go?"

"Not too far," I said, "or we'll spend all our time travelling. I'll think about it, Sheila, perhaps ring a few hotels, see where we can get booked in at short notice."

"And you'll talk to Lizzy," Sheila said, looking a bit awkward. "Explain that it's just a little holiday."

"Yes, I'll tell her," I said. "Don't worry, Sheila. You haven't seen Lizzy and James together yet. They are close friends and it would have upset them both had you wanted to take her away."

"I knew she would be all right with you," Sheila said, her awkwardness vanishing. "I told you to put her in a home if you didn't want her, but I knew you wouldn't."

"No," I said. "I would never do that."

"So all's well that ends well," Sheila said. "I can give you money towards her keep now, Emma."

"Perhaps you can send her some pocket money," I replied. "I'll leave that to you and Lizzy."

"You're a glutton for punishment," Sol exclaimed when I told him I was taking two days off for a short holiday with Sheila and the children. He frowned at me. "She'll let you down again, Emma. You would be a fool to trust her."

"No, I don't think she will do anything to harm me or Lizzy," I replied. "Sheila had a bad time during the war, that's all. She sent Lizzy to me when she went off with Todd because we were friends, and that shows she trusted me to look after her. I think she will be straight with me now."

Sol shook his head, clearly unconvinced.

My mother was even more forthright when I telephoned her with my news.

"Have you lost your wits, Emma? That woman used you before, and she will do so again. You should have more sense!"

"What Sheila did hasn't harmed me. I've loved having Lizzy live with us. And the rest of it is water under the bridge, Mum. Anyway, how are you – and Bert?"

My mother's second husband was the best thing that had ever happened to her. After enduring years of unhappiness tied to my father, she had married her first love just before the start of the war. Unfortunately, Bert Fitch had been having bronchial trouble for the last few winters, which had left his chest a bit weak, and I knew Mum worried about his health.

"He's a little better this morning," she said. "But he's not the man he was a few years back, Emma. He gets a terrible tightness in his chest, and the coughing pulls him down sometimes."

"I was going to ask if you wanted to come when I take the children on their proper holiday next month. You and Bert – or you on your own, though you won't feel like leaving him, will you?"

"We'll see," she said. "I wouldn't mind a holiday, and it would do Bert good to be by the sea for a few days. Where were you thinking of going?"

"I thought I might take a house somewhere in Cornwall."

"I see." She sounded interested; Sheila had been forgotten. "A house in Cornwall . . . that would be lovely. All of us together as a family. I'll definitely give it some thought, Emma."

I was smiling as we hung up. Mum had been feeling a little down recently. Her own health had never been really good, though she'd been much better since she married Bert. She came to stay with me in London sometimes, and I took James down to stay with her in my home town of March. There wasn't much going on in the small Cambridgeshire market town, but I liked visiting my friends, and there were the three shops to consider.

My father's sister looked after them for me on a day-to-day basis. She had discovered a talent for shopkeeping after her own mother died, and I never bothered to do more than check on our stock levels so that I knew what to send to Madge Henty, my partner in the dress shop and to the next-door children's clothing shop. Gwen ran that, and the newsagent and tobacconist shop that had been my father's, like clockwork.

I would have asked Gwen if she would like to come with us to Cornwall, but I knew she would be too busy. Besides, she preferred to live her own life, and I knew she had made a lot of friends in March. She had her own little car now, and Mum had hinted that she might be courting. She had already told me that she was going to close the newsagent for ten days in July while she had a holiday in Yarmouth.

It was a long time since I'd taken the children anywhere other than to my mother's or to stay in Hunstanton at Pam's sister's boarding house. They were excited at the prospect of going away for two days, though Lizzy had pulled a face when I told her that her mother was coming with us.

"I don't want her to come," she said, a look of apprehension in her eyes. "I want to stay with you and James. Don't let her take me away, Emmie. I don't want to leave you."

"She won't take you away," James said fiercely, but with an anxious look in my direction. "We shan't let her – shall we, Mum?"

"Lizzy's mother doesn't want to take her away," I reassured them with a smile. "She has just come on a short visit, and she wants to have a little time with Lizzy. We'll all be together. I'm not sending you on your own, Lizzy."

Lizzy came to me, clinging to the full skirt of my dress. "I love you, Emmie, and James. I never want to leave you."

"Not even when I punish you by not letting you go to the pictures?"

She gazed up at me, her eyes wide and earnest. "Not even then. I like living here with you and James."

"Then I expect you will stay with us," I said. "But you might change your mind when you see your own mother again, Lizzy."

She shook her head, a look of determination on her face.

"Lizzy can't go away. I want her here." James had that mutinous expression in his eyes, and a hint of accusation hung about him, as though he were blaming me for something. It did not seem to matter how often I showed my love for my son, there was always that little bit of uncertainty in his mind.

It was my own fault, I knew that. I had allowed him to learn to love Jack Harvey and he would always blame me for sending his "Daddy" away. Looking back I saw how hard that must have been for him. And of course I was not always around when he needed me.

"I want her here, too," I said, "but Sheila is Lizzy's mother. She has a right to see her sometimes, darling. Lizzy isn't your sister; she is your friend. You must accept that, even though she lives with us, she might have to leave one day."

James didn't answer, but his mouth had set in a hard line. I knew there would be trouble if Sheila did try to part them.

However, I need not have worried. I had booked into a small but prestigious hotel in Southend-on-Sea, and we took the children down on the train. Sheila bought them sweets, colouring books, crayons and a box of puzzles for the journey, which kept them amused. By the time we arrived Lizzy's hostility towards her mother had faded.

We spent the next two days spoiling them both. We took them on the pier, letting them play with the penny slot machines as much as they liked. We bought them fish and chips wrapped in newspaper to eat on the beach, with ice creams and sticks of peppermint rock to follow. James went on the donkeys, but Lizzy thought they were smelly creatures and would only watch from a safe distance.

During the day, our time was devoted to the children. The weather was kind to us, the sun warm enough to make it pleasant to sit in a sheltered spot on the beach or pier. We took the children shopping on the Friday morning. Sheila bought Lizzy some pretty shoes and a new dress, and I bought James a new engine for his train set, which was so magnificent that it took up half the floor of the playroom at home.

When they were safely in bed on the Friday evening, Sheila and I sat in the hotel lounge and talked. The years seemed to roll back as we laughed about the time we had gone to the church social, me with Dick Gillows and Sheila with the man who was to become her first husband.

"That all seems part of another world, like something out of the dark ages," Sheila said. "My life is so much better these days, Emma – and it's all due to you."

"Why? I should have thought it was for an entirely different reason."

"Oh, yes, it's because of Todd, too," she agreed, catching the teasing smile in my eyes. "I really care about him, Emma – and he loves me. He's so jealous. I daren't look at another man."

"I shouldn't have thought you'd want to!"

"No, of course I don't – but you know what I mean." She looked a bit like the cat that had found the cream. "I'm so lucky now – and I might never have met Todd if you hadn't made me help out at the social club during the war."

"According to Pam, you didn't do much helping," I said, and laughed. "But I do know what you mean, Sheila. It's funny how things work out, isn't it? You've helped me, and I've helped you – that's what friends are for."

"Yes, I suppose I did help you a bit when you were having a bad time with Dick," she said. "But I know I owe you, Emma. If there's ever anything I can do . . ."

"I'll know where to come," I replied. "All I want is for you to let Lizzy stay with us, at least until the children are older. James would be so upset if you took her away."

"I told you, Todd doesn't know about her," Sheila said. "I couldn't have her with me even if she wanted, but" – she

28

looked at me oddly, slightly apprehensive, as if unsure of my reaction – "I wouldn't mind doing this again one day. And I would like to send her things now and then . . . if you don't mind?"

"No, I don't mind," I said. "I think it would be—"

The words died on my lips as I glanced across the room. Three men had just entered, and I knew one of them well. The sight of him made my heart beat wildly. He was every bit as darkly handsome as he'd always been. He looked older, a sprinkling of silver at his temples, but all the power, all the magnetism was still there.

"What's wrong?" Sheila asked, looking at me in concern. "You've gone as white as a sheet." She turned to look over her shoulder, then nodded as she saw the reason for my shocked expression. "The man in the grey striped suit – that's Jack Harvey, isn't it?"

"Yes." I felt breathless. "Yes, that's Jack."

The protests were drumming in my brain. What was Jack doing here, in this hotel? Why couldn't he have chosen somewhere else? How could Fate be so cruel as to let him walk in here just when I'd chosen to come for a couple of days?

I prayed he wouldn't see me. I hoped desperately he would leave again without glancing towards the settee near the window where we were sitting, but my prayers were in vain.

Jack was looking straight at me. He was frowning, his expression cold as ice. I thought he seemed angry, unforgiving. He stared at me for some seconds, our eyes meeting briefly before mine dropped, then he turned and spoke to one of his companions.

I watched from beneath lowered lashes as the three men walked out of the room together. Jack did not look at me again as he left. For a moment I felt as if I had been struck across the face.

"Well, that was a bit rude of him," Sheila remarked. "He might have come across to say hello."

"We had an argument before he left to go back to America,"

I said, feeling sick and shaken. "It was after the invasion of Europe, but before the war was really finished. He said then that there was nothing left to say – obviously he still doesn't want to speak to me."

"He might have nodded or something," Sheila said, looking concerned. "Are you all right? He has upset you, hasn't he?"

"Yes." I took a deep breath to stop myself shaking. "It was just the shock of seeing him like that. I had no idea he was in the country. I haven't heard from him – or of him – for years."

Sheila hesitated, then ventured, "So you didn't know he was married?"

"Married?" My heart twisted with pain. There was no reason why Jack should not have married, of course, but it was a shock and I hadn't expected the news to hurt so much. "No, I hadn't heard." I swallowed hard, my throat dry. "When . . . how long?"

"About three months ago," Sheila said. "Before we left America for our European tour. In April, I think. I'm sorry, Emma. If Jane Melcher didn't tell you, I probably shouldn't have . . . I didn't mean to hurt you. It wasn't done out of spite, believe me."

"No, of course not," I said. My head was beginning to clear a little. "I would rather know . . . I *would* rather know."

That wasn't quite the truth. Alone in my hotel room that night, I found myself unable to sleep, and tossed restlessly on my pillows as the thoughts tumbled in my mind.

Jack was here in England. I had no real need to wonder what had brought him to Southend. Knowing Jack, it would be business. He was a wealthy, powerful man and had always been caught up in some deal or other even during the war.

I switched on the bedside lamp, reaching for the library book I had brought with me. It was F. Scott Fitzgerald's *The Beautiful And The Damned*, which I had wanted to read for a long time, but I was too disturbed to settle to it. Sheila's news had shocked and distressed me, and the words blurred on the page.

Jack married . . . What was she like, his wife? Was she pretty? She would be, I knew that. Much prettier than me. Did he love her? Were they as good together in bed as Jack and I had been?

The stupid, petty jealousies were like needles in my flesh. I wanted to scream or cry, but there was no sense in giving way to my feelings.

I had thought I was over the pain of losing Jack, but it was back, cutting me to the bone. I was still in love with him, as much as ever, and very aware of what I had thrown away.

This was madness. I must not let myself think this way.

"You made your bed, lass, now you must lie on it."

I seemed to hear my beloved Gran speaking to me down the years. She had been a very wise lady, and I knew she would scold me for letting myself look back with regret.

"No regrets, Emma. Look to the future."

I had made my choice. I had chosen Jon and sent Jack away. I knew I would do the same if I were forced to make that choice all over again . . . so why did I feel like weeping?

I prayed that I would not bump into Jack again. We were leaving Southend on the Saturday afternoon, and the children wanted to go on the pier once more before we caught our train. With any luck I would not be forced to see Jack again. I could push the memory of him back to a corner of my mind, where it could not hurt me – at least, not as much as it was hurting now.

"Mum, when can we do this again?" James demanded as we walked back to the hotel, loaded down with our parcels. Sheila had enjoyed spending money on both children, and I had not tried to stop her, so they had lots of good things to take home. "It was fun. I want to stay in a hotel again one day soon."

"I was thinking I might take a house in Cornwall for a few weeks next month," I replied. "Grandma and Bert could come with us – and Sarah. It would be more fun like that . . . don't you think so?"

James did not reply. I thought he was considering my

31

question, but when I glanced down at him I saw he was staring at a man who was walking along the street towards us.

"Daddy," he yelled and started to run. "Daddy . . ."

My son had grown out of calling me "Mummy" just after he started school, but Jack was still his "Daddy". That hurt somehow. My heart caught as I wondered how Jack would react. I watched as he suddenly became aware of the young boy charging eagerly towards him. For a moment he hesitated, then he started to grin and took swift steps to meet James, catching him up and swinging him off the ground.

"Hello, son," he said, his manner natural, welcoming. "Well, this is a surprise. I was coming to see you in London next week. I've got a present for you."

Sheila looked at me as I paused uncertainly.

"Go on," she hissed. "Now's your chance. Make him crawl, Emma. Tell him to get the hell out of your life."

"I can't," I said. "James adores him."

I walked towards Jack, my heart jerking, Lizzy still clinging apprehensively to my hand. "Hello, Jack," I said as I reached him. "I'm sorry about this."

"Why?" His brows rose, and I could see him looking at Lizzy. He seemed angry, but was trying to conceal it, probably for James's sake. "Because of last night, I suppose. Well, I won't deny it was a shock. I was with colleagues and thought it best not to intrude. I was going to call next week . . . to see James, as I promised I would next time I was in London." He ruffled James's hair, something that would have made my son squirm if I had done it, but which he seemed to enjoy coming from Jack. It was quite clear that whatever place Jon had in his life, Jack was his father. I doubted that he had thought about the meaning of the word. Jack was the "Daddy" he recognised and loved.

I met Jack's intense gaze. "You haven't been back to London since the war."

He shook his head. "No, I've had other things to keep me busy."

"Yes, so I believe." I raised my head, hoping no sign of my

inner turmoil showed as I looked into his eyes. "I understand congratulations are in order?"

"You mean because I'm married?"

I nodded, and Jack's expression became even colder, if that was possible.

"Emmie . . ." Lizzy tugged at my hand. "Can I have an ice cream, please? Just one more before we go home?"

"I'll take her," Sheila offered. "You'll find us in the café over the road, Emma." She held out her hand. "You coming, James?"

He shook his head. His expression was tortured. It was obvious he wanted that ice cream, but he wanted to stay with Jack more.

"No, I want to be with Jack," he said. He had remembered he was grown up now, his expression slightly apprehensive as he looked at his "Daddy". "Are you really going to come and see me next week, sir?"

"Yes, I really am," Jack said. "I promise. I'll take you out somewhere – if your mother says it's OK." I nodded, and he gave James a little push towards Sheila and Lizzy. "Go with your friend," he said. "I want to talk to your mother now for a few minutes."

James was silent, still hesitant, then he nodded and ran off to join Sheila and Lizzy. For a moment Jack and I stood absolutely still, just staring at each other.

"I'm sorry," Jack said. "I was rude last night, Emma. I should have come over and said hello."

"You were surprised to see me," I said. I was desperately trying to stay calm. "It was a shock for me, too, seeing you walk in like that. We only brought the children down for a couple of days. Sheila has been in America since the war. She came over to visit Lizzy, who lives with me, and book the hotels for her husband's tour. She married Todd Jansen, the jazz singer."

Jack nodded, his expression thoughtful. "Yes, I sort of recognised her. We met once at a charity concert in New York. I vaguely remembered she was a friend of yours once."

"We are friends," I replied. "We don't see each other often, but we're still friends."

"Am I still your friend, Emma?"

My throat was tight with emotion. "Do you want to be?"

"It might be easier . . . for the boy's sake." Jack's eyes were intent on my face. "I would like to see something of him while I'm here – and keep in touch in the future." He frowned. "I thought he might have forgotten me by now. It was my intention to bring him a present and then go quietly away again if he didn't remember me."

"James has never forgotten you."

My heart was aching. I had not forgotten Jack either, but I would not let him see that if I could help it.

"In that case, you won't mind if I call to see James?"

"No, I don't see any reason why you shouldn't." I hesitated, then raised my gaze to meet his. "I am fetching Jon home from hospital tomorrow. He doesn't know about—"

"About us being lovers?" There was a faint smile in Jack's eyes. "No, I didn't imagine he would. I'll be careful, Emma. All your husband needs to know is that I'm James's friend. I'll tell the boy I prefer to be called Jack now he's grown up."

"Yes, that might be best . . . more tactful. James does call Jon Father occasionally, though only out of politeness. He clearly still thinks of you as his Daddy." I took a deep breath. "Well, I ought to be going. We have to catch the train at two thirty this afternoon."

"I shall see you next week, then," Jack said. His gaze narrowed. "Thank you for being so reasonable, Emma."

"Why should I be anything else?" I asked. "I did what I had to do, Jack. I never meant to hurt you."

"No," he said, and there was an odd expression in his eyes now. "I believe you did what you thought was right . . . and perhaps it was. Who knows about these things?"

"You wouldn't have met your wife if I had left Jon."

"No." Jack smiled, a mocking, challenging look that made me flinch as if he had struck me. "I wouldn't, would I, Emma?"

"I wish you every happiness, Jack."

"Thank you, Emma. Believe me, I am as happy as I deserve to be."

I nodded, and turned away to cross the road.

"Are you happy, Emma?"

His question held me. For a moment I paused on the edge of the pavement, glancing back at him. "I'm as happy as I expected to be," I said, then I ran across the street and did not look back.

Three

"Well, what did he have to say for himself?" Sheila asked when we were sitting on the train. The children were bored with playing with their toys and had gone out to walk up and down the corridor. "I hope he apologised for his rudeness?"

"Yes, he did," I replied. "He says it would be better if we could be friends – for James's sake."

"I would have told him to get lost," she said, pulling a wry face. "You're storing up trouble for yourself. You were always too forgiving, Emma. People take advantage." She laughed as she realised what she'd said. "Including me."

"Everyone does what they have to do."

"I could pay you the money back now – the five hundred pounds you let me have when . . . I needed it."

"I don't need it," I said. "If I ever do, I'll ask. Just let the past go, Sheila. I'd like us to be friends, really friends. Even if we don't see each other much."

"We'll keep in touch," she promised. "I always meant to come back one day. It may be a long time before I can visit again, but I shan't forget. You or Lizzy."

I nodded. There wasn't much need for words. Sheila's visit had removed a nagging worry from the back of my mind. I had always wondered if she might return to claim Lizzy, but now I knew she wouldn't. Lizzy might choose to leave us one day, but that was a long way in the future.

A future that was about to change. It would seem very strange to have Jon actually living with us all the time. There would be adjustments to make . . . not least the presence of my husband in my bed every night.

*   *   *

I was thoughtful as I drove down to fetch Jon from the small military hospital the next day. Sheila had gone off to finish making arrangements for Todd's tour, and things were back to normal again – or almost.

It wasn't as easy as I'd hoped to dismiss my chance meeting with Jack, or the knowledge that he would be coming to the house to visit my son. A part of me wanted to forget, but another part of me was tingling with anticipation, excited at the prospect of seeing him again. It seemed that neither my son nor I had been able to forget Jack.

Don't be a fool, Emma! I scolded myself mentally. I had fought long and hard for my peace of mind, and now I was in danger of letting Jack destroy it all over again. It would be foolish of me to allow him back into my heart and mind. I must keep reminding myself that Jack was now married.

He must love his new wife. Of course he did! He had forgotten me, forgotten the way it had been between us . . . and yet something in his parting words had seemed to deny that. "Believe me, I'm as happy as I deserve to be." What did that mean? I felt a surge of hope – ridiculous, selfish, glorious hope – that he still loved me. I squashed it swiftly. It would be wicked of me to hope that Jack was not happy, that he had never truly forgotten me.

I made a determined effort to put all such thoughts from my mind. This was a special day. It was the last time I would need to fetch Jon home. From now on we would be living together, all the years of pain and struggle behind us.

Sister Jones was waiting in her office. I had brought her several small gifts of flowers, fruit and chocolate – I had discovered over the years that she had a passion for Fry's dark chocolate bars. We were friends now, and she smiled ruefully as I handed her my gifts.

"I'm going to miss your visits, Emma – and so will the boys. They all look forward to seeing you."

"I shall miss you, Vera – but you must visit us in London whenever you come up. Let me know, and I'll arrange seats at the theatre."

"Always so generous." She smiled. "I might just come

one day. And now, I mustn't keep you any longer. Jon is in the games room. He and some of the others are having a few beers. Jon insisted on giving a little party."

I nodded my understanding. Jon was more fortunate than some of his friends. His scars had responded to treatment, healing fairly well over the years, as had his injured hand, but there were other men who would never leave this place, because they were either too ill or too afraid of the world outside.

I stood on the threshold of the games room and watched. Jon was talking to a man in a wheelchair. Robert's spine had been shattered and he would never walk again. His wife had visited him once, then written to say she could not face coming back. His situation was not uncommon amongst these heroes of the peace.

"Emma!" Jon's face lit up as he saw me. "Don't stand there, darling. Come and say goodbye to everyone."

"I brought a few things," I said as I kissed his cheek. "Pam made cake and biscuits." I put the tin down amongst the debris of glasses and empty bottles. "I'll leave them for your friends."

"We're going to miss you, Emma," Robert said, grinning at me. "Your pretty face makes a change from Sister's ugly mug."

"I heard that," Sister Jones said from the doorway. "That's an extra enema for you, my lad!"

"Sorry, Sister! I'm drunk – not responsible for my actions. Or words, come to that. Not that I ever am, of course."

There was a chorus of laughter from the men. Sister was smiling. She was accustomed to their insults, which were meant only in jest and helped to relieve the tedium. Life here wasn't all pain and misery, thanks to the devotion of people like Vera Jones.

I stayed for over an hour talking to the men I had come to know so well. Then the moment came to leave for the last time. We said our goodbyes and went out, but I sensed something in Jon as we walked to the car – apprehension, perhaps, or a certain sadness.

"What's wrong?" I asked. "You're not sorry to be leaving, are you?"

Jon glanced at me, a rueful expression in his eyes. "You know me so well, Emma. No, I'm not sorry to leave, but I am sorry for Rob and some of the others. And there is a slight fear of facing up to the future . . . and of life outside."

"You've no need to be afraid," I said, meeting his troubled gaze. "I know there's still a weakness in your chest. You can't work, Jon, but we've talked this over. You don't need a job."

"Because my wife keeps me?" He frowned, and I sensed his pride was bruised.

"I've been lucky," I said. "Things have worked out with the shops. Besides, you can help me with the accounts if you feel like it."

"You don't need my help," he replied, frowning. "I thought I might try to write, Emma. I may not be any good, but—"

"Write?" I was surprised and pleased as I realised he was serious. "You haven't mentioned this before. What will you write – poems?"

"I've written a few," he admitted, "but I'm thinking of trying a play. Actually, I wrote something for the radio. Just a little story, but they're going to read it on air."

"That's wonderful, Jon." I turned to kiss his cheek, but his arms went round me, embracing me. His lips touched mine, soft and tender, but also with a hint of sexual intent. As I gazed into his eyes, I knew Jon had turned a corner in his mind. He meant to live as normal a life as possible. "I'm so pleased, my darling."

"They've asked me to go for an interview," Jon said. "They want to discuss some ideas I put forward. I wrote to them from the hospital, so they will be expecting me to look a bit odd. It won't shock them too much."

"You don't look odd." I reached out to touch his scars, which were shiny and smooth to the touch, but had long since ceased to give him pain. "Your face just looks lived in, Jon."

"Slightly battered and the worse for wear," he said and

laughed. He had come to terms with his appearance long ago. "It doesn't worry me, Emma. You've gone on loving me, and that's all that matters. I'm so much luckier than some of the others . . ."

I saw the reflection of pain and sadness in his eyes, and felt the guilt strike me. How could I have allowed myself to think of Jack again when I knew how much Jon needed me?

"I'm lucky to have you home," I said. "I've got some news for you, darling. I've been thinking of taking a house in Cornwall for a few weeks during this summer. We could all go down as a family – and we might think of having a look round while we're there. We could buy a house in the area."

"I thought you wanted somewhere nearer London?"

"Well, yes, if we were going to live there all the time. I was thinking more of holidays. And it would be nice for you if you wanted some peace . . . somewhere to write. You'll need to be in town when you're meeting people, won't you? So it makes sense to stay where we are for the moment – doesn't it?"

I hoped so much he would agree. Was I asking for too much?

Jon nodded, a thoughtful expression in his eyes. "Yes, it might be a good idea. Let's think about it for a while, Emma. I'm in no hurry to make changes at the moment. I'm just looking forward to being with you and the children."

"We could buy a house for holidays in France, if you prefer."

"We need time together," Jon said. "I know we've talked, but we couldn't make plans while I was still spending most of my time in the hospital. Let's see how things work out."

"Yes, of course," I agreed. "There's plenty of time."

I started the car engine.

"Time to go home," he said, looking as if he could not wait to leave.

"Yes, my darling. It's time to go home."

We didn't go straight home that afternoon. Jon's mother had asked if I would take Jon for a short visit, and so we stopped at the house in Hampstead for twenty minutes or so.

"Thank you for coming, Emma." Dorothy Reece was scrupulously polite with me these days. "I know you are busy."

Her expression was faintly wistful, her eyes carrying a veiled accusation. I had tried to call on her and Pops every so often right through the war, but whatever I did, it was never enough for her. Even despite an outburst of anger against me in the hospital the day she'd seen Jon's scars for the first time, I had continued to visit when I could afterwards. She had blamed me that day for not preparing her for the shock of Jon's changed looks, but the truth was she disliked me. In fact, I thought that deep down she hated me.

However, we usually kept up an armed truce, and I had visited at least once a month until Pops died the winter before last. Since then, I had merely telephoned occasionally. I still missed Jon's grandfather, who had been the sweetest of men.

I had wondered what Dorothy would do after her father died, but she had continued to live in the large old house, and now had a female companion.

"I suppose we had to call," Jon said to me when we left, "but I shan't do so very often, Emma. It wasn't too bad when Pops was alive, but . . ." He looked at me ruefully. "You were very good to them. Pops came to see me in the hospital a couple of times on his own. He told me about all the things you did for them during the war."

"I loved Pops, you know I did. I'm afraid I haven't been to visit Dorothy much since he died, but I do telephone – and Miss Carter is very good. I've told her to let me know if she ever needs help with money or anything else."

"Pops left the house to me," Jon said. "Did you know that?"

"Yes. He told me that was his intention – with the option for Dorothy to live there for as long as she wants."

"I should have thought she would rather have a nice modern apartment," Jon said. "I'll have to ask her about that one day. That house is much too big for her, and I shall never live there. I could sell it and use the money to buy something more useful."

41

"Well, that's up to you," I said. "As long as she doesn't think it's my idea, she might agree."

Jon reached out for me in our bed that night. I snuggled closer to him, relishing the warmth of his body and his presence beside me. I had missed that while he was away. I did not enjoy sleeping alone.

He stroked my back through the thin silk of my nightgown, his mouth seeking mine in the darkness.

"I love you, Emma."

"I love you too, darling."

"I've missed you so much."

His hand caressed my breast. He pushed back the nightgown, kissing me in the sensitive hollow between my breasts. His hand moved down to stroke my thigh.

"You know I want to make love to you, Emma. I want to be a proper husband to you."

"Yes, I know."

"It just won't happen. The desire is there, in my mind, in my heart . . . but my body won't function."

"You've been ill for a long time."

"It may never happen." There was a catch in his voice. "I may never be able to—"

"Hush, my darling." I kissed him, my fingers becoming tangled in the soft hair at the nape of his neck. "Give it time. If it happens, that's good, but if not . . . Just hold me, Jon. Hold me and love me, that's all I ask. It's lonely without you here. We can share so much. Let's be grateful for what we have."

"My precious love."

Jon continued to stroke and kiss me for a while, then he turned over and closed his eyes. I knew he wasn't sleeping. Nor could I doze off for a long time. His caresses had aroused a need in me that was unsatisfied.

I tried not to think of Jack. I tried not to remember the nights of passion that we had spent together during the war, but they crept into my mind, intensifying the hunger I felt. I still wanted him, loved him . . . but I had no right to feel that way.

It was so unfair of me! A betrayal of the love I felt for Jon. He had endured so much for my sake. All this talk of writing was as much for me as for himself. He wanted to make some sort of a living, to allow me to feel that I was not supporting him, that I did not need to work for his benefit.

I understood his pride and his need. The fact that I would have wanted to work anyway helped a little, but Jon had always been sensitive. He was a good man, a gentle one, and I'd never wanted to hurt him.

I had resisted Jack when we first met, refused to admit that I was attracted to him. Only my belief that Jon had been killed in an air crash had made me vulnerable to Jack's determined pursuit.

I decided I would put Jack right out of my mind, turned over and went to sleep.

At some time during the night Jon must have left our bed. I did not stir, nor was I aware that he had gone until I woke soon after dawn and discovered that the bed was cold beside me.

I was out when Jack came to collect my son a few days later. He had telephoned the previous evening to ask if it was all right, and I'd deliberately arranged to be working. I had decided it was safer not to see Jack. Better, too, for my peace of mind.

James showed me the present Jack had given him when I went up to say goodnight to him that evening. It was a rather smart camera, American, and more advanced than anything I had seen on sale in this country.

"Jack showed me how to use it," my son told me, glowing with pride. "It's easy. I think I'm going to make movies when I grow up, Mum. I'm going to live in America and be a famous director of motion pictures. And Lizzy will be my star."

"Where did all this come from?"

He wasn't nine yet! Already he was talking of leaving home. My heart caught with fear. I blamed Jack for putting ideas into my son's head, and in that moment I almost hated him. Why had he come back into our lives?

"It's not easy to do something like that, darling. Besides, you might not like it when the time comes."

James was looking at me oddly. "You love going to the pictures, Mum. You always buy the latest magazines, and you tell me about the film stars you like all the time. Why shouldn't I be interested, too? Don't worry; when I'm as rich as Jack, I'll have a big house with a swimming-pool and you can come and live with me and Lizzy. You won't have to work all the time. I'll look after you and Lizzy."

"Thank you, James. That's very kind of you."

"Don't laugh at me!" James said, giving me one of his scowls. "I'm really going to do it. I told Jack. He didn't laugh. He promised to help me get started when I'm ready."

His statement took away any desire I might have had to laugh. Was Jack deliberately trying to set my son against me by filling his head with dreams? All this talk of big houses and swimming-pools could only have come from one source, even though James's love of the cinema might be partly my influence. If James went to live and work in America when he was older, it would be sweet revenge for the lover I had spurned.

"I'm not laughing," I said. "If you really want to be a film director, then perhaps you will."

"Jack says I can do anything if I try hard enough. He says all it takes is guts, determination and hard work."

"I'm sure he's right . . . but you don't have to think too hard about it just yet."

"Will you buy me a book about photo – ography for Christmas?"

I smiled inwardly as James stumbled over the long word. He was so serious, so grown up for his age, but he was still only a child. I had no need to worry that he would be leaving home just yet.

"I'll buy you a book long before that," I promised. "Photography is an exciting hobby. It is something you will always be able to enjoy, whatever you do when you're older. You can take lots of pictures when we go on our holiday."

James nodded, looking pleased by the idea. I was smiling

as I kissed my son goodnight and left him to play with his new toy. He would probably grow tired of it as he did with most things he was given. This idea of going to live and work in America was quite likely to be forgotten very soon – but I would speak to Jack when he next came to take my son on an outing.

I would very politely request him not to fill James's head with foolish dreams.

"Why is it such an impossible idea?" Jack frowned at me as we faced each other across the sitting room a week later. "I know it sounds a rather grand scheme for a child of eight to come up with – but if he has that kind of imagination at his age, who knows what he might achieve? After all, his mother isn't exactly an ordinary woman. Is she, Emma? If you can become rich and successful in a matter of a few years, why can't James do the same?"

"I had a lot of help from friends." The colour burned my cheeks as I remembered that a large slice of that help had come from him, through the investments he had made on my behalf.

"So? What's wrong with that when it comes to your son?" Jack's brows rose. "I told you once – when James is older, I shall help him do whatever it is he needs to do."

"That was different . . . things were different then."

I bit my lip, feeling helpless. Jack was such a powerful force. I had always found him difficult to resist. Why should my son be any different?

"How were they different?" Jack gave me a hard stare. "My feelings towards James haven't changed."

"Don't try to take him away from me, Jack. I would hate you if you did that." I glared at him angrily. "I gave permission for you to see him. I didn't expect you to—" I stopped, unable to continue as I realised how I must sound: like a jealous, panic-stricken woman.

"I can't stop James loving me. The bond between us was formed that summer we all went to the Cottage, Emma. He's my son in all but name and blood. We can none of us change

45

that. James knows what he wants . . . he's like his mother in that way, if not in others."

"What do you mean?"

Something in Jack's tone seemed to imply a lack in me. I felt hurt as I waited for his reply, but before he could speak the door opened and Jon came in. He halted, looking surprised.

"Forgive me, Emma. I didn't realise you had a visitor." He was staring at Jack, as if searching for an elusive memory. "Excuse me . . . surely we've met before?"

"Yes." Jack walked towards him, sure, smiling, confident as always. "I was General Harvey then, known to my friends as Jack. We met soon after the invasion of Europe. I came down to the hospital to talk to some of the men there."

"Yes, of course!" Jon shook his hand warmly. It was obvious his recollection of their meeting was a good one. "I didn't realise you knew Emma – or did you come to see me?"

"I was in business with Sol during the war," Jack replied easily. "We still have some interests in common. However, I've actually called to take James out for the day. He and I became good friends during the war. I was just about to leave." He looked at me, eyebrows raised. "That's if the boy is ready?"

"I'm sure he is," I said, my heart racing.

This was awful! I had dreaded the moment when the two men met. They had done so already, of course, as Jack had explained, but that had not been in my presence. Would Jon sense anything between Jack and I? Would he guess that we had been lovers? I prayed he would not, for his sake as much as my own.

I looked at Jack. "If you ask Mrs Rowan, she will take you up to James. I think he has something he wants to show you before you leave."

Jack nodded. His manner was polite, friendly, but if he was feeling any sort of emotion it didn't show. "It was nice speaking to you, Mr Reece – and you, Emma. Excuse me now, I mustn't keep James waiting."

Jon looked at me as he went out into the hall. He seemed slightly puzzled, though not suspicious.

"I had no idea you knew anyone like that, Emma."

"He wasn't a general when we first met," I replied, keeping my voice level. "He and Jane Melcher are great friends. She gave parties for the children. One was in the summer and we held races. James and Jack won the three-legged race together. I suppose something like that stays in a child's mind. James . . . sort of adopted him as an uncle."

Jon accepted my excuse at once. "Yes, I can see how that might happen. He needed a father, Emma – and I wasn't here. It's not surprising that he doesn't see me in that light, even though he gives me the title of Father. He surely doesn't remember me from before the war, and we have hardly had time to get to know each other as yet."

"It wasn't your fault you weren't here, Jon. You never wanted the war in the first place."

"No, I didn't," Jon said. His eyes held a thoughtful expression. "The war is to blame for a lot of pain and hurt, Emma – but it is over now. We need to look to the future. This holiday you were talking about . . ."

"Yes?" I was surprised he should mention it. I had thought he wasn't too keen on the prospect.

"You should go ahead and book a house, Emma. It will be an ideal chance for us all to relax as a family. That's what we need, darling. It will help to break down James's resistance to me, help us all to get to know each other."

"Yes. I did think it might help, with Mum and perhaps Bert there too."

Jon smiled at me. "We all of us have to live with what we have, Emma. The past is over now. We have to try and find a life together – a way of living that suits us all."

I went to him then, reaching up to kiss him on the lips. This was the man I loved so much, the caring, decent, thoughtful man that still lived on despite all that he had endured.

"That's what I want, Jon."

"Yes, I know." He touched my face. "I love you, darling. I want us all to be happy. If that's possible." A wry look crept into his eyes. "Perhaps that's asking too much. Peace and contentment might be more achievable."

"We can be happy, Jon. I know we can."

I heard the sound of my son's eager voice in the hall, and the deeper tones of Jack answering.

"At least James is happy today," my husband said. "It was good of Mr Harvey to take the trouble to visit him. Not many men of his status would bother about a young boy."

"Jack is fond of him. He wouldn't harm him . . . he's not one of those odd men who interfere with children."

Jon laughed, seeming amused. "Good grief, no! I didn't think that for a moment, Emma. No, that was the last thing on my mind."

Something in Jon's eyes made me catch my breath. Was it possible that he was beginning to suspect the truth? Or was it just the knowledge of my guilt that made me think so?

"Were you going to tell me something when you came in just now?" I asked, anxious to pass over the awkward moment.

"Yes! It slipped my mind for the moment," Jon said and laughed. "I've had news . . . about my play."

"Have the BBC taken it?" I sensed his excitement. He had subdued it when he discovered Jack here, but now it was in his eyes. "They have, haven't they?"

"It was just a short piece," Jon said. "It's a trial for a series, Emma. They've paid me an advance of fifty pounds."

"Fifty pounds!" I was surprised. It seemed a lot of money for one short script. "They must have been impressed, Jon."

He looked oddly shy, almost embarrassed. "Well, yes, I think they were. If it goes down all right, they will want me to produce twelve scripts for the first series."

"That sounds like a lot of work." I looked at him anxiously. "The doctor said you shouldn't do too much, Jon."

"I'm not an invalid," Jon said, a hint of annoyance in his voice. "I know what I'm capable of – and what I'm not."

I heard the bitterness and it shocked me. I had known that Jon deeply felt his inability to make love to me, but until now he had hidden his anguish from me. Now it was there, raw and ugly.

"I wasn't nagging you, Jon."

"No, of course you weren't." He smiled apologetically. "Forgive me, Emma. I suppose it's nerves. I was anxious that they wouldn't like my play, now I'm anxious in case they don't want to go on with the series. It's foolish, I know, but it means quite a lot to me. I want to feel that I'm doing something worthwhile."

"Yes, I understand that. I shan't interfere with your work, Jon – but you won't tire yourself too much, will you?"

"No, I shan't," he promised. "I've already done a lot of the background stuff. I just need to polish it up a little. I can work during the night when we're on holiday. I seldom sleep much anyway. That's when I wrote while I was in hospital . . . at night, when I couldn't sleep. It's a habit, I suppose."

"So that's where you go! I had wondered." I nodded as he smiled slightly ruefully. I had woken more than once since that first occasion to find the bed cold and empty beside me. "Well, if it's what you want, of course you must do it, my darling."

Jon's news left me with mixed feelings. He had been paid a considerable sum of money for his play, and I was pleased at his success, but the doctor's warning echoed in my mind. A warning given me only weeks before he left hospital.

"Your husband is unlikely to live to middle age, Mrs Reece. He seems better for the moment, but his condition could suddenly take a turn for the worse. He shouldn't try to do too much."

How could I forbid Jon the chance to make a success of his life? If I forced him to become an invalid, he would resent me. It would have been easier and kinder to have left him in the hospital if I was going to make his life intolerable.

Jon had always been understanding of my own need to work. I could not be less understanding of his.

That evening, James told me he wouldn't be seeing his "friend" for a while.

"Jack has to go to Paris tomorrow," he said, giving me an

oddly unchildlike look. "Angie is buying clothes. He left her there while he came over. Now he has to fetch her. They are going to stay at the Cottage."

I felt as if an iron hand had taken hold of my heart. Jack was taking his wife to the lovely old house we had stayed at together during the war. We'd had such a wonderful time there! It hurt me that he could think of taking *her* there. I had treasured the memories of that time, but now they would be spoiled.

"Well, that will be nice for them."

"Why didn't you marry him, Mum?"

James was staring at me intently. How much those eyes seemed to say! I had always known he blamed me for sending Jack away, but now he seemed to have a new understanding.

I took a deep breath. "When I thought I might marry Jack, I believed Jon was dead," I said. "Please try to see it my way, darling. I didn't want to hurt you or Jack. I was still married. My husband – your father – was badly injured. I couldn't walk away from that. I couldn't leave Jon. It would have been cruel."

I spoke of Jon as my son's father, because in law he was. Jon had given James his own name to protect him, and deserved the title if only for that.

James nodded and looked thoughtful. "That's what Jack told me. He said you had done the right thing, that it was sometimes very hard to do what was right – and that only very brave people ever manage to do it. He said I should respect you for what you did, Mum."

"Did he?" My throat felt tight and I was close to tears. "He was angry with me at the time."

"He was at first, but isn't now." James frowned. "He said he was unfair to you – that he was the selfish one, to have demanded too much of you."

"Oh." I felt confused and hardly knew what to say. "Well, I suppose he doesn't mind so much now that he's married. You do know he is married, don't you? You spoke of Angie . . . she must be his wife."

"I saw her picture," James said. "She was sitting by a swimming-pool at Jack's home in Newport. That's in Rhode Island. Jack works and lives in New York but his wife will stay there most of the time. She's pretty, Mum. Her hair is blonde and she's only nineteen. Jack says she's too young for him, but he couldn't resist her because she loves him."

Had Jack deliberately fed my son this information to hurt me? He seemed to be telling the boy rather a lot. Too much for my comfort!

"Why did he tell you that?"

"Because I asked. Jack says I should always ask him whatever I want to know. He says I'm old enough to understand about life and he will always tell me the truth."

"I see." I smiled at him, resisting the urge to ruffle his hair. It was a little long and beginning to curl at the nape of his neck. "You are very fond of Jack, aren't you?"

His eyes were wide and serious. "I love him. I can't stop loving him because you did, Mum." He spoke the words without the embarrassment he would have shown had I asked him to express his love for me. It was another proof of the hold Jack had over him.

"No, of course not." I felt a lump in my throat. If only he knew the truth, but I could never tell him. "I'm glad you love Jack. I just hope you won't be too upset when he goes away again."

"Oh, no; I'm older now," James said. I could see the new maturity in his eyes. At eight years old, my son was thinking almost like an adult. When had that happened? Was it all due to Jack? "Besides, he isn't going away for long. He and Angie are going to live in London. Jack has bought a big house and . . ."

The rest of James's chatter was lost on me. I had expected that Jack's visit would be of short duration, but he and his wife were going to live here. That meant he would continue to visit James. I would be bound to see him from time to time.

I was not sure whether that made me happy or miserable.

Four

That night, Jon tried unsuccessfully to make love to me. I went eagerly to him. I wanted it to happen so much. Jon needed to feel he was a complete man again – and I wanted to forget my own needs in his arms. I ached for the release of physical love, and when Jon turned away in frustration I could have wept. For myself as well as for him.

I lay awake for hours. Neither of us spoke, and I sensed the hurt Jon was feeling. I wasn't surprised when he left our bed. I was restless too, but could not seek relief in work. My accounts were done, and I needed to sleep to be fresh for the morning.

The lonely nights seemed to stretch ahead of me down the years. I had believed I could accept Jon's condition and be grateful for all I had, but it was harder than I'd imagined. Jon's frustration was a part of it. At first, he had seemed content to be with me, to touch me and kiss me, just to be able to talk and live life normally as husband and wife, but he was beginning to resent the fact that we could not have sexual relations.

I'd never really thought about the act of sexual intercourse in isolation before. To me it had always been the natural end to the pleasure of foreplay, the kissing and touching as important as the sex itself. Now I began to realise that all the rest meant very little to Jon if he could not participate in the act of intercourse.

Was it the same for most men? I supposed it must be, though I suspected that most women would feel as I did. Jon had always been a considerate lover – though never as inventive or as playful as Jack. I had never reached a true climax in Jon's arms, though I had known content at the start of our marriage.

That was before I had discovered what true fulfilment could be, before I had found myself in Jack's arms. Perhaps I would still have felt empty if Jon had been able to make love to me as he wanted. The thought shocked and chilled me. What had I done?

Jack had tried to warn me. He had told me bluntly that my marriage could never be more than an empty sham, and he was right. I had sent him away, and for what? The comfortable, happy marriage I'd shared with Jon before he was wounded seemed out of reach.

I had been so determined to bring Jon home, but what good had come from my giving up my own needs if all I had done was to cause my husband to leave our bed in frustration?

Jack had accused me of being cruel and selfish. He'd insisted it would be kinder to let Jon go, not give him hopes of a normal life, but I had not listened. I had thought *him* cruel, but now I began to see that perhaps I had been, if not cruel, then at least thoughtless to force Jon to come back to the real world – a world in which I knew now he could never be truly at home.

Tears stung my eyes but I would not let them fall. I refused to give way to self-pity. I had made my choice. I would stick by it no matter what.

Yet it would be much harder, knowing Jack was living in London. I dreaded the day when I saw his wife for the first time. Angie was only nineteen, and beautiful. The thought of Jack making love to her was almost unbearable.

Jon brought me yellow roses the next day. He offered them with a rueful smile and apologised.

"Forgive me for what happened last night. I'm not going to put you through that again, Emma. I've been thinking about the problem, and I'm going to get a fresh opinion – from a specialist. Until this is sorted out, I'm going to move into the spare room. I've bought a desk and a portable typewriter. I can work in my room without disturbing you or anyone else during the day – and at night I won't use the typewriter."

"Oh, Jon." I looked at him sadly, my heart aching. This wasn't what I wanted. "Please don't."

"It's for the best," he said. "Just until I get this problem sorted out."

He seemed confident, cheerful, as though coming to a decision had eased his frustration. What could I say? Jon had made up his own mind. I could not force him to sleep in my bed.

"If it's what you want . . ."

"I love you, Emma," he said and kissed my cheek. "I always shall love you – please believe that – but I can't lie beside you and know that I'm unable to give you what you need. I have to see a doctor I've been told about. He will help me overcome the problem in time. Then we can be together again."

What if there is no cure? The question was in my mind, but I did not speak it. I could see there was no alternative. Jon was full of hope. I did not want to destroy that.

The thought of lying alone every night was distressing, but I knew it was the price I must pay.

"I'm going upstairs to work," Jon said. "I'm sure you have lots to do, Emma – especially if we're going away next month. You'll want to make sure everything is going as it should with the shops."

"Yes, I need to check stock levels," I said. "I must get ahead with reordering before we go." My heart was aching. At that moment I had no interest whatsoever in how many dresses had been sold this past week, but I knew the grief would pass. "And I have to buy a book for James."

I found what I needed in the book department of Philip Matthews' store, which was situated just off Oxford Street. There were three rather interesting volumes I thought might be useful. One was almost all pictures, with brief footnotes about lighting and focus. Another was very technical and far too complicated for James to understand by himself, but we could talk about it together – and the third was actually written for children. I bought them all, and a Rupert annual for Lizzy. I was about to leave when I heard a voice I recognised and turned.

"Emma!" Philip Matthews cried, looking at me in delight. "What are you doing here?"

"Buying some books for my son. He has taken up photography. He says he's going to be a film director when he grows up."

"That's a very grown-up statement." Philip smiled. His hair was sleekly oiled and I could smell a light, refreshing perfume. "How old is he, Emma? Seven or so?"

"He's eight," I said. "And a few months. He has seemed to grow up fast lately."

"My sister tells me they do when they go to school. Of course, I'm not married." He hesitated, looking at me uncertainly but with a hint of eagerness. "I'm having a party next month to celebrate my fortieth birthday. I wondered if you and your husband would like to come?"

"That would have been nice, but we're going away to the sea. My mother, Jon . . . all of us." I glanced at my watch. "I have to go now. I have an appointment. A new firm of costume makers has asked to show me their range of Scottish plaid. I thought I might try a few this winter – if they are stylish and well made."

"You work too hard, Emma. A woman like you shouldn't need to work." His eyes seemed to convey so much more than his words.

"I enjoy my work." I laughed at him, teasing him a little. "You're so old-fashioned, Philip. I don't want to stay at home and be given things, I want to earn lots of money for myself. I like using my wits – and getting a good bargain from the salesmen!"

Philip's eyes gleamed in appreciation. "How would you like to run my dress department?" he asked suddenly. "My present buyer is leaving. I've been wondering whether to look for a new one or put the business out to an independent source. We might even be partners. I'd want good quality merchandise. Your own showrooms could provide about half of the day dresses, as you do now – but I'd like some French lines. Since Dior brought out the New Look, that's all the customers want – something with a French influence. You could pop over to Paris yourself. Buy whatever you think we could sell."

I stared at him, surprised by the offer. It was along the lines of something I'd been thinking of for a while. I'd even discussed the idea with the owner of another store, though a slightly smaller, less prestigious shop than this one. With all the passing trade of Oxford Street, this was a huge opportunity for me.

"Are you serious?"

"Yes, of course. When it comes to business, I never say what I don't mean, Emma."

His suggestion had set my mind racing with possibilities. "Let me give the idea some thought. We'll talk about it again when I come back from my holiday, Philip."

"I'll take you to dinner one evening."

"Make it lunch," I said. "I'll telephone you when I'm ready."

"I shall look forward to it, Emma."

"Yes, so shall I, Philip. I feel quite excited."

His eyes lit up with pleasure. I was thoughtful as I left the store. This might be just what I needed. Something new and challenging to help take me out of myself. A trip to Paris would be thrilling. I would enjoy buying the kind of stock Philip was talking about – not *haute couture*, of course, but well-made, top-quality clothes for those who had a little more money to spend than the average woman.

Yes, it would be something to look forward to. I knew, of course, that Philip was hoping that the relationship between us would develop into more than just business. However, I believed I could handle any offers of an intimate nature he might make. I liked Philip, and I believed our partnership could work – providing the contract was all sorted out properly first. There was no possibility of anything else. I respected Philip as a businessman, but I wasn't interested in having an affair with him.

Despite the difficult situation between Jon and myself, I

had no intention of sleeping with anyone else. And if I were ever tempted, it would not be Philip Matthews who would make me change my mind. There was only one man I wanted, and he was beyond my reach. If I could not have Jack, I did not want a substitute. I would prefer to sleep alone, as I had for several years now.

However, the business venture with Philip did interest me. I would consider the idea carefully while I was on holiday with my family.

I had found us a suitable house for the holiday in Mousehole. Set halfway up the steep cliff path, it was large enough to accommodate us all. We had come down in two cars, Sol driving my mother, Sarah and Bert, while I'd brought Jon and the children. Pam had chosen to stay at home.

"I'll see to things here, Emma. My sister wants me to visit her, so I'll go down for a couple of weeks when you get back."

"You could do that and still come with us. Are you sure you don't want to?"

"Not this time."

I was not able to persuade her, so I gave in. Besides, she would be company for Sol when he returned after spending the weekend with us.

"I'm not much of a one for the seaside and holidays," he'd told me when I'd asked him to come with us. "I'll drive down for the weekend, and I'll return to pick up your mother and Bert when they're ready – but don't expect me to stay and build sandcastles."

"Surely you can't say you don't like this?" I asked as we stood in the gardens overlooking the bay that Sunday morning. "Look at that view, Sol! Isn't it magnificent?"

"Too rural for my liking." He pulled a face. "I'm a town lover, Emma. Give me more than two days of this fresh air and I get homesick for the smoke of London."

I laughed but I knew what he meant. I was looking forward to the holiday with the children, but I would never want to live so far away from the bustling city that had become my home.

"You must admit it's a lovely old place, though," I said. "This village is steeped in history, Sol. The Phoenician tin merchants first came here two thousand five hundred years ago."

"Been reading the guide books, Emma?" His eyes gleamed with amusement.

I answered in the same light, bantering tone. "Yes, of course. You know what James is. He will want to know everything there is to know about Cornwall, the tin mines, smuggling, anything! He asked me what Stargazy Pie was this morning, and when he could try it."

"Did you know the answer?" Sol laughed as I nodded. "Of course you did! You shouldn't be surprised that James has a thirst for knowledge, or a bold imagination. You only have to look in the mirror to know the reason why."

"I suppose I've always thought the best way to get on was to find out as much as I could."

"You're ambitious, Emma. I knew that from the first day you came to my showroom, and admired it in you. As I admire you for all your other qualities."

There was something in Sol's eyes at that moment, something that made me lower my gaze and feel oddly uncomfortable. We had always been friends, and I knew he cared for me, but just for an instant I had sensed more – a much stronger, deeper emotion.

"Well, anyway, I'm going to have my work cut out keeping up with James and Lizzy. They are both adventurous, both strong-willed."

Sol nodded but didn't say any more. My mother called just then from the house to say that she'd made a pot of tea and our tête-à-tête was at an end.

Sol left early the next morning. I missed him, of course, but there wasn't enough time in the days that followed to think about that look in his eyes or wonder what it meant. Nor did I wish to. I preferred to keep everything as it always had been.

For the next three weeks I hardly ever seemed to sit still. James and Lizzy wanted to explore everywhere. Sarah and

I were forever taking them somewhere different, though my mother and Bert often preferred to sit in the garden and look at the view on warm afternoons. It was a restful, peaceful time for them, and they had the pleasure of the children's company for at least a part of every day.

Despite the hectic nature of my outings with the children, I also enjoyed a few quiet moments sitting in the garden with my mother, talking to her about experiences and hopes we had shared.

"Do you remember when you found those gold coins, Emma? Your father's secret hoard . . . after all that searching, there they were in the most obvious place. If we'd known that sooner, we could have taken them and run away, and you wouldn't have had to marry Dick Gillows."

"It would only have made Father angry," I said. "And they came to me in the end. I hardly ever think of any of that now, Mum. It's all so far away; it seems like a dream – as if the girl who was forced to marry Dick Gillows was someone else. This is another kind of life."

"Yes, you've done well for yourself," my mother said. "And what's more, you've done it all your own way."

"Well, I had help, and those coins started me off," I said, "but I have worked hard."

"And now you've reaped the rewards." She looked about her. "Who would have thought you would ever be able to afford to take a lovely, big house like this for three weeks, Emma? Much nicer than staying in a boarding house or a hotel, and someone paid to come in and clean for us, too! I've never had a holiday like this before – and it's all due to my clever daughter."

"You deserve it, Mum. I'm just glad you and Bert came with us on the holiday."

This was a very different holiday to the one the children and I had spent in Southend with Sheila. There we had spent a lot of time shopping and visiting the pleasure beach; here we spent a part of every day walking and visiting various beauty spots. The Cornish countryside had a wildness, a raw exciting atmosphere that appealed to my son.

James wanted to take a thousand pictures. He never left the house without the camera Jack had given him. A part of the present had been what seemed a never-ending supply of films, but as the days passed I realised I would soon have to buy more. Far from becoming tired of his plaything, James's enthusiasm grew ever stronger.

"This is wonderful, Mum," he told me, his eyes glowing with excitement. "The best holiday ever – except for that summer with Jack. And this camera is the best present I've ever had."

My heart twisted with regret. I had not thought when I sent Jack away how much my son would miss because of my actions. Nothing I could do would ever quite make up for the loss of his "Daddy". I had given James everything I could, but there were some things I had not been able to provide. My son wanted a father and the father he had chosen was Jack Harvey.

At least he was enjoying this holiday. He was always taking pictures of Lizzy. Wherever we went, Lizzy was required to pose in front of sweeping scenes of cliffs, sea and sky, or quaint cottages and abandoned fishing boats. She did so with infinite patience, seeming to find no fault in obeying her hero's latest whim.

"Why not take a picture of Grandma and Uncle Bert?" I suggested one afternoon after poor Lizzy had been made to stand for ages as James tried to get the precise angle he wanted. He was an exacting taskmaster! "Let Lizzy have a rest, darling."

"She isn't tired," James said carelessly. "She likes having her picture taken – don't you, Lizzy?"

"Sometimes," she said. "Let's do something else now. Can we go down to the village and buy ice creams, Emmie?"

"Yes, of course. Be careful, though; keep away from the edge of the cliff. James, make sure you take care of her."

"I always take care of Lizzy," he said. "She's going to be my star when I'm a famous director."

"Yes, darling. You told me so." I smiled as I watched them go off together. James had his beloved camera in a leather case, the long strap slung over his shoulder. "Don't be too long."

It was growing late in the afternoon and the children had not yet returned. I was beginning to feel anxious. The cliff path was steep in places and could be dangerous to a young child.

"I should never have let them go alone," I said to Sarah. "It's almost six o'clock. It was just after four when they went to get those ice creams – that's two hours."

"Perhaps I should go and look for them?" Sarah was anxious, too. "James is sensible, but Lizzy can sometimes be reckless."

"You go to the village," I said. Personally, I was not sure that Lizzy was the reckless one. "I'm going to try that cove James likes so much – the one that is hidden away from the port, with all the rocks and trees on the cliffside. He was talking about going back there again before we leave."

"Should I say anything to Mr and Mrs Fitch?"

"No – not yet. I'll just tell them I'm going for a walk. We don't want them to worry for nothing."

I was worried myself. I had not thought anything very terrible could happen in this tranquil place. Besides, James was so independent. I knew he hated being watched over all the time, and it was only a short distance down the hill to the café where the children usually bought their ice creams. The cliffs were sheer in some places, but they had been warned not to go near the edge in those areas. Nevertheless, I should have gone with them.

Had something bad happened? Supposing one of them had fallen? James would never leave Lizzy if she was frightened or hurt. Had Lizzy the sense to come home for us if it was James who had fallen?

What if they were both hurt? Why hadn't I taken them to get their ice creams myself?

The beauty of the softly wooded slope leading down to the secluded cove was lost on me as I made my way to the beach. The air was scented, warm and gentle on my skin as the sky changed colour, the sun sinking into the horizon. I was blind to the peace and tranquillity of the scene, however, my pulse racing as I scrambled down the steep incline. All I could think of was that the children might be in danger, might even be dead – and then, when I was close to desperation, I saw them.

Lizzy was sitting on a rock at the edge of the water, a gorgeous sunset behind her turning the sea to orange and black. She was naked, her clothes a little further up the beach. James was taking yet another photograph!

As I watched, Lizzy stretched out on the rock, arching her body like a little sea siren at the behest of her director. My instinct was to shout at them, but I controlled it. There was nothing evil about what they were doing. I was quite sure that James was thinking only of the art of the pictures he was taking and did not realise what he had done by persuading Lizzy to pose like this.

"James," I said as I went up to him. "What on earth do you think you are doing? Lizzy will catch a chill – and that rock could be dangerous. If she slipped she might hurt herself."

James looked round at me, and I caught a flash of guilt in his eyes.

"She's all right, Mum. It's not cold."

"You shouldn't have asked Lizzy to take her clothes off, James. It isn't right."

"Why? There are lots of naked girls in that book you bought me."

He was right, of course. It hadn't occurred to me that James would want to copy the poses he saw in his book – but I should have known my son.

"Yes, I know." I hesitated, not wanting to make too much of the incident. "But they are much older than Lizzy. She might feel upset or embarrassed about the pictures one day. I think you should throw the film away, and I don't think you should ask Lizzy to do something like that again. Not until she is grown up and understands what she's doing. It's not fair to her, James. Photography is your hobby. Lizzy always wants to please you, but she might be cross about it one day."

I called Lizzy. She came at once, pulling her clothes on

hastily. I knew she was anxious, afraid that I was going to punish her or James, and ready to accept the blame to save him.

"I didn't mean to be naughty, Emmie."

"It wasn't naughty, Lizzy. I would just rather you didn't do it again – not until you're grown up and understand what it means."

"I told James it was rude," she said. "But he said it was art. And that I would be famous one day."

"Some people would think it was rude," I agreed. "Others would agree with James. I don't think it's rude, just not right for you, darling. When you're older you will understand."

"Are you cross?"

"No, I'm not cross, but Sarah and Grandma might not understand. They might think it was naughty, so we'll keep it a secret between us three, shall we?"

Lizzy nodded. She had obviously been reluctant to pose naked, but had given into James, as she usually did eventually. His own expression was a mixture of guilt and annoyance that he had been caught. I now suspected he was well aware that he should not have asked Lizzy to take her things off, and he was also disappointed that he hadn't managed to get the pictures he wanted.

For the first time, I began to believe that James really would achieve his ambition one day. There was a certain ruthlessness in him that could have come from Paul Greenslade – but then, hadn't I taught him that when you wanted something you went after it?

I wished I could share my secret with someone. James's behaviour had shocked me at first, but only for a moment. Afterwards, I was secretly amused. I had told James he must destroy the film, and he had given it to me the next morning.

"There's nothing on it, Mum," he said. "I've let the light in so the pictures won't come out."

"Thank you, darling."

I threw the film away, relieved that the pictures of Lizzy

on that rock would never be seen. My mother would not have been amused by the incident, nor would Sarah. I might have told Jon if we had ever been alone together, but we never were these days.

Jon had spent some time playing cricket with James and Lizzy on the lawn. He was unable to drive the car because of his hand, which although better than it had been did not allow him to use the gears, but he accompanied us to various beauty spots, and seemed to be enjoying the outings. However, at other times he went for long walks on his own. Often he was gone for hours.

"It's beautiful here," he said to me when we were eating warm scones, clotted cream and strawberry jam at a pleasant little restaurant. It was a fine afternoon and the last we would have to relax in before packing up to go home. "I've had lots of ideas down here, Emma. I think you were right about buying a holiday home. I might come down again after we go back . . . use the trains and local buses to get about. See if I can find somewhere suitable."

"You haven't seen anything yet?"

"No – have you?"

I shook my head. We had been away for almost three weeks. I was ready to go home; the last thing on my mind was buying a house, even though I had suggested it.

"Poor Emma," Jon said and smiled at me in his gentle way. "You're not really happy here, are you?"

The children were playing on some nearby swings. I looked at Jon, struck by something in his tone.

"Why do you say that? I've enjoyed our holiday."

"Yes, but it wouldn't suit you to live in the country or by the sea," he said. "Even somewhere as beautiful as this would bore you before long."

"I like coming to the sea for holidays." I was defensive, nervous, unsure of what he meant.

"Do you ever think of that estate – the cottage – where we spent our honeymoon? I should like to go back this September. Scotland is beautiful in September."

"Yes, I remember you telling me." I frowned. "I'm not

sure I can manage September, Jon. We're always busy then with the autumn stock coming in."

"You don't need to come, Emma. I was thinking about the house. It's probably best for me to buy something that suits me. You won't be there that much, but I think I shall. I've found my writing comes much easier down here. If I'm somewhere not too far from a mainline station, I can come and go as I please – and you can visit at weekends."

He was talking about us living separate lives. I felt a chill at the nape of my neck. Was this the way it would be in the future?

"Why, Jon? I thought you wanted us to be together?"

"I do, Emma. Of course I do – most of the time. But I also need somewhere I can come to be alone. I'm sorry. I know this sounds selfish, but I can't live with you all the time, my darling. I love you, and I'm grateful for the way you've stood by me, but I have to do what's right – for us both."

"I want to be with you."

"And you will, sometimes," Jon said, his eyes intent on my face. "I know you love me. But you don't need me, Emma. You have the children and your friends – and your work, of course. I'm only a small part of all that. Don't force me to live *your* life, my darling. Let me go. Please? Let me go and come back to you when I can."

My heart felt as if it were being torn apart.

"I do need you, Jon. The children need you."

"You know that's not true. I'm just a guest in your house as far as they are concerned. It was too long, Emma. For years I was just a vague memory for James. Other people took my place in his affections. I understand that. It's no one's fault." Something flickered in his eyes. "It might have been better if I had never come back."

"Please don't say that," I begged, my throat threatening to close up. "We were going to be a family again."

"We still can be," Jon said, reaching out to stroke my cheek. "Don't look so hurt, Emma. I'm not abandoning you. I'm just asking you to understand that I need my own place. I need to take things at my own speed." He smiled to ease my pain. "You and James have so much energy. I can't keep up with you. Forgive me, please?"

"There's nothing to forgive."

"I'm not saying I want us to separate." He ran his thumb over my mouth. "It won't be so very different from the way it has been, darling. We'll still see each other often, just as we did when I was in hospital."

"Yes, of course. You must do whatever you want, Jon."

I was close to weeping, but I held back the tears and the protests. I had to let go if that was what he needed, but it was a painful end to our holiday. Much of what Jon said was true. I had the children, my friends and my work – but that still left a gaping hole at the centre of my life.

At that moment I had no idea how I was going to fill the emptiness inside me.

Five

"I'm not sure this partnership idea is such a good thing," Sol said that morning. I'd been back from Cornwall for two weeks and I was meeting Philip Matthews for lunch at the Savoy that day. "I should think long and hard about this if I were you, Emma."

"Why?" I stared at him in surprise. "I thought you approved of Philip?"

"He's a good customer," Sol admitted. "But I'm not sure about him as a man, Emma. I can't tell you why – there's nothing obviously wrong – but just be careful."

"Yes, of course. I shall ask you to look through the contract before I sign."

"It's not just business." He shook his head as I raised my brows. "Perhaps I'm speaking out of turn . . . but does Jon know about this?"

"I mentioned the possibility," I replied, not quite meeting his eyes. "Jon wasn't interested. He says what I do with my business is my own concern."

Sol looked anxious as he picked something up from my tone.

"You haven't quarrelled with him, Emma?"

"No, we haven't quarrelled." I sighed wearily. "Jon just wants to find his own way. We're not exactly separating, but Jon won't be here often in the future. Not once he finds a suitable house. He'll come to town now and then, and I'll visit the house—" My throat caught on a sob. "But that's about it."

"I'm so sorry, my dear." Sol seemed disturbed. "I had suspected things weren't right between the two of you,

67

but I thought you might be able to work them out in time."

"This isn't my idea – and it has nothing to do with Philip. I'm not interested in him other than as a business associate."

"Well, you know best, Emma. I wouldn't dream of interfering – but be careful of Philip. I'm not sure I trust him."

"I promise I shall be careful," I said and smiled at him. "I trust *you* Sol. Completely. If I have any reason to suspect he's not being fair to me, I'll come straight to you. I give you my word."

Sol nodded and the subject was dropped.

As I went upstairs to change for my lunch appointment, I wondered why my friend of so many years was against my taking up Philip Matthews' offer. Recalling that unguarded moment in Cornwall, when I had glimpsed something in his eyes, I suspected jealousy. Could Sol be jealous because he thought I might turn to Philip in my disappointment at Jon's rejection of our marriage?

That would imply that Sol's feelings were much stronger than the friendship I had believed he felt for me. Was that possible? He had loved Margaret so much. While she lived, Sol had treated me almost like a daughter – but had his feelings for me changed?

I was not sure how I would feel if that were the case. I loved Sol as a friend, but that was all. There was still only one man I wanted to make love with, and that was Jack Harvey.

I had been willing to live as Jon's wife in every way, but that was not possible. The physical relationship Jon needed would never happen – we both knew that in our hearts – and now that Jon had decided to find a home of his own, we would probably drift further and further apart. I found that thought very depressing.

Perhaps if my marriage had been happier, I would not have bothered to keep that appointment with Philip – but in any case, it might make little difference. There were times when I felt overwhelmingly lonely, moments when I had no interest in whether my shops were successful or not. Yet somewhere inside me a strong ambition still burned.

Philip's offer had set me a challenge, and it was in a spirit of adventure that I went to meet him that day.

"I've always admired you," Philip said as the waiter hovered. "Would you like some more wine, Emma? Or a brandy, perhaps?"

"Thank you, no," I said. "I wouldn't mind coffee."

"We'll have it in the lounge." He nodded to the attentive waiter, who drew back my chair solicitously and handed me my bag. "A pot of coffee – and petit fours, please."

We made our way into an elegantly furnished lounge. Philip spotted a vacant table in the corner. It was partially separated from the others by a tall, fronded plant in a jardinière, and very suitable for a private conversation.

"So we're in broad agreement about the contract," Philip said as we settled ourselves down. "I'll have my lawyers draw it up and send it to yours. Any small differences can be ironed out by them."

"Yes, I think we can go that far," I replied. "I shall talk it over with Sol, and if he feels everything is satisfactory I see no reason why we shouldn't go ahead."

"In the meantime, how do you feel about a preliminary trip to Paris? You could make contacts, have a look round, then when we're ready to sign the contracts you can move straight into action."

"That sounds sensible," I agreed. "I'll make my own arrangements and go as soon as I can. I've already applied for my passport and travel documents."

"You don't intend to let the grass grow under your feet!"

"There's no reason why I should."

Philip looked pleased. Our coffee and a dish of fancy little sweets arrived. I poured for us both, but declined the comfits. Philip ate several. I had noticed that he was becoming a little fleshy in the face, and I wasn't surprised if he ate sweets on top of the substantial meal he had just finished.

"Did you enjoy your holiday?" Philip asked, deciding to

talk of other things now that our business was done for the moment.

"Yes, very much, thank you. Jon liked the village where we stayed. He is very fond of Cornwall, and is going down again soon to look for a house for us, though not necessarily in the area in which we stayed."

He looked startled, displeased. "I hope you aren't thinking of moving away?"

"Oh no. It will just be for holidays – though Jon may spend more time there. He needs time and peace for his writing. There is always so much going on at home."

"You intend to stay on in London – in the same house?"

"I'm settled where I am." I frowned, not quite sure of his meaning. "Why do you ask?"

"I just wondered. People sometimes speculate . . . about your relationship with Solomon Gould."

"We are friends and business partners, that's all. Three other women live in the same house, and two children."

He realised I was annoyed and shook his head. "I'm not questioning you, Emma. I know some people think the situation a little odd – since his wife died – but I'm not one of them."

Something in his manner told me that was a lie. I was irritated by the implication, but tried not to let it show.

The fact that I lived in Sol's house might seem strange to anyone who did not know our story. There had been nothing unusual in the situation when Margaret was alive, of course. Perhaps I ought to have considered moving after she died, but it had not seemed necessary – and it did not now.

"Sol is my friend," I repeated, feeling slightly annoyed. "Nothing can change that."

"No, of course not. Forgive me. I shouldn't have mentioned it."

"I'm married," I said, pressing the point. "Even though Jon may not always be around, I'm still his wife."

"Yes, of course. I wasn't suggesting there was anything wrong. Good grief, Sol must be more than twenty years your senior!"

"Yes." I changed the subject, speaking of the trip to Paris and asking what percentage of stock he felt should come from the French suppliers we were intending to do business with.

We talked for a few minutes longer, then I left Philip to finish his coffee and petit fours. I was thoughtful as I went outside. I had intended to catch a bus part of the way home and then walk, but it had turned chilly. Seeing a taxi passing, I hailed it, opening the door and jumping in as soon as it drew to a halt.

I was startled when a man followed me in, and turned to voice a protest – but the words died on my lips as I saw who it was.

"You won't mind if I share, Emma?"

"We may not be going in the same direction."

My heart crashed wildly against my ribs as I looked into Jack's eyes. Oh, why did he always make me feel like this? Why couldn't I be indifferent to him?

"I want to speak to Sol about something."

"Oh, I see. In that case . . ."

Jack gave the driver the address and slid the glass panel between him and us shut. I settled in my seat, glancing at him as he sat back, my heart still beating faster than normal.

"I might have been going to one of the shops."

"Were you?" I shook my head and he grinned. "That's all right, then. Don't look so annoyed, Emma. It was a spur-of-the-moment thing."

"How long have you been back in London?"

"You mean after my trip to Paris?" Jack took out his cigarette case. It was gold on silver and engraved with his initials. It looked new, and I thought it might have been a wedding present – perhaps from his wife. He offered the contents to me. His cigarettes were flat and expensive. Father had once sold them in his shop to discerning customers. I shook my head.

"Do you mind if I do? . . . And the answer is a few days."

"No, I don't mind. I smoke occasionally, but not often."

Jack lit his cigarette. His eyes were intent on my face.

71

"You were dining out with a friend? I saw you in the Savoy foyer and followed you out."

"I was having a business meeting."

"Ah yes, of course. You're a successful businesswoman these days. May one enquire what you are planning at the moment?"

"I'm not sure." I hesitated, then explained about Philip's offer. "It sounds good – almost too good to be true, perhaps. I like the idea of buying stock in Paris."

"Are you going alone or with Matthews?" Jack frowned. "Not my business, of course. But I should warn you, Emma. Mixing business and pleasure doesn't work."

"It's strictly business!" I glared at him. "And you're right – it isn't your affair."

"If I were you, I would stay clear of the whole thing," Jack advised, ignoring my outburst. "It stands to reason – Matthews wants you. He's using this to get you into his bed."

"How dare you?" I hissed. If we had been alone I might have struck him. "You may have a low opinion of me, Jack – but Philip admires and respects me."

"What kind of a man is he?" Jack looked amused. "At least I was always honest with you, Emma. I wanted you from the start – as a matter of fact I still do."

"What?" I stared at him as the breath left my body. "I thought you despised me?"

"At first I came close to hating you," Jack admitted. The expression in his eyes mocked and challenged me. "However, once I saw you again I knew I still wanted you. I'm married now, but so are you. You made me an offer once – now I'm making you one, Emma. Whatever Matthews is willing to give you, I'll treble it."

I recoiled, feeling as if he had punched me in the stomach. How could he say such a terrible thing to me?

"I'm not for sale, Jack."

"I wasn't attempting to buy you, darling – just prevent you from making a big mistake."

I was silent as the fury churned inside me. I wanted to

lash out at him, to hurt him as he had hurt me, but if I let my feelings loose at that moment there was no telling what I might do.

"You always imagine you know best," I said at last. For those few seconds, I hated him as fiercely as I loved him. "Thank you for your offer – but I think I prefer Philip's."

"That's your final word?"

I nodded, not trusting myself to speak again. Jack leaned forward and slid the glass panel back.

"Stop at this corner, driver. I shall get out. You can take the lady on – she will pay you."

He smiled at me as he got out.

"Enjoy yourself in Paris, Emma."

I wouldn't give him the satisfaction of an answer.

The stupid thing was, I had almost decided to turn Philip down until Jack made me that outrageous offer. I hadn't liked the way Philip had hinted that there was something odd about my living in Sol's house. If Jack hadn't got into my taxi, I might have changed my mind about the Paris trip, but now I was determined to go through with it.

Why should I give up this chance just because Jack disapproved? He obviously believed I was willing to have an affair with the first man who offered. Damn him! The pain rippled inside me, but anger was taking over. Why should I care what he thought?

Besides, my marriage was virtually over. If I wanted to have an affair with Philip or any other man, that was entirely my own business.

Jack Harvey could go to hell for all I cared!

I spent a restless night, unable to sleep, my mind chasing round and round as I tried to reconcile my feelings.

I was so angry with Jack, and yet I could not forget his words to me in the taxi. Had he really meant that he would like us to have an affair?

I had turned him down, but in my heart I was beginning to regret it.

*   *   *

"We need some more dresses for the six to seven-year-olds," Gwen told me over the phone the next morning. "They've sold well this summer, Emma. And those sailor suits for three-year-olds – could you get some in larger sizes?"

"Yes, I think so. I'll order them today. I'm going to Paris next week – but I'll try to come down when I get back."

"Paris? That sounds exciting!"

"You wouldn't like to come with me?"

"Me? No thank you," Gwen said and laughed. "I don't fancy crossing all that water. Besides, I'm too busy. You go and tell me all about it when you come down. I might have some news of my own for you then."

I smiled as I replaced the receiver. My mother had hinted that she thought Gwen might have a special friend.

"I'm not saying there's any funny business going on," Mum had said. "But they've been seen out together on several occasions."

I wondered if Gwen's news was about the gentleman my mother had mentioned. I rather liked the idea of my aunt having an admirer. She had devoted her life to her invalid mother until Mrs Robinson died, and was in her early fifties now – but there was no reason why she shouldn't enjoy the friendship of a man.

I was brought out of my musings by a sudden interruption.

"Emma – these have just arrived for you."

Pam came into the study carrying a bouquet of pink carnations and roses. She offered them to me. I sniffed their perfume and took the attached card, feeling curious. Who had sent them?

"Forgive me. Can we still be friends? Jack."

I stared at the card for a moment or two, then tore it in half, feeling angry. How dare he send me these?

"Return them to the florist, please."

"I didn't see the delivery van," Pam said, looking at me anxiously. "What's wrong, Emma?"

I sighed, then shrugged. "Nothing . . . not really. I suppose it doesn't matter. Just throw them away."

"That would be a pity. May I have them in my room?"

"Yes, of course, if you want them." I smiled at her. "Don't worry, Pam. I'm just cross. Jack Harvey sent them. I'm annoyed with him, that's all."

"Oh . . . Jack Harvey. I see." Pam looked relieved. "He does seem to have a habit of making you cross, doesn't he?"

Her tone made me realise how ridiculous I was being and I laughed ruefully. "Yes, he certainly does," I said. "Just take them away, Pam."

"There are some letters in the hall," she said. "I had to sign for one of them. It may be the documents you've been expecting. Shall I fetch them for you?"

"You'd better put those wretched flowers in water. I'll have a look at the post."

I went into the hall as Pam departed. My temper had cooled quickly. Jack had obviously thought better of his behaviour the previous day, and the flowers were a peace offering. I supposed I would have to forgive him. I still wanted to punish him, but in a small, secret part of my heart, I was pleased that he had admitted to still wanting me. Even as his mistress.

In a way, it was my own fault he had made me that outrageous offer. It was because of what I'd said to him when we'd quarrelled just after the invasion of France. I'd said something about our sleeping together whenever he was in London – just after I had told him I was staying in England with my husband. I hadn't thought about what I was suggesting. I had just been so desperate at the prospect of losing him that I'd spoken impulsively. It was only afterwards that I had realised the enormity of what I'd said.

Jack had accused me of using him. He had been so angry, so bitter.

"You're a selfish little bitch, Emma. You want to keep me on your string . . . prolong the agony. You don't care that you've broken my heart."

His words and the manner in which they had been spoken were still fresh in my mind, despite the years between. He had left me in anger and now it seemed he had relented. Or had his offer been meant to insult and wound me?

Surely it must have been? If he had spoken in earnest . . .

My mind reeled dizzily at the realisation of what that might mean.

No, I was chasing butterflies. Jack was married to a young and beautiful girl. He must love Angie. Why else would he have married her? Unless it was out of pique, because he hadn't been able to forget me . . .

Such vain, foolish thoughts! It was wicked of me to hope that Jack still loved me. I shut the tantalising thoughts out of my mind as I went through the pile of letters in the hall.

There were three for Sol; the other four were for me. One was from my friend Mary. I knew it would be full of gossip from the town of March and the busy life she and her family led. I put it aside for later.

Two of the letters were from manufacturers: one concerned buttons and zips, and the other was from someone who wanted to sell me some material containing nylon – still a very new fabric as far as I was concerned, though it had been invented in America in 1938. We'd seen very little of it during the war, but now more of it was beginning to become available, though the stockings made from it were still like gold dust and hard to find. I thought it very exciting and believed it would be increasingly popular as time went on.

My fourth letter was a bulky package from the solicitors Sol and I both employed in all our business ventures. I opened it, saw it was a draft contract, and took it into the sitting room to read. I had a feeling that I might need to study this very carefully.

"I'm not sure about this clause," Sol said, tapping the contract with his finger. "It appears to mean that if you cease to be Matthews' partner, you cannot work for anyone else within a radius of five miles for five years afterwards."

"Philip didn't mention that!" I frowned over the documents. "I do wish lawyers would put things more simply. I certainly wouldn't want to be tied down by a clause like that."

"I told you to watch him, Emma. I should give this some more thought if I were you."

"Yes, I shall." I looked at him thoughtfully. "I shan't cancel my trip to Paris, though. Even if I don't take up Philip's offer, I may still buy some stock for my own shops. He was right about that part: everyone is going mad over the New Look." I wrinkled my brow. "What about that dress I suggested – is it selling? The one with the midway skirt length."

"Very well," Sol replied. "Better than the ankle-length version, actually. It's because it takes less coupons, but still looks new and exciting – and we're competitive on price. I saw someone else has had a similar idea, but is selling for five shillings more than us."

"If I bring in some French designs, we may be able to take some ideas from what they are doing over there. I've wondered if we should consider taking on a designer of our own, Sol."

"We're the bread-and-butter end of the trade," he argued. "We may change the length of the skirt or sleeves, but our lines are classic – they sell year in, year out."

"Yes, I know. I'm not suggesting we should stop producing our usual lines, just that we might try to move upmarket a little. Be a little adventurous."

"Well . . ." His gaze narrowed. "It would be a risk, Emma."

"It might be worth having a go. We could try a few samples for a start, see how things work out – but first we need a designer we both like. Someone with fresh ideas, but nothing too outrageous at first."

Sol was considering the idea. We did very well with the lines we sold currently, which we had based on half a dozen classic styles with variations of collars, sleeves and so on. Like most other manufacturers, we were experts at copying anything the important designers came up with. We were followers of the latest trends, but never set them ourselves.

That had always been good business, but for a while now I had been thinking that we could do with some new ideas. Women were becoming more demanding these days. Their natural desire to wear beautiful clothes had been repressed during the years of rationing. We were still suffering from these restrictions, but it couldn't go on for much longer. When the upturn came, there was going to be a big change in the way ordinary women dressed. New materials would make clothes cheaper to produce, and therefore more accessible. I believed we ought to be preparing for the change.

"We'll see," Sol said at last. "You find a designer who is willing to work for the sort of wages we can afford to pay, and I'll go along with you." He laughed. "I might as well agree now and have done with it. Otherwise, you will go ahead and do it on your own anyway."

"I wouldn't go against you, Sol. We might have had our disagreements in the past, but I don't know what I would have done without your friendship. Whatever happens in the future, I want us to continue to be friends and partners."

Sol nodded, his eyes warm and amused. "You know I would do anything for you, Emma. And don't worry about that contract. I'll talk to our lawyers before I let you sign anything."

"What would I do without you?"

"I've no idea," he said drily. "Fortunately, the feeling is mutual – so you won't have to. As long as I am around, I'll always do my best to look after you, Emma."

"My best of friends." I kissed his cheek. "Thank you. In that case, I can go off to Paris and enjoy myself. The only thing I have to worry about now is whether the French Jon taught me when I used to visit him in hospital will get me through . . ."

Six

It had been a productive day! I had spent most of the morning wandering in and out of the dress shops and large stores with clothing departments. My object was to discover what was selling, which designers were most popular – and where I could buy similar clothes at wholesale prices.

I had brought a few addresses with me, of course, but I wanted to research the market thoroughly before I got down to establishing contacts. And there was a showroom I wanted to visit this very afternoon. I particularly liked their designs, which appeared to be on the rails of all the best shops, and the showroom itself was situated right in the centre of the city – just off one of the fashionable avenues leading from the Champs Elysees.

There was a lively feel to the fashions I had seen. The French clothing industry seemed to have thrown off the effects of the war much more easily than we had at home. Of course, some of the fashion houses had continued to function right through the war, making *haute couture* clothes for wealthy patrons – including the ladies who had visited escorted by German officers.

I knew feelings still ran high in certain quarters over this, but as far as I was concerned the war was over. Now that I had had a good look at the clothes on sale in France, I was all the more determined to have some of their merchandise on sale in my shops if I possibly could.

I had by now decided to turn Philip's offer down, even if he would agree to change that clause in the contract. After careful thought, I had come to the conclusion that it would not suit me to be in business with him. Besides, before I left on this trip, Sol had offered to finance a shop in Oxford Street for me.

"If you want to move up there, why not have your own business?" he had suggested. "I can lend you the money, Emma. I'm not talking about a little shop like the others . . . I mean a large store, selling everything from underwear to shoes."

"That would need a lot of money," I'd said, looking at him uncertainly. "It's what I really want, Sol. I'd thought I would have to wait a few years, then sell those I already have, but if you're sure . . ."

"I wouldn't offer if I wasn't," he said. "Let me write to the lawyers, tell them you are not prepared to accept the contract as it stands. We'll let Matthews down lightly. He won't be best pleased when he discovers what you're going to do – but we'll cross that bridge when we come to it."

I put the inevitable meeting with Philip Matthews out of my mind. I would have to tell him personally, of course, but I would invite him to dinner at the house so that Sol could be with me. I suspected that Philip might have a temper when roused.

For the moment, I was more concerned about making contacts with French manufacturers. I left my taxi outside the showrooms of Marie Bourdeille, and paused to look in the window before entering. As I did so, I heard a terrific row going on inside; then the door was opened and a young woman was thrust out of the door. She caught the heel of her shoe on the step, and would have fallen had I not moved swiftly to support her.

Without looking at me, she turned to glare at the much older woman who had pushed her out, and let loose what could only be a torrent of abuse. It was answered in kind, and the older woman spat at her, then slammed the door in disgust.

"Are you all right?" I asked once the door was closed. "Pardon, mademoiselle. I am sorry, but my French isn't good enough to ask whether you were hurt or not."

She looked at me, and smiled suddenly. "I'm English

– well, at least, my father was. My mother was French, that's why I speak the language so well . . . I can swear like a trooper! And that bitch in there got what she was asking for." Her cheeks went red. "Forgive me for being rude, and thank you for helping me. I might have hurt myself – not that *she* would care. She would rather I was dead, then she could get away with stealing my work." She spoke with a slight French accent, but her English was perfect. "But I'm not going to let her have those designs for nothing. Either she pays or I'll make sure she's sorry."

I stared at her in surprise. "Stealing your work – are you a dress designer?"

"Yes, and a good one, despite what *she* thinks!" The girl looked angry. "I sent her three designs last Christmas. She returned them to me, said they were not professional enough for her to use in her workshops – and now they are selling all over Paris."

I felt a tingling of excitement at the base of my spine. "What were they like? Was one of them by any chance an ankle-length full skirt with a plain top and a little jacket to match the skirt?"

"Yes . . . how did you know that was one of mine?" She looked surprised. "She wouldn't have told you – she denies ever having seen my sketch."

I studied her for a moment in silence. She was a pretty girl of perhaps twenty with honey-blonde hair, which she wore dragged back into a chignon, and green eyes.

"I didn't know – but it was the style I liked best of all Marie Bourdeille's designs. I was about to order six of each size for my shops – but now I don't think I want to do business with her very much."

"Her clothes sell well," the girl said and frowned. "I'm Francine White, by the way. You shouldn't let me put you off buying from the old . . . well, what I mean is, she is one of the best designers in the middle price range."

"But if you designed the set I liked best . . ." I smiled at her as my idea began to take shape. "Why don't I buy you a drink,

Francine? My name is Emma Reece, and I have something to suggest to you."

"Did you say you had a dress shop?" she asked, a flicker of interest in those green eyes. "Only I thought I might try for a job in London, working in a dress shop. I could work on my designs in the evenings, and maybe I can find someone to take a few of them in London. Someone who will actually pay me for them. That mean old – so-and-so – didn't have to steal them. I wasn't asking for more than a hundred francs. It wouldn't have hurt her to pay me something."

"I think I can do better than give you a job as a sales assistant," I said. "Let's go and have that drink, Francine, and I'll tell you what I have in mind."

I was feeling very pleased with myself as I entered the hotel that evening. Francine had not yet agreed to design exclusively for me, but she was considering it. She had resolved to come to London very soon, and I had promised to show her the showrooms and workshops. Francine was obviously ambitious. I suspected she was playing hard to get, which wasn't surprising after the way she had been treated, but I was confident of talking her round once she got to know me.

"Oh, Madame Reece," the receptionist said as I went to the desk to collect my key. "Your room has been changed. Here is your key."

I looked at the number and frowned. "But this is on the top floor. I don't understand. Why has the change been made? My single room was adequate. I don't need a suite."

"But your husband arrived this afternoon, madame. He asked for the change to be made."

"My husband?" I was very surprised. I had not expected Jon to come out and join me. Indeed, when I left London he had still been in Cornwall. He must have returned and flown out to be with me.

"I see." I smiled at the receptionist, feeling pleased. "Thank you. I didn't realise he was coming."

"He ordered flowers and the best champagne," the girl

went on. The expression in her eyes told me that she thought it was all very romantic.

I nodded and smiled but said nothing as I went on by and into the lift. Jon was being very extravagant. Maybe he had something to celebrate. He might have found a house he liked – or perhaps he had sold another of his plays.

I unlocked the door of the suite and went in, feeling astonished as I saw its opulence. There were sumptuous sofas, gleaming glass tables, and a huge display of exotic flowers as well as a basket of fruit and champagne cooling in an ice bucket. This wasn't like Jon, even if he had sold a play. Fifty pounds wasn't going to pay for all this! What on earth had got into him?

"Jon," I called as I laid my shopping down. "Where are you, darling?"

I could hear water running. It sounded as though he had been having a bath. I went through to the bedroom, and looked in the wardrobe. My clothes had been moved from the single room and were hanging neatly on the rail.

A man's shirt lay on the bed, and there were toilet articles strewn beside it. A large pair of scissors was on the bedside table, and some cufflinks. I frowned as I saw them. Were they Jon's? I certainly hadn't seen them before. He must have bought them recently.

I took a thin dressing gown from the wardrobe, then began to remove my blouse and skirt. It had been a warm day, and I had spent most of it trudging the streets. I could do with a wash when Jon had finished in the bathroom. I slipped off my things, and put the robe on, turning as the door from the bathroom opened.

"Jon . . . this is a surprise—" The words died on my lips as I saw the man who had walked in. He was wearing a silk dressing gown in a rather lurid pattern of crimson and gold, and he wasn't my husband!

Instinctively, I wrapped my robe more tightly around my body. "Philip! What are you doing here? I was told my husband—"

He gave me what passed for a smile, but struck me as being

more of a sneer. "I thought you would rather I pretended to be your husband, Emma. For the sake of discretion. No one has to know any different while we're staying here."

"Oh, yes, they do," I said, and walked towards the telephone. "I'm going to ring reception immediately and tell them to move my clothes back where they belong. How dare you do this, Philip? You had no right . . . no right at all!"

"I thought it would make you laugh," he said, looking a little annoyed. "Surely you can see the advantages?"

"I see none for me." I glared at him. "I have no intention of sharing a room with you – or a bed!"

"Come on, be nice," he said, his voice soft and persuasive. "It isn't so very different from the arrangement you have with Sol, is it? Or that American you went around with during the war."

"Sol is my friend – and my feelings for Jack are none of your business." I felt cold and a little sick. This was a shock, and not a pleasant one. "Now, if you don't mind, I would like to get changed and pack my things."

"You weren't like this when we talked before," he said, eyes narrowing, expression sulky. "I thought you understood this was part of the bargain?"

"You forgot to mention it," I said, my tone crisp and cutting. "Just as you forgot to mention the exclusion clause. As it happens, I have decided not to go through with the contract, Philip. Even if I had wanted to be your partner, this would have changed my mind. I am not and never will be interested in you as a man – you aren't my type."

"Well, that's a shame," he said, "because you are very definitely mine. I've made this trip for your sake, Emma – and I don't intend to lose out on my investment."

Something in his tone – and his face – put me on my guard. I had seen that look in a man's eyes before: it was the kind of look Dick had given me sometimes . . . at the times when he had come close to raping me in our marriage bed. I backed away, looking for an avenue of escape.

There was no point in screaming. Even if someone heard, it might be ages before anyone came to investigate. As far as the management was concerned, this man was my husband. They would think long and hard before interfering.

"Don't you dare touch me," I said, trying not to give way to fear. A man like Philip enjoyed seeing fear in a woman's eyes: it gave him a feeling of power. I saw him for what he was now. What on earth had ever made me consider the idea of going into business with him? I had been a complete fool! "If you do—"

"What will you do, Emma? Scream? There's no one to hear you up here – and if they did, they would turn a blind eye. The French are very understanding of these things . . . they know women like you scream when they are enjoying themselves."

What did he mean, women like *me*? I was beginning to feel very frightened, but I knew I had to hide my fear.

"Keep away from me, Philip. I'm warning you."

"I'm stronger than you." He was sneering at me, utterly confident of his power to persuade or bully me into doing what he wanted. This wasn't the first time he had forced a woman to obey him. "When I've finished with you, you'll never want another man near you, you little whore. I know how to make women like you crawl."

I gasped, feeling the fear shoot through me as I saw the expression in his eyes. He wasn't like Dick. Dick had been tortured by his jealousy – this man was evil, mad!

He made a grab at me. I struggled and pushed him off. He hit me across the face twice, so hard that I tasted blood in my mouth – then punched me in the stomach. I fell to the floor in a heap, retching. I was terrified, but also angry. No man had ever done that to me, and I didn't intend to let this one get away with it.

Before I could move, Philip dragged me to my feet and pushed me so that the backs of my knees were against the bed. I could feel my legs giving way, and knew that once I was trapped beneath his weight, I would have no chance of getting away. That wasn't going to happen. Self-preservation made me throw off my fear. I gave a yell of rage and went for his face with my nails, scratching his cheek so hard that the blood ran. He jerked back, staring at me in disbelief and cursing.

Before he could attack me again, I darted forward and caught up the pair of scissors from the table beside the bed. He had clearly been using them earlier, though I had no idea what for, and the sharp blades were open wide. I held them in my hand, prepared to stab him to the heart if necessary.

"Come any closer and I'll kill you, Philip," I said, hardly knowing what I was doing. "I swear I'll kill you."

I could see he did not believe me. He tried to reach out for me and I plunged the scissors into the fleshy part of his upper arm. He gave a yell of pain and sprang back, clutching the deep wound.

"You bloody bitch," he muttered. "I'll make you pay for this."

"I warned you," I said, standing my ground. I was fighting for my life, a tigress. I could see the blood dripping from his arm into the carpet. "Get out now, or I'll put these through your chest."

"You're mad," he said, but he was backing away, believing me capable of carrying out my threat. At that moment he was right to believe it. The tables had turned; he was afraid of me now, his face white with disbelief. I doubted that any woman had ever stood up to him before, and it had shocked him. "You led me on."

"No, I never did that," I said. "You led yourself on. You're not my type, Philip. I don't even want to work with you. You make me sick to my stomach. Now get out of here, before I decide to stab you again. I'm going to pack my things, then I'll be gone. You can come back and collect yours later."

"But I'm wearing my dressing gown." His voice carried a whine now, as if he were about to burst into tears. Like most bullies he was a coward underneath. "You can't turn me out."

"Just get out." I lifted my arm threateningly. "I mean it, Philip."

"I'll ruin you, Emma Reece," he muttered sulkily. "You won't get away with this, believe me. I'll ruin you and

Solomon Gould. By the time I've finished with you, you won't have a penny left between you."

I dashed at him with the scissors and he bolted, out of the bedroom and through the sitting room into the corridor. I bolted the door behind him, then went back into the bedroom and double-locked the door. Then I slumped down on the edge of the bed. I was shaking, the dizziness sweeping over me. All at once, I felt the vomit rise in my throat and I made a dash for the bathroom, retching over the toilet as the bile spilled out. Afterwards, I was left with a bad taste in my mouth.

The horror of what had just happened was churning inside me. If Philip had not left those scissors on the bedside table, he would have succeeded in raping me. Without a weapon to defend myself, I would probably not have been able to prevent him from carrying out his threats. The thought made me vomit again, and I leaned against the basin feeling weak.

I stared in the mirror on the wall, seeing my pale reflection. The things he had said to me kept running through my head, making me feel ill. Even though he had not succeeded in carrying out his threats, I felt dirty, violated. He was depraved, evil!

Suddenly, I could not wait to get out of the hotel. I ran into the bedroom, swept my clothes into my cases, picked up the bag containing my documents and money and rang for the porter.

"Are you leaving, madame?" the receptionist asked, sounding surprised.

"Yes. I'll pay for the room I booked; the suite will be paid for by Mr Matthews. That man was not my husband. He attacked me. I want a taxi waiting for me when I come down, and have my bill ready – otherwise I shall leave without paying. And I may ask my lawyer to take action against you for moving my things without my permission."

"Not your husband?" She sounded shocked. "But he said—"

I slammed the receiver down on her. Anger had replaced

the fear. I was furious with the hotel for moving my belongings without checking with me first, disgusted with Philip Matthews for his vile behaviour – and angry with myself for having fallen into his trap.

Sol had been right to warn me – and so had Jack. I only wished I had listened.

My face looked a mess. I glanced at my reflection in a compact mirror as the taxi drew up outside my home. I had applied powder but there was no way I could hide the dark bruises on my cheek, and I was still sore from being punched in the stomach. I could conceal that, but how was I going to explain my looks?

I paid the taxi driver and went into the house. Mrs Rowan came out to greet me, the words dying on her lips as she saw my swollen lip.

"Oh, madam," she cried. "What happened to you?"

"I had a little accident," I said. "It's all right. Nothing serious. Please don't make a fuss."

I left her staring as I went through into the sitting room. There was no point in hiding myself away. I might as well get it over with.

When I went in, I discovered that Jon was with Sol. They were having a drink and laughing over something, but as they turned and saw me the laughter was silenced.

"What happened?" Jon asked. "You've been hurt, Emma."

"I walked into a door," I began, but saw the disbelief in their faces. "All right, I might as well tell you – Philip Matthews tried to rape me."

"My God!" Jon went white. "Have you been to the police, Emma? Tell me; it's important."

"No – and please, don't make me," I begged. "I said he *tried* . . . I fought him off. In fact I stabbed him with a pair of scissors. His face probably looks worse than mine. I scratched that with my nails."

"What happened exactly?" Sol asked, eyes narrowed in anger. "I warned you about him, Emma. I told you not to trust him."

"Yes, you did – and I should have listened. If I had I might have been on my guard," I said. "As it is, I wasn't expecting it . . . He changed my room to a suite on the top floor. The receptionist told me my husband had made the arrangements." I caught back a sob as the horror I had felt then swept over me once more. "I walked in thinking Jon was in the bathroom and took my clothes off. When he came out I was only wearing a thin robe."

"The devil!" Sol growled. "I'll kill him. I mean it. I'll kill him."

Jon took my arm and led me to the settee. He made me sit down, looking at me anxiously as he knelt at my feet and took my hands in his.

"Take your time, darling," he said gently. His expression was one of concern, but his eyes were hard, angry, unlike the Jon I knew. "Tell us exactly what happened."

"I was going to ring down for my things to be moved. He laughed, said he thought it was amusing and that I would like what he'd done. When I told him he wasn't my type and that I wasn't going into partnership with him . . . he attacked me. He wasn't like a normal man, Jon. The look in his eyes, the things he said: filthy, disgusting things. He made me feel sick. He hit me several times, punched me in the stomach . . . then tried to force me back on the bed. I scratched his face hard. It stunned him for a moment, and I grabbed some scissors he must have been using. I stabbed him in the arm. I was so angry I told him I would kill him. He said he would ruin me – and Sol."

"He might try," Sol muttered. "But he won't live long enough."

"Don't," I begged, tears squeezing from the corners of my eyes. "I've caused enough trouble as it is. I don't want you to kill for my sake, Sol. I don't want you to hang or go to prison."

"No, of course not," Jon said, giving Sol a quelling stare. "It was just an expression of anger, Emma. We shall have to talk about this, Sol, decide what to do to protect Emma – but no talk of killing. It upsets her – and she's upset enough as it is."

"I should think she is." Sol was still furious. I could see he would have liked to punch Philip Matthews in the face, or perhaps take a horse-whip to him – but murder was a different matter. "Sorry, Emma. I didn't mean it, of course – but I'll sort him out. I'll speak to Jack. He'll know what to do."

"No, don't tell Jack," I whispered, my throat closing as the tears gathered then spilled out in noisy sobs. "I'm sorry. I'm going upstairs. I want to be alone for a while. Please . . . forgive me."

I ran from the room, past a startled Pam and on up the stairs. Once in my bedroom, I locked the door. I was feeling sick again, the nausea washing over me in waves. I went into the bathroom and turned on the taps. I had washed several times since Philip attacked me, but I didn't think I would ever feel really clean again.

For almost a week I didn't leave the house. Everyone was considerate of my feelings. No one mentioned the Paris incident, and Jon was especially gentle and caring. He talked about everything except what had happened in Paris, telling me he had found a house he liked, not in Cornwall but just outside Torquay in Devon.

"When you're feeling better I'll take you to see it," he promised. "I've told the owners I'm interested, but I want you to have a look at it before I buy."

"Thank you." I smiled at him. "You are so thoughtful, Jon."

"That's because I love you, Emma."

When I was with Jon or Sol I didn't feel too bad, but at night I often lay restless. I kept remembering Philip's threats, and the look in his eyes. I believed he was just mad enough to take some sort of revenge on me for stabbing him.

I realised now that Philip was the kind of man who actually hated women. He needed them, but he also needed to humiliate them, to prove he was superior. He was not likely to forgive a woman who had stabbed him and forced him to wander about the hotel in his dressing robe. He would also have found it embarrassing to explain the situation to the management. No, I did not think he would simply forget and leave me in peace. He would do something.

I told Sol that I was worried.

"Just what do you imagine he could do?" Sol asked. "He might damage us a little by cancelling his last order, but there's not much more he can do. Anyway, I've had a word with Jack. He will sort Matthews out if he tries to harm you."

"Oh, I wish you hadn't told Jack." I looked at Sol reproachfully. "I particularly asked you not to, Sol."

"Jack is a good friend," he replied, an odd expression in his eyes. "Forget about reprisals from Matthews, Emma. They aren't going to happen."

His words were reassuring, but I was still uneasy. Then, towards the end of that week, I had something else to think about.

I had been lying without sleeping for hours that night. It wasn't just the incident in Paris. For some reason my mind kept going back to the time when my father died. The doctor had been satisfied that his death was due to natural causes, but I had suspected that it had at least been hastened by poison. I would never be entirely certain, but some months later my first husband had confessed to adding pills that contained small amounts of arsenic to Father's medicine.

Why was I remembering that now? It was all so long ago. There was no reason it should be in my mind – except that I'd felt the same unease then as I did now.

Knowing I would never sleep, I got up, pulled on my dressing gown – not the one I had been wearing in Paris! – and went downstairs. I warmed some milk in the kitchen, then carried my cup into the sitting room. As I reached out to open the door, I heard a noise like glass rattling.

Jon was standing fully clothed by the tray of decanters and glasses. He was trying to pour some brandy into a glass, but his hand was shaking so much that he was in danger of dropping the glass.

"Jon – what's wrong, darling?"

I set my cup down on the table as he swung round to face

me. He looked ashen, his eyes a little wild. For a moment he stared at me as if he did not know who I was.

"Are you ill?"

I noticed that his jacket was slightly damp. I had heard the rain beating against my bedroom window earlier, when I lay sleepless: it had stopped now. Had he been out for a walk? He did that sometimes when he couldn't sleep.

Jon took a deep breath, then forced a wry smile. "I've been having a panic attack, Emma. I've no idea why. It's ages since I had one – a couple of years or more."

"Oh, Jon, I'm so sorry." I knew he'd once suffered from what Sister Jones called "the shakes".

"A lot of the men have them every so often," she'd told me when I'd begun to visit Jon in hospital. "It's not unusual after what they've been through, and we don't really know why they happen. The best way to cope is to be understanding and not make too much fuss."

I had thought Jon was over all that now, however. He was facing up to his injuries and getting on with his life. The surgeons had helped him in so many ways, even restoring some mobility to his left hand, something that had seemed impossible at the beginning. It wasn't easy for him to use it, but he could just about manage – except when he was suffering from nerves. He couldn't drive, of course, and there were other small tasks that were too difficult for him, but he'd worked out how to do most things for himself. He had no trouble in dressing or tying his shoelaces, which was something I had thought he would never be able to do – but with practice and determination he had managed. But at this moment he couldn't hold a glass or pour himself a drink.

I went to him, pouring his brandy and one for myself. He smiled as I joined him on the settee. He had managed to control the shaking now, and was obviously feeling better.

"Couldn't you sleep either, Emma?"

"No." I sighed. "It's not what happened in Paris, Jon. Not really. I'm getting over that, and my face is almost back to normal. I suppose I just feel unsettled."

"Natural enough. Shall we go away tomorrow?" His fingers brushed my cheek. "Just the two of us. We'll look at the house, walk by the sea, take things slowly. You never had a chance to rest when you were with the children, and you work so hard. They will be all right for a few days without you."

"Yes, of course they will." I leaned over and kissed him softly on the mouth. He was such a gentle, kind man. "Thank you, Jon – and thank you for not telling me that what happened was my own fault. I know it was, but I didn't expect—"

"Of course it wasn't your fault!" Jon said, a grim expression in his eyes. "The man deserves to be punished. You should have gone to the police in Paris and had him arrested at once."

"I didn't want all the embarrassment and fuss," I said. "Besides, it's all over now. It shook me for a while, but I'll get over it. Believe me, I shall."

"You are very strong," Jon said. He was smiling now, a tender note in his voice. "And I am sure you are right, darling. It is all over. The best thing you can do is to put the whole incident out of your mind. The man isn't worth worrying over."

"I shall forget about it," I promised. "We will go away together, Jon. I should like that – if you are sure you feel well enough?"

"I'm fine. Really, Emma. That nonsense just now – it's something I have to live with. My hand won't obey me sometimes, that's all. The attacks don't come often. They don't bother me as long as they happen at home. If I'm out it can be embarrassing."

I accepted his assurances – he didn't want a fuss – but it reminded me of how much he had suffered. My own upsetting experience had somehow brought us closer together again. Jon had been so protective of me, so understanding.

It made me remember why I loved him.

Seven

"Will you be away long, Emmie?" Lizzy slipped her hand into mine. She gazed up at me with her large, seeing eyes. "Is your poor face all better now?"

"Yes, much better," I said and bent to kiss her. Lizzy was such a loving child, and sometimes I felt closer to her than my own son. She had so much love to give, and she was so generous with it. "I was very silly to walk into that wardrobe door. I need a little holiday, darling, but it is only for a few days."

James directed a sullen stare in my direction. He hated me going away without him, and I had only recently been to Paris.

"Why can't we come? We don't have to go back to school yet."

"Because I want a few days alone with your father," I replied. "You had a lovely holiday, James – and I'll take you both on some outings when I come back. We'll go to the pictures and the zoo."

"Jack is taking me to the science museum," my son said. "I like to know how things work – and he promised to take me inside a factory where they make lenses for cameras."

"Well, you will enjoy that," I said. "You'll hardly know I've gone – and I'll bring you both a present back." I was glad James was going somewhere with Jack; it eased my guilt at leaving him again so soon.

I left the children and went downstairs. Pam was hovering. I could see she wanted to talk to me, but Jon was already having our cases taken out to the waiting taxi.

"Look after everyone for me, Pam?"

"Yes, of course. Enjoy yourself, Emma. Have a good

rest." She kissed my cheek impulsively. "You've looked tired recently."

"Is something on your mind, Pam?"

"No. Nothing for you to worry about." She smiled, but looked somehow uncomfortable. "We'll talk when you come home. It's not important."

"Pam—" I broke off as Jon called to me. "When I come back. You must tell me then. Promise?"

She nodded. I smiled at her, then went out to join my husband in the taxi.

Jon bought a pile of newspapers and magazines for the journey. He gave me half of them, then settled down to the crossword in *The Times*. I read the copy of *Vogue* he had given me.

After a while, a waiter came to tell us that coffee and toast was being served in the dining car.

"Would you like some?" Jon asked.

"Yes, that would be nice."

We gathered up our paraphernalia. I picked up the paper Jon had been reading earlier, noticing an article about a bomb going off in a car in London. I glanced at the headline, then tucked the paper under my arm as I followed Jon out into the corridor.

It was only after we had enjoyed our hot buttered toast and marmalade that Jon asked for his paper. I looked through the pile, my eyes drawn towards the article again – and my blood ran cold.

"Have you seen this?" I looked across the table at my husband. "Did you see what happened? It's Philip Matthews. He was killed late yesterday evening. His car had been tampered with . . . some kind of an explosive device—"

"Yes, I did read it, Emma." Jon's expression was grim. "I didn't mention it because I knew it would shock and upset you, and I want you to forget all that. This has nothing to do with you. Pay no attention to it, darling. The man was clearly a rogue."

"The journalist calls it a 'gangland killing'," I said.

"Apparently, the police were about to launch an investigation into Philip's business affairs. They seem to think he may have been connected to London's criminal element."

"So I read." Jon frowned. "And he seemed so respectable. I only met him once, briefly, but I thought him an inoffensive sort of chap – until I found out what he tried to do to you. It shows one should never judge by appearances. It's as well you didn't sign that contract, darling. You might have been caught up in all this nastiness."

"Yes." I frowned over the article, feeling numbed. Philip had frightened me and I had hoped never to see him again, but this was a terrible way to die. I shuddered. "Do you suppose it was really a gangland killing, Jon?"

"Of course. What else could it be? It takes experience and a certain kind of skill to set up something like that, Emma." He gave a strange, harsh laugh as he saw my frown. "You're not imagining that Sol did it? No, my darling, you can put that right out of your mind."

"But he was so angry. He threatened to—" I bit my lip. "You know he did, Jon. You were there."

"That was merely an expression of anger, because you had been hurt," Jon said in a reasonable tone. "Believe me, Emma. Sol wouldn't be capable of doing something like that. He might have thrown a few punches at the man if he had come across him in the street – but this car bomb was a professional job by the sound of it. Probably Matthews had been poaching on some little gangster's territory."

"Yes, I suppose so. It's what the police seem to think."

Jon's explanation made sense. I knew there was a sinister criminal element flourishing in London. It would be impossible to live and work in the city and not be aware of what went on. Amongst the petty gangsters and bully-boys there were frequent squabbles, which led to beatings, knife fights and the occasional murder. All kinds of rackets went on under the noses of the police: illegal gambling, vice clubs, protection schemes. If Philip Matthews was caught up in all that, it was not surprising he had met a violent death.

I didn't know whether Sol had ever paid protection money.

I had never been approached, but Sol had lived and worked in London much longer than me. I thought he would pay and keep his mouth shut.

Despite Jon's assurances, I continued to worry and wonder as the train clattered relentlessly along the line. I stared unseeingly out of the window at the changing scenery: woods and fields, smoky buildings and a patchwork of tiny back yards. During the war, Sol had been involved in a few slightly shady deals. He obviously knew people who operated close to the edge. He probably knew of the criminals who ran London's underworld, at least by name and sight.

If he had wanted Philip Matthews dead, he would not have had to carry out the assassination himself. Pound notes would buy anything amongst the criminal fraternity. If one were prepared to pay, a car bomb would be easy enough to arrange.

Sol had spoken to Jack about the threats Philip had made against me. Was Jack ruthless enough to arrange something like that?

The thoughts went round and round in my head. I wanted to dismiss them as nonsense. I wanted to believe that my friends were above taking such a terrible revenge on the man who had attacked me, but I couldn't.

I had ignored their advice about getting involved with Philip. He had tried to rape me. Now he was dead. I was very much afraid that I was the reason behind the brutal attack that had led to his death.

The house Jon had chosen was perfect. A substantial, whitewashed property, it was set on a gentle hillside amongst beautiful trees. The view from the garden was breathtaking, looking out over the sea, cliffs and the bay.

"Do you really like it, Emma?" Jon asked after we had spent almost an hour looking round the house and large garden. "The furniture and curtains are included. We can make changes when we're ready, of course, but they're not too bad as they are – are they?"

"Some of the curtains are a bit faded," I said, "but that doesn't matter. I think it's lovely, Jon. You were very clever to find it. We are private up here, but it's an easy walk to the town – and a short taxi ride from the station. It's exactly what we want. I can visit when I like, and the children can come down for holidays."

"I'm so glad you like it as much as I do," he said, looking pleased. "I'll go ahead and buy it, then."

"Do you need any help financially?"

"No, I can manage. Mother has decided to move into a flat. I've had an offer for the house in Hampstead, and after I've bought Mother's flat I'll have sufficient left for this."

"She has made up her mind, then?"

"I think she's had enough of running that huge place on a shoestring. It will be much better for her in a modern flat."

"Yes, I expect it will." I smiled at him. "So when do you expect to move in?"

"Next month." He looked thoughtful. "Providing you don't need me in London. You know I'll stay for as long as you want me, Emma? If you are still upset over that business . . ."

"I'm all right now. Really I am."

The two days we had already spent in Torquay had relaxed me. We had been for slow, restful walks round the cliffs, stopping now and then to sit on a rocky ledge and drink in the views, which became more breathtaking the higher you went. Or perhaps that was the effect of the steep paths that wound on and on, ever upwards?

We had also been to the cinema and the theatre.

"It's more lively than some seaside resorts," Jon had said when he was showing me the town. "The children will have plenty to do on their holidays – and I know you like to go shopping! There's a nice little town, darling."

I liked Torquay. It had both beauty spots and a bit of life, and there were lots of interesting places to visit in the area. By the time Jon took me to the house – which he had saved until last – I had already decided that I would be happy to spend some time here.

I had made a determined effort to shake off my doubts and anxieties. The papers had carried several articles about the assassination of Philip Matthews. It seemed that he had been linked to a gambling racket, and also to prostitution. He owned several houses that were known to be brothels, and was clearly a very unpleasant character altogether.

My fears would appear to have been irrational. The police were convinced that it was a gangland killing. Philip had upset some powerful members of the criminal fraternity.

It was clearly foolish for me to go on worrying. Neither Sol nor Jack had been involved. I had been wrong to imagine either of them would kill for my sake. Why should they? I had been hurt – and humiliated – but I was getting over it.

I was enjoying my few days at the sea with my kind, gentle husband. Jon was always so considerate of me. He did everything he could to please me, though he had not once attempted to make love to me. I believed his specialist had told him it was a vain hope.

So we were friends and loving companions, just as we had been before our marriage. It was not an ideal situation, but it was better than I had expected when Jon suggested that we should live apart some of the time.

I was not quite sure what had changed, but Jon was different. He did not seem as apologetic as before. He was more confident, more sure of himself – and very tender towards me. I supposed the transformation was because he knew where he was going with his life, and because he was having some success with his writing.

His consideration for me over those few days helped me banish the feeling of humiliation that had been so strong on my return from Paris. I could think of Philip's attack now without wanting to scrub my skin until it stung. After all, it was not so very terrible. I had driven Philip off – and I was strong enough to subdue any irrational fears that his attack had planted in my mind.

It was a pleasant interlude for both Jon and myself. I began to feel better than I had for a while.

By the time we were due to return to London, I was almost back to normal and ready to go on with my plans for the future. Sol had offered to lend me the money to open a big, new shop of my own, and I had lots of ideas for our wholesale business. The future had begun to look bright once more.

After our return to London, events seemed to overtake me. The summer was almost gone. I had time to take the children on a few outings, and then they were back to school.

James was going to a new school this term, a school for boys only, where his talent for singing would be nurtured. I had dreaded the moment, but to my surprise he accepted it calmly. My son was growing up very fast. It was Lizzy who wept in my arms.

"It's just part of growing up," I told her. "Don't worry, darling. You will still see James every evening and weekends."

"I don't want to grow up, Emmie. I like things as they are."

"We all have to grow up," I said and kissed her. "Believe me, Lizzy, there are nice things in store, too."

I wasn't sure she believed me, but she went off to school and within a few days she had got used to the changes.

It was then that Pam shocked me by telling me that she was leaving us to go and live with her sister in Hunstanton.

"Oh, Pam, you can't!" I cried, dismayed at her announcement. I had come to rely on her and she had seemed to like living with us. "Why? Are you unhappy here? What's wrong?"

Pam was flushed and uncomfortable, her fingers restlessly pleating the material of her dress.

"Please don't look like that, Emma," she begged. "I hate letting you down, but my sister needs me. I've promised I'll help with the boarding house. Her husband bought it when he came back after the war – but he leaves all the work to her."

Somehow I sensed she wasn't telling me the whole truth.

"Why do you want to go, Pam? Have I done something to upset you? Please tell me."

"No, of course you haven't. You've been good to me. It's just—" She lowered her gaze. "It's not you, Emma. It's Sol."

"Has he done something? Been rude or sharp with you?"

"No." Her gaze swept up to mine. "It isn't his fault, either.

I'm in love with him. I know it's silly. He would never look at me. I know that, of course I do. I just can't help the way I feel."

"Why wouldn't he look at you? Have you ever told him how you feel?" I wrinkled my brow, sensing more was on her mind. "I'm sorry. I don't understand."

"Sol loves you," Pam replied. "You probably haven't noticed the way he looks at you, Emma. He worships the ground you walk on. I understand that. I'm not jealous or upset. I just think I would be happier living somewhere else."

"Oh, Pam." I felt sad as I looked at her and realised what she had been going through. It was hard to love someone who did not return your feelings, especially if you saw them every day, lived in the same house. I understood now why she wanted to leave. "I'm so sorry. I shall miss you very much."

"I shall miss *you*, Emma. I shall always be grateful for what you did – bringing me here, making me a part of your family – but it's better if I go now."

I could not persuade her to change her mind, and I supposed that if she really wanted to make the break and start again, it would have been wrong to try too hard. I was sad that she felt she needed to leave, especially as it was because of her love for Sol. She was older than me, a little tired looking these days perhaps, but younger than Sol. It was not surprising that she had felt drawn to him. He was an attractive man, and I knew he had a habit of teasing her. I was sure he had no idea of her feelings for him, and would be sorry if he guessed he had hurt her feelings. Of course I would never tell him.

I insisted on taking her down to Hunstanton in the car, then took a detour to March and paid a short visit to my mother and friends before returning to London.

Mum was worried about Bert, who had a nasty cough, but Gwen was very happy.

"Richard is very kind and gentle," she told me. "He's a widower with two sons and lives on his own. We're not going to get married just yet – but we see each other two or three times a week."

"I'm so pleased, Gwen. I'm glad you've got someone special."

"I wanted to tell you first – though I suspect that Greta has guessed." Gwen laughed. "Your mother doesn't miss much, Emma."

"No, she doesn't," I agreed. "She's worried about Bert, though."

"Yes, that's a nasty cough," Gwen agreed. "And he was such a strong man until this trouble started. It's a shame for her – and for him, of course. I go round when I can, but there's not much anyone can do."

I was thoughtful as I left March and began the drive back to London. What would Mum do if anything happened to Bert? She would miss him dreadfully.

I shook the morbid thoughts off. I didn't want to think about death – especially violent death. Sometimes I still wondered who had arranged that bomb in Philip's car. The police seemed no nearer to finding the assassin than they had when it happened, despite having questioned members of the gangs they suspected were involved. Whoever had done it had left no clues. He must be very clever, and had covered his tracks well.

Jon had been right to say it was a professional job. The police were inclined to think the culprit had once been in the explosives division of the army – someone who knew exactly what he was doing.

No, I wouldn't let myself be haunted by what had happened. It was all in the past. I was already making plans for my new shop. I had found suitable premises and the contract for the lease was proceeding. Sol had arranged to lend me six thousand pounds, which was all I needed. I had some capital of my own, and the loan would enable me to stock my shop generously without over-stretching myself.

"Are you sure it is sufficient?" Sol had asked. "I'm prepared to let you have more if you need it."

"I have the money I've been saving ready to make this

move," I told him. "Besides, you may need more yourself if we buy that property next to the showroom and expand our workshops. Especially now Francine has agreed to work with us."

Francine had arrived on my doorstep a couple of days after the children went back to school.

"I'll be honest with you," she said, a bright challenge in her eyes. "If I wasn't broke, I probably wouldn't have come. I want my own business, and I would prefer to work as an independent designer, but I need a job for a while. I won't promise to stay with you if I find something better."

"Come and try working for us," I suggested. "We'll pay you a fair wage, and ten pounds for every design we use. And if your designs sell well, I'll pay you five per cent of the profits we make on your range at the end of the year. And we'll put your name on the label. If you're not happy we'll have a month of severance time, then you'll be free to work where you please."

"That sounds fair enough."

"I shan't try to cheat you like Marie did, I promise."

"I like the sound of my name on the label – but Francine White? No, it doesn't sound quite right." She shook her head. "Francine de Paris. The customers will like that. French fashion is hot news in London at the moment. I've discovered that since I've been here."

"Shall we call that a deal?" I offered her my hand and she laughed and took it. "Good. We'll have a contract drawn up to keep things straight between us – but I'm glad you've agreed to join us, Francine. I like you, and I like your designs."

"I like you, Emma," Francine said. "I wasn't sure I could trust you when we first met. The offer you made me seemed too good to be true. I mean, you didn't know me when you asked me to come to London. I could have been lying about Marie stealing my designs. You hadn't even seen my drawings."

"But I have now," I replied, smiling at her. "It was such a chance, I just grabbed it. If your designs hadn't matched my expectations it wouldn't have mattered – but they do. I am thrilled with the latest ones, Francine. You are exactly what we need."

In the short time she had been with us, Francine was already revitalising our stock, adding lots of new touches that made old styles look fresh and exciting. She had a flair for colour and a slightly zany sense of humour that showed up most in her own designs.

As well as Dior's New Look, an ankle-length hobble skirt by Jacques Fath had recently been introduced. An American designer had also brought out a similar look. It was proving more popular than I had expected.

I hadn't particularly liked the idea at first. I thought it would be difficult to wear, and unflattering to women who didn't have the perfect hourglass figure needed to show it off to its best effect. However, Francine had come up with a variation that I thought was more attractive and comfortable to wear. The long straight skirt was as tight as the one designed by Jacques Fath, but it had a little V shape of pleats at the back. When the wearer was standing still, it looked as though it was just a split, but when she walked the pleats opened out rather like a little fish tail. It was amusing and different, and when we put out three samples the orders came rolling in.

Sol had been very quiet when I introduced Francine to the workshops, but after a few weeks he was completely convinced.

"She's a jewel," he told me privately. "Don't let her know I said so or she will be wanting more money. I'm not sure how you managed to get her here, Emma, but I'm glad you did. Trade has picked up all round."

Francine herself was still a bit of a mystery to us. She was always friendly, always willing to talk about design, fashion and anything of a general nature, but I knew very little about her as a person.

"My father left us when I was twelve," she had told me when we were discussing her move to England. "I was brought up by my grandmother so that my mother could work as a seamstress."

"Did she work for one of the famous fashion houses?"

Francine hesitated, then shook her head. I thought she might have been hiding something, but I did not press for details.

"Where is she now?"

"She died just as the war ended." Francine's eyes held a look of pain. "It was an accident."

Again, I sensed something hidden, but asked no questions. Francine's past was her own affair. If she had secrets, so did I. Most people did. All that mattered was our working relationship, and that was more than satisfactory.

Once again, I was caught up in my work, though I took three days off at the beginning of October to see Jon settled into his new home. We had arranged for a cleaning woman to come in each morning, and he would either cook simple meals for himself or eat out.

"I can walk into town and buy fish and chips if I'm hungry." He smiled at me. "Don't worry, Emma. I learned how to survive in France during my time with the resistance movement. I am still capable of many things . . . things you might find surprising."

"Like what?" I asked, teasing him. "Can you light the fire?"

"Yes, of course. I can skin a rabbit. Even sew on a button if I'm obliged."

We both laughed at the idea, though of course in the forces men were required to do that kind of thing. It just seemed strange that he should have to – it was usually a wife's task. "You can always ask Mrs Martin to do that for you." My laughter was stilled as I looked at him. "Are you sure you won't be lonely? You can always come home. You know you will always be welcome."

"This *is* my home now, Emma. I rather like being alone some of the time – but I expect to make friends. And I shall come to London for Christmas, if not before."

"Yes, of course."

Jon's writing was going well. His plays were being produced as a series for the wireless. I'd read one or two of

105

them now and I had been surprised. I'd expected them to be rather serious, emotional stories, but in fact they were full of a gentle humour.

When I left Jon in Torquay and returned to London on the train I felt sad, and a little guilty. If I had been a better wife perhaps he would not have wanted to live alone. If I had been content to stay at home and look after the children – but Jon and I had no children of our own, and it was unlikely that I would have another child now.

Such thoughts could only make me restless. I had tried to dismiss them many times, but they kept coming back to haunt me. As always, however, I held my vague feeling of unhappiness at bay, throwing myself into all the new ventures I had begun.

I heard that Philip Matthews' cousin had sold Philip's shop to a foreign buyer. Within a few weeks it had been turned into an investment bank. Things were changing fast now as London began to lick its wounds and shake off the scars of war.

All over the city there were boarded-off areas where houses and shops had once stood. Many of the sites were still derelict, weeds growing through cracks in the concrete, but some were gradually being cleared ready for rebuilding.

"Did you know that one of Jack's companies is involved in clearing the bombed-out areas?" Sol asked me as we were talking over coffee one November morning. We had just heard on the wireless that an unexploded bomb had been found. Police were warning people to stay away until it had been made safe. "You need people with special skills for that, Emma. Jack set up the company with ex-army officers."

I thought about that piece of information for a moment. So he would employ men who not only knew how to defuse a bomb, but also how to set one off.

No, of course Jack hadn't paid for Philip Matthews to be killed! It was ridiculous of me to feel this faint shadow of guilt. I hadn't wanted Philip dead – or at least, only for a few seconds in that hotel bedroom. Besides, the police still believed his death was a gangland revenge attack.

"It must be a dangerous job," I said, looking at Sol thoughtfully. "Someone was killed the other day dealing with a live shell . . . somewhere south of here, I think."

"That's the trouble with explosives," Sol said. "They can cause trouble for years afterwards. But don't worry, Emma. Jack set up the company, but he won't be there himself."

"No, I don't suppose so." I pulled a face at him.

Was I so transparent to this friend of mine?

As it happened, Sol was wrong. I went to the pictures with Sarah a few nights later and the Pathé News was reporting the incident. They had filmed the area as the experts dealt with the bombs – two had been found under the debris – and the reporter spoke to the man in charge of the operation.

My heart raced as Jack answered the reporter's questions. He explained that the task of clearing London's bombed-out areas was likely to take a long time and could be dangerous in some cases.

"We know there are more unexploded bombs waiting to be found," he said. "But it has to be done. We fought the war so that the British, amongst others, could live in peace and prosperity – and now we are building the peace."

"Bloody Yanks!" I heard a jeering voice call out behind me. "They took their bloody time coming in, and now the buggers think they did it all themselves."

There were some murmurs of agreement from the audience, combined with hissed warnings to be quiet. I was angry. The man who had spoken had no idea of all Jack had done for our country during the war! I wanted to turn round and tell him, but I suddenly discovered that I was crying. I fumbled for my handkerchief and wiped my eyes.

The news had moved on, and was now showing more pictures of the royal wedding, which had taken place a week earlier.

Princess Elizabeth had married her Prince Charming – Lieutenant Philip Mountbatten, who had been given the title of the Duke of Edinburgh by the King on the day of the wedding. I had seen the pictures in the paper, of course, but the princess looked even lovelier on the screen.

Her dress was wonderful: it was an ivory colour, and had been specially designed for her by Norman Hartnell. There were yards and yards of material in the skirt, which was embroidered with flowers of pearls and beads. Her tulle veil hung from a circlet of diamonds.

"Is something wrong?" Sarah whispered. "I didn't think you cried at weddings?"

"No, of course not. I think I might have a cold coming on, that's all."

It was a lie. Seeing Jack so unexpectedly on the screen, knowing that he had risked his life along with the men he employed, had made me realise how much I still loved and missed him. I had forgiven him the incident in the taxi. I was lonely despite all the hours I spent working, and I wished I could see him again.

Sol knew where to contact him, of course. I had only to telephone and arrange to meet . . . but I knew I couldn't do that. I was married to Jon and even if we didn't live together I still cared for him. It was best that Jack and I didn't get involved in an affair that could lead only to more unhappiness.

Eight

Lizzy and James were home for the Christmas holidays. I took them to a pantomime at Olympia, and to the big stores in Oxford and Regent Street to visit Father Christmas. Lizzy was enchanted with the fairy grottoes and working models of gnomes and reindeer, but James was apparently bored by the whole thing.

"It's all made up anyway," he said as we left the store that afternoon and went to Lyons for delicious little marzipan cakes. "No one comes down the chimney. All the presents are bought by mothers and fathers."

"Don't spoil it for Lizzy," I told him, "or this mother won't be buying one ungrateful boy anything."

James grinned at me. "You've got everything stacked in your wardrobe already, Mum. Me and Lizzy looked the other day when you were at work. We saw parcels with our names on."

"I can still give them to someone else," I threatened. I raised my eyebrows at him. "So if Christmas is all nonsense, you won't want to help me decorate the tree with sugar mice and all things nice?"

"I do," Lizzy said quickly. "I don't care what James says, Emmie. I love Christmas. You always make it so special for us."

"I try, darling."

I smiled at her. Lizzy was very dear to my heart. She was a beautiful girl, her eyes so serious and yet at times lit by an enchanting mischief. I was so lucky to have her.

Sometimes I wondered that Sheila was content to leave her with me. How could she bear to be parted from her daughter?

If Lizzy had been my own child I could never have given her away to someone else. Yet Sheila's letters were always bright and breezy. She and Todd had returned to America after their European tour to even greater success for Todd. His record sales were booming in America as well as here, and it looked as though she had everything she had ever wanted.

I liked Todd's records myself. I had bought most of them for my own collection, and some of the ballads for Mum because she liked any soft, romantic music. She was a big fan of Paul Robeson, and had once seen him on stage in London when she was a young girl. I had bought her a new gramophone as a birthday present and she now had all his records.

"As long as it's restful, Emma. None of that terrible jazz!"

My mother was coming to stay over Christmas, and so was Bert.

"He's a little better at the moment, and he did enjoy that holiday you gave us so much. He's always talking about it."

Francine was coming to dinner on Christmas Day. I had invited Gwen and Pam, but neither could manage to get away. It didn't matter. Jon would be there, and I would have my family around me.

I felt quite excited as I dressed that evening. Sol was taking me to a dinner-dance at a prestigious hotel. It was a business thing, of course, but I hadn't been out in a dress like this for a long time.

I was wearing a dark blue satin gown I had made from a design Francine had created especially for me. It had thin shoulder straps with *diamanté* embroidery, and a square neckline. The skirt was narrow but had a little train at the back, and there was a matching wrap also embroidered with *diamanté*.

My hair was rather long at the moment. I had been growing it for a while and I'd swept it up into a large and glossy swirl, which I had fastened with marcasite clips in the shape of butterflies.

"You look beautiful, Emma," my mother said. "It's a pity Jon isn't here to see you dressed up like that."

"He is coming tomorrow. I can put it on for him. I might wear it again for Christmas night." I glanced down at my dress. "It is rather lovely, isn't it?"

"You are," Sol said. "I don't think I've ever seen you look better, Emma." He presented his arm. "Ready, my lady?"

I laughed and took his arm, feeling rather special. I thought it was going to be an enjoyable evening.

The very first time I'd gone to a reception with Sol I had felt lost and out of things, but it was different now. I was more sophisticated, well able to hold a conversation with anyone. Besides, I knew almost everyone who would be there that evening.

Our taxi sped through the city. It was nice to see that some of the stores had lit their window displays for Christmas. I had a feeling of anticipation as we went into the hotel.

We mingled for drinks, then moved into the dining room. The tables were wonderful, set with red cloths and white Christmas roses, and a silver gift-wrapped gift of sweets for each lady. I put mine in my bag for Lizzy.

Sol held my chair out himself. I glanced across the room as I sat down and my heart stood still. Jack had just come in. A pretty woman dressed in white was with him. Her gown had a full skirt, was strapless and like mine was embroidered with beads. She had a white fur wrap draped over her shoulders, but slipped it off as she sat down.

So this was Angie! She was very pretty. A fragile, sweet, helpless girl who looked nervously at Jack all the time, as if seeking his approval for everything she did.

No wonder he had married her. What man could resist her? She smiled at her husband, and I saw her whole face light up. She was obviously very much in love with him.

Jack had seen us. He frowned and said something to his wife that caused her to look our way, then got up and came over to our table.

His manner was friendly, though perhaps a little reserved. "Emma – it's good to see you. I had no idea you would be here this evening. Sol, nice to see you. Perhaps we could have a chat later?" His eyes came to rest on me. "You must meet Angie later, Emma. I am sure you will like her."

I tried desperately to match his coolness. "She is very lovely, Jack. I should like to meet her. Thank you."

He nodded, turned and went back to his table. Angie smiled at me. I had to smile back. How could I have ignored her attempt to be friendly?

I'm not sure what we ate that evening. It all tasted the same. I sipped my wine, picked at my food, and wished I had not come.

After dinner, everyone moved gradually into the next room. Music was playing, and people were beginning to dance when Jack brought Angie to us.

"Emma – this is my wife, Angie. I've explained that your family made me welcome during the war. She knows I take James out sometimes. In fact they have already met – haven't you, darling?"

I found myself playing the part he had drawn for me. "My son won the three-legged race with Jack one summer. I don't think he ever forgot it. And of course there was the pedal car. Your husband is very good at giving presents, Angie. James is convinced he's going to be a famous film director thanks to Jack."

Angie laughed but looked puzzled. I explained about the camera and my son's obsession with taking pictures.

"Oh, I see. I dare say he will get over it. Children do, don't they?" She looked at me shyly. "Where did you buy your dress? It's lovely."

"Thank you. I made it myself. From a design someone created specially for me."

"Would the designer do something for me, do you think?"

"Yes, I'm sure she would," I replied. "But can you find someone to make it up for you?"

"I was hoping you might? Jack told me your firm makes dresses."

"Not this kind," I replied. "But I'll speak to Francine. She might take it on herself."

"How do you like living in London, Mrs Harvey?" Sol asked. "Does it seem strange after New York?"

"I like it in England," she said. "Especially at the Cottage. We're going down for a while after Christmas."

The musicians had just struck up for a waltz.

"Would you like to dance, Mrs Harvey?"

Angie looked at Jack. He nodded his approval. She smiled and accepted Sol's arm.

"Your wife is charming, Jack," I said as they moved away. "You must be very proud of her."

"Yes, I am proud of her. She is a sweet girl, and very pretty." He raised his eyebrows. "Would you like to dance, Emma?"

I did not think I could bear to be that close to him.

"No, not for the moment, thank you."

His gaze narrowed. "Are you still angry with me for what I said in the taxi?"

"No. I forgave you months ago. It was my own fault – besides, you were right. I should not have considered that partnership. And you were only offering me what I once offered you. I understand why you did it."

"Do you, Emma?" The question was quietly spoken, but there was such a look in his eyes! My heart stopped for one fraction of a second, then raced madly on. "I very much doubt it. I doubt you even suspect how much I regretted the words I said to you that day we parted. I should have swallowed my pride and taken what you offered."

My throat was so tight I could not speak. I could only stare at him – but perhaps he understood the words I could not form. He had always known what was in my mind when we were together.

"Jack." I managed the word at last, but it was too late. Sol and Angie were leaving the dance floor, coming towards us. "I wish—"

But I could not speak the words in my heart as I saw the way Angie smiled at her husband. I had given up the right to Jack's love. I must not try to take it back.

* * *

113

"This is the best Christmas we've ever had," Bert said as he kissed my cheek the morning he and Mum were due to leave. "The holiday in Cornwall was good, but I've really enjoyed seeing the children with their toys."

"Yes, it was fun, wasn't it? They were so lucky. I've never seen so much torn wrapping paper! Everyone spoiled them this year – and Jack went over the top with the new bicycles for them both."

Bert looked slightly disapproving. "They can't ride them much in town, can they?"

"I think it's safe enough round the square, but we shall probably take them down to Jon's later in the year and leave them there. The children won't mind that once the newness has worn off, and there's plenty of space there for them to ride to their hearts' content."

"A good idea," Bert said. "Before he left, Jon asked me and Greta to go and stay with him in the spring. I think we shall go. It will be a nice quiet holiday for us."

"Yes, you go," I said. "It will do you both good."

Mum came into the sitting room then to tell us the taxi was waiting to take them to the station.

"Thank you, Emma," she said and hugged me. "It was lovely. We've both enjoyed ourselves."

"We must make it a regular event."

"Yes." She glanced at her husband and I saw something in her eyes . . . a faint wistfulness. "Yes, perhaps we shall. Well, this won't buy the baby a new dress, Emma! We ought to be off."

"You sounded just like Gran then," I said and laughed. "She used to say things like that."

"Don't remind me I'm getting old." She pulled a wry face. "I know it well enough."

"Of course you're not old. You just remind me of her sometimes."

"I shall never be the woman she was. I still miss her, Emma. I never appreciated her until she wasn't there any more."

I nodded but didn't say anything as I went to the door to see them off. My mother and Gran hadn't always got on, but

I knew they had always cared underneath – and both of them had always tried to protect me.

I waved until the taxi was out of sight, then went back to the sitting room. Sol was sitting in his usual chair, reading a newspaper. He laid it aside and looked at me.

"So it's just us again, Emma. Feeling a bit low now they've all gone?"

"No, not really." I smiled at him. "Have you time for a coffee, or must you go straight away?"

"Ring for coffee," Sol said, his eyes intent on my face. "Then sit down and tell me what's on your mind."

"You know me too well," I said ruefully. I sat on the sofa opposite him. "It's just . . . well, it's Jack."

"Of course it's Jack," Sol said, a smile flickering in his eyes. "When you look like that it's always Jack – but what has he done now?"

"He sent me a diamond bracelet for Christmas. I couldn't show it to anyone. It's far too valuable. Everyone would have known it came from him. Jon gave me a silk scarf and perfume."

"What is really causing that frown?" Sol wasn't smiling now. "Are you seeing him again?"

"No . . ." I hesitated for a moment, then confessed, "He has asked me to have lunch one day. He has taken Angie to the Cottage for New Year. She wants to stay there for a while, but Jack has to come back next weekend for a meeting."

"And he wants to take you to lunch. You know that isn't all he wants, don't you?"

"I'm not sure."

"Don't fool yourself, Emma. I've no idea why he married that pretty child, but he isn't in love with her. She irritates him. He tries to hide it, but sometimes it shows. Angie is too young, too insecure and too gentle for a man like Jack Harvey. If he isn't careful, he will crush her."

I knew Sol was right. "Yes. I thought she seemed very anxious to please the other evening, over-anxious in fact. Jack likes people who stand up to him. He only respects those he can't walk right over."

"You were the woman for him, Emma. I didn't want you to leave London, but I wish you had married him. I don't like to see you unhappy." His eyes met mine. "If you want to sleep with him, do it. I shan't blame you."

"Sol!" I laughed at his bluntness. "You are encouraging us both to commit adultery."

"So? As long as Angie doesn't know, it won't hurt her. And I imagine Jon expects it to happen sooner or later."

"What do you mean?" I stared at him in surprise. "He doesn't know about Jack. I've never told him. I didn't see the point of hurting him when it was over. I never expected Jack to come back. How can Jon know?"

"He knows," Sol said. "He has known for a long time. Not from me. I wouldn't have told him. I like Jon, and it must have caused him considerable pain. I should think it was probably his mother."

"Dorothy never liked me. In fact, I think she hates me."

"You need look no further for the culprit, then," Sol said and pulled a face. "I cannot understand a woman who could do that to her own son – but I'd bet on it having been her."

"Yes, I agree."

If Jon knew then it must have been his mother who had told him. She had done it to spite me, not realising that she was hurting Jon by her actions.

It made sense of Jon's sudden decision not to try and make love to me, and of his need for a home of his own. He was hurt, of course, but he hadn't blamed me for what I'd done during that time when I had believed he was dead. He hadn't stopped loving me. He had simply given me my freedom. He had stood back so that I could find happiness with someone else. I would not feel so much guilt on Jon's account if he had given me his blessing.

I felt humbled, sad and yet excited. If Jack wanted us to be together, perhaps . . . but how could we? No, of course we couldn't. It wasn't right.

Sol had said it wouldn't hurt Angie if she didn't know, but it would take something very precious away from her. And it would be morally wrong.

I tried to put the temptation out of my mind. I had a week to think about it – a week in which I was going to very busy at the shops. It was January sale time, and that meant I would have no time to fret about anything else.

I was shocked as I heard the tearful note in Mum's voice that morning. She couldn't stop crying and I realised something terrible must have happened.

"It was so sudden, Emma. He'd been coughing a bit, and I took him a cup of tea. He smiled the way he does . . . Oh, Emma, I can't bear it! I went through to the kitchen for five minutes. That's all it was . . . and when I came back he was dead. He'd gone just like that, sitting in his chair."

"Oh, Mum, I'm so sorry," I said. My knuckles were white as I gripped the telephone receiver. It was only four days since they had gone home. This was terrible news, unbelievable! Bert had seemed so well the day they left. "I'll come down today. I can get a train this morning. I'll be with you as soon as I can."

"Would you, Emma? I know you're busy with the sales, but I can't seem to think straight. Gwen came round. She's . . . seeing to things. She knows what to do, but I do want you to come. I need you."

"I'll pack a few things and be with you in a few hours. There's nothing I can do from here. Ask Gwen to stay with you until I get there."

"Yes, she said she would. She has been very kind, but I need you."

"I love you, Mum. I'll be with you soon. I promise."

I replaced the receiver as the tears came to my eyes. We had all been so happy just a few days earlier. Now Bert had gone. He had been ill for a while, but none of us had expected this. Not so suddenly. It was hard to believe it had happened.

Sol was stunned when I rang him at the showroom. Bert was only a couple of years his senior.

"That's such a shame," he said. "He was a decent man – and good to your mother. Yes, you go down straight away."

"Will you do something for me?"

"You want me to tell Jack where you've gone, don't you?"

"Yes. Tell him I will ring when I get back."

"I'll tell him. Is there anything else I can do? What about the new shop? Weren't they coming to finish the fittings this week?"

"Yes. Would you take care of it for me?"

"Yes, of course. Take care – and tell your mother I'm sorry."

"I will. I'll let you know when the funeral is. You will come down?"

"I couldn't do otherwise. Bert was family."

I was crying again as I replaced the receiver, then rang Jon.

"I'm sorry," he said. "I'm not sure when I can get down. I've had a bit of a chill myself – but I'll come for the funeral, of course."

"No, don't come if you're not well, Jon. Mum wouldn't want you to. Telephone her this evening, and send flowers. That will be enough."

"Are you sure? I don't want to offend Greta."

"She won't be offended. She is very fond of you, Jon. She wouldn't want you to risk your own health. Nor would I."

"Then I shan't come. I've been in bed for a couple of days. Mrs Martin has been very helpful. I've been well looked after, Emma. She has made me soup and hot drinks."

"I could come down after the funeral."

"No, that's not necessary, darling. Take care of Greta. She will need you. I am not ill – just unwell. You don't need to make a fuss."

Everything else that had been playing on my mind was forgotten as I tried to comfort my mother. She was distraught with grief. In fact, she cried so much that I thought she would be ill and fetched the doctor to her.

"She needs sleep," he told me. "I'll leave her a sleeping draught. It should help, but I wouldn't recommend it as a habit."

"No, of course not. She will be better tomorrow."

Mum slept after she had taken the medicine mixed with a glass of warm milk. I sat with her until she drifted off, holding her hand, then I slipped under the cover beside her.

"I can't bear to sleep in there," she had told me when we passed the room she had shared with Bert. So we were both sleeping in the guest room.

During the night, Mum moaned once or twice. She spoke Bert's name and then cried out, "No, Harold! Don't hit me . . . please don't hit me."

She was having a nightmare from the past. I stroked her hair back from her forehead. "It's all right, Mum. He can't hit you. He's dead."

She quietened again, but I felt sad for her. She'd had so many years of unhappiness with my father, and just a handful of good ones with Bert. It wasn't fair that she had lost her husband so soon.

In the days that followed, we talked about Bert a lot. Mum told me things about when she was a young girl and courting her true love.

"I was sixteen when he first noticed me," she said. "I knew he fancied me, Emma, but I played hard to get. I kept him dangling for nearly two years, then I let him kiss me after we'd been to a fair. We neither of us meant it to go so far, but after we'd started – well, we couldn't stop. The wonder of it is that you're not Bert's child, but it just didn't happen."

"You've always been sure?"

"Oh, yes. I hadn't seen Bert for three months before I married Harold. You were born eight months and three weeks later, and you were early because I'd had a fall. At least, that's what the doctor said."

"Then Father must have known I was his all the time."

"In his heart I'm sure he did, but he couldn't forgive me for not being a virgin on our wedding night. I tried to tell him it was over – but you know all this."

It was so sad that she had married the wrong man.

"I sent Bert away and I've always regretted it," she said. "Maybe I didn't deserve these years of happiness, but I've been lucky. You're lucky too, Emma. Jon really loves you.

You shouldn't forget that, love. Not many women have that much."

I glanced away. "We're not living together, Mum. You know that."

"It's an odd arrangement," she agreed. "But at least you are friends. Your father and I were never that."

I nodded, but didn't say anything. Mum wouldn't approve of my seeing Jack again. She was fond of Jon. She respected him for what he'd done in the war, and would think I was letting him down. If I did have an affair, I would have to keep it from her.

"What are you thinking, Emma?"

"I was remembering something Margaret once said to me . . . about taking your chances of happiness when they come."

"Yes," she said, thinking I was talking about her and Bert. "I'm glad that we had that holiday last summer. Bert really enjoyed himself, and at Christmas too."

"Yes, at least he had that."

We talked on, remembering the good things. I knew that Mum was beginning to get over the first, sharp pain of losing Bert, though she would continue to grieve for a long time. I decided that after the funeral, I would take her back to London with me.

"Come back with me, Mum," I pleaded. "At least for a few days. Give yourself a chance to get used to the idea of living alone."

"It's best to start as you mean to go on," she said. "If I ran away from it now, I wouldn't be able to face coming back."

"But you don't have to, Mum. You can stay with us for as long as you like. We should all be glad to have you."

She shook her head. "No, Emma. I'll come and stay sometimes, like always – and Jon has asked me to visit him. I think I shall go down next week. He doesn't sound at all well to me."

The look she directed at me was reproachful.

"I offered to go down. He said it wasn't necessary."

"You should go anyway. He is your husband, Emma – though I think you sometimes forget it."

"That's not fair, Mum. You don't understand. Jon doesn't want me to go at the moment. Really, he doesn't. If he did, he would have said something."

"Well, I think someone should, and if you won't, I shall."

Her tone and manner were accusing. We were close to quarrelling. I was shocked. We hardly ever argued.

"I'll telephone Jon, ask him if he wants me there – but if he says no, I shan't go."

"Do it now, then."

I obeyed for the sake of peace. The telephone was answered by Mrs Martin.

"Mrs Reece. What a shame!" she said. "Mr Reece went out for a walk a few minutes ago. He will be sorry to have missed you. Is there a message I can give him?"

"No, no message. I was just ringing to see how he was."

"Oh, much better. Yes, almost his old self again."

"He's much better – that's good news. I'll ring again one evening next week."

Mum looked unconvinced as I replaced the receiver. "Well, I still think you should go, but I can't force you. I don't know what your plans are for the future, Emma – but Jon doesn't deserve to be hurt."

"What does that mean?" I felt defensive as I looked at her. She blamed me because Jon had chosen to live alone.

"You've allowed Jack Harvey back into your life."

"You seemed to approve of Jack during the war."

"That was when you thought Jon had been killed. I didn't want you to spend the rest of your life alone, but things are different now."

"Are they?"

I almost told her the truth about my marriage then, but kept it inside. It wasn't Jon's fault that he couldn't be a proper husband to me. The least I owed him was to protect our private life.

"What are you saying, Emma?" Her gaze narrowed in

suspicion. "I just don't understand what's going on between you two. If it isn't because of Jack Harvey—"

"It's Jon's writing," I said. "He needs peace to write, and apparently he finds my life too exhausting."

"Well, I suppose that's understandable," she said. "I'm sorry if I've wronged you – but I wouldn't like to see you hurt Jon. He was always good to you. He helped you a lot when you were going through a bad time."

"Yes, I know that. I haven't forgotten. I don't want to hurt him either."

The subject was dropped. We talked about inconsequential matters until it was time for me to leave, then she came and kissed my cheek.

"We won't part in anger," she said. "You know I love you – but sometimes you're inclined to go your own way no matter what. Think before you leap, love."

"Yes, I shall," I promised. "And I'm not angry. I love you, too. Take care of yourself – and don't be lonely. Come to us whenever you like."

I was sorry that she had chosen to stay at the cottage. I knew she was independent, but she would feel Bert's loss more after I left.

I mulled over what my mother had said as I sat staring out of the train window going home. She was right, of course. Sometimes I did act without thinking of the consequences for others.

It wasn't only Jon I had to consider; there was Angie, too. She wasn't just Jack's wife, a faceless woman I could pretend wasn't there. I had met her, spoken to her – liked her. How could I deliberately destroy her marriage?

Two weeks passed and I did not telephone Jack. Instead I threw myself into my work, trying to blot out the sharp longing I felt every time I thought of him.

My new shop was just about ready in time for the grand opening. I was there long before anyone else that morning, checking every detail so that everything was as perfect as I could make it. As I walked through the different departments on three floors, I could not help feeling a rush of pride. What I had here was a highly individual store that would provide women with everything they needed for personal wear.

I had a lingerie department, hosiery, beachwear – with a rather exciting display of bathing costumes for mother and daughter – knitwear, pretty blouses, costumes, dresses for day and evening, jackets and coats. And a rail of nothing but tailored slacks! There was a whole floor devoted to hats, gloves, bags and shoes, and also a department for the enthusiastic needlewoman.

A woman looking for a special outfit would be able to buy everything she needed, matching gloves to shoes, hats to dresses, all under one roof. The major department stores already provided a similar service, of course, but they sold other goods, too, and the different departments were often too far apart to make matching colours easy. My shop was devoted to the fashion-conscious woman.

I intended to sell exclusive designs that could not be bought elsewhere, as well as the normal, less expensive ranges. It was something new and exciting. Having borrowed to finance my new business, I knew I was taking a risk. If the customers did not return again and again to buy, I could lose much of the capital I had invested.

I refused to think of failure. All my other shops had done well. I could only trust that my luck would hold.

I asked all my friends to the champagne opening. We cut a blue ribbon and had displays of flowers throughout the shop.

There was a steady stream of customers through the front door the first day. They came to look, and a few bought bits and pieces, but it was not a wonderful day for business.

"Don't worry," Sol said to me that evening. "It's different, Emma. You knew that when you opened. You have to give it time to work."

"Yes, I know."

I was a little disappointed that night, but the next day the sales were better. They improved gradually day by day. My idea wasn't a raging success, but it was beginning to work. If I could hold on long enough, the upturn was bound to come.

Nine

It had now been three weeks since Bert's funeral. I still hadn't telephoned Jack. I imagined Angie must be back in town, and thought the time of temptation had passed. When Jack rang to ask if he could take James out that weekend, I agreed to be at home when he came to fetch him. After all, what harm could it do just to see him, here in the house?

"I have to talk to you, Emma."

My heart was racing wildly, but I replied in a calm, flat tone. "Yes, we should talk."

"On Saturday then?"

"Yes, why not?"

I was waiting for him an hour before he arrived. I had changed my dress three times, and was extremely nervous. When he came into the sitting room my heart stood still. He had brought me a huge basket of hothouse flowers, their perfume filling the air.

"They are lovely, Jack." I smiled at him, the familiar desire beginning once more. "There was no need to bring me a present, though. And you shouldn't have given me that bracelet at Christmas. I shall never be able to wear it."

"You can always sell it."

His tone was so harsh that I gasped.

"What's wrong, Jack? What have I done?"

"Nothing . . . of course you haven't done anything, Emma. It's all my fault. I'm the only one to blame."

"What have you done? Are you in trouble?" Had he arranged to have Philip killed? Had the police found out?

He smiled oddly. "How can you ask, Emma? I've ruined

everything. I admit it. I know that your marriage is only in name. If I had been patient – if I'd waited—"

"Jack! Stop talking in riddles. We are both married, but if we both want . . . It isn't right, but—" I stopped as I saw the look in his eyes. There was something more, something he was finding it difficult to tell me. "Just tell me. Please."

"When we spoke at that dance – in the taxi – when I sent you the bracelet and asked you out to lunch—" His hands clenched at his sides as if he were trying to control them. "I intended to ask you to have an affair with me, Emma. I knew you wouldn't leave Jon and I couldn't divorce Angie just yet, but I thought in time – when she was a little older and wouldn't be so hurt . . . We might have had a chance of being together properly one day."

"Why shouldn't we, Jack? If we're careful – if we don't hurt anyone – why shouldn't we have a little happiness for ourselves?"

"I want you so much, Emma. I know what I was planning was wrong, but I couldn't keep away from you." He cursed softly. "I wish to blazes I'd never married her!"

"Why did you – if you didn't love her?"

"She was pretty and gentle, and I knew she loved me. Or thought she did, poor child. She didn't know what she was getting. I thought she might help me to forget you – but it didn't work. As soon as I saw you again the hunger was back."

I recognised the desperation in him and my heart leaped with excitement.

"Jack," I said, and moved towards him. I wanted to touch him, to feel his mouth on mine. "I've never stopped—"

"Don't!" he warned. "Don't say it, Emma. It's too late. I was going to ask, but now . . ."

"I don't understand. What has changed?"

My throat was tight. I couldn't speak. I just had to stand there and listen as he tore my foolish hopes to pieces.

"Angie is having my child."

His words were like a knife thrust in my heart. Angie was

having Jack's child . . . something that I had wanted so much and knew I would never have.

"I see."

"Do you?" He frowned. "She has been ill; she has a weakness in her heart. The doctor told me she could lose the baby if she is upset . . . she might even die. I can't risk that, Emma. Even for you." His eyes sought mine as if to ask for forgiveness. "You wouldn't desert Jon when he needed you – how can I desert Angie knowing that it might kill her?"

Of course he couldn't. It would be too cruel. She was young and vulnerable – and she was carrying his child. Besides, I knew it was unlikely that I could ever give him such a precious gift – if he lost Angie he might lose all chance of ever having a child of his own.

"You can't hurt her, Jack. We mustn't . . . do anything to upset her."

His eyes were bleak as he looked at me. "I knew you would say that. You are kinder to me than I was to you."

"I love you, Jack. I always have and I always shall."

"Emma! My God!" He moved towards me and the desperation was in his eyes. "How can I leave you again? I love you. You are a part of me. I can't get you out of my system . . . I never shall."

He reached out for me. I went into his arms, drawn by the fierce hunger I sensed in him, a hunger that matched my own. We kissed again and again, our hands running over the other's face, stroking, touching, trying to absorb the beloved features, knowing that when we parted this time it would be for the last time.

He gazed longingly into my face and I sensed what he was about to ask of me.

"I love you so much," Jack said. "Just once, Emma . . . come to me once more before we part. Please?"

It was what I had asked of him when we'd parted during the war. He had thrown my words back in my face with such anger that they had haunted me ever since, but I understood his hunger, his need – because it was my own.

"Where is Angie?"

"At the Cottage. I'm going to fetch her tomorrow, and we fly home to America in a couple of days."

"So it really will be just once." I raised my head, looking into his eyes. "She need never know. No one will know. We shan't hurt her or the child."

"You will come?" He looked disbelieving as I nodded. "To our place, Emma? I bought Jane's house – did you know that?"

"No, I didn't know."

"Angie has never been there," he said. "I let friends stay there – but the studio is kept locked. I couldn't let anyone else in there . . . but I go there sometimes and remember."

"Oh, Jack," I whispered as the tears stung my eyes. "You foolish, foolish man."

"Foolish for loving you?" he asked, then shook his head, his smile tender and loving. "No, I don't think so. Foolish for leaving you . . . for hurting you . . . yes, I was that. I know I'm being unfair to you now—"

I touched my fingers to his mouth.

"No, Jack. For this one night we will pretend it is still wartime. We'll pretend that the years between never happened – that there is no Angie and no Jon."

I told Sol that I would be staying with a friend that night. He did not need explanations, but promised that he would make my excuses should my mother or Jon happen to ring.

When I kissed James goodnight, he told me that Jack was going back to America.

"He has to go – it's business. But he says he will write and that I can go and stay with him when I'm older."

"That's good, darling."

I left him clutching the leather-bound photograph album that was Jack's latest gift to him and went down to the waiting taxi. I was wearing a dress I had not worn for years. It was very old, and had belonged to Margaret before it was mine. It was a blue velvet gown that had a slightly medieval look: the gown I had been wearing the night Jack and I met.

It fitted me as well as it had then, and although old it still looked beautiful, at least in the softer lights of evening.

Jack smiled as he saw me step out of the taxi.

"You're so lovely, Emma. I always did like that gown."

"I wore it for you. I've never worn it since . . . the party at Jane's. The night we first made love."

He drew me into his arms and kissed me, then took me by the hand, leading me out into the courtyard behind the house, down the stone steps to the little studio apartment where we had always made love.

During the war we had always had to leave the shutters closed because of the blackout, but Jack had pushed them back so that we could see the sky and a sprinkling of stars. He had filled the garden room with flowers, so many that their perfume was overwhelming.

"I always wanted to give you diamonds," he said, as we stood for a while looking out at the sky, his arms around my waist, his body close to mine, so close that his breath tickled my neck. Now that we were together, we were in no hurry. This was a night to savour, to remember for the rest of our lives. "But you would never let me give you more than a few trinkets."

"All I wanted was your love, Jack."

"That will be yours for as long as we both live," he vowed. "When I've gone I shall always think of you here, like this, my arms about you, wearing that dress."

I turned and put my fingers to his lips.

"No, Jack. No regrets."

"I want you so much . . ."

"Let's go upstairs."

I smiled, took his hand and led him up to the bedroom.

It was as if we had never been apart. Our bodies fitted together so well. Every caress was a memory deeply imprinted into our hearts and minds. We touched and kissed, exploring each other hungrily, the pleasure as fierce and sweet as it had always been when we lay together.

We did not sleep all night. Sleep would have been a waste of those precious hours. Instead, we lay entwined, beating heart to beating heart, as we talked, made love, talked and made love again . . . and again.

Jack had brought champagne and an ice bucket. We sipped our champagne, ate chocolate truffles and strawberries.

"Where on earth did you find strawberries in February?" I asked as he dipped one in the champagne and fed it to me with his lips.

He laughed and touched his finger to my nose. "That's my secret, Emma. If I told you, you would be horrified . . . but they came from a long way away."

"You are so extravagant!" I scolded, kissing him as I swallowed the delicious fruit. "They must have cost as much as diamonds to get them here."

"Worth every penny," he murmured, his mouth moving down my navel, to the strawberry he had placed in a very odd position. "I wanted to cover you with diamonds, my darling. I wanted to give you so much . . ."

"You have," I said, pressing my body closer to his as I felt the desire stir between us once more. "When I thought you hated me it broke my heart – but I can bear anything now."

Jack hushed me with kisses. We would not think of the parting that must come after this night. We would make it last for ever.

But it could not last. Morning came too soon, and we knew it was over. Nevertheless, we both tried to laugh and make jokes as Jack cooked bacon and mushrooms for me, just as he had after our first night together.

At last, I knew I must end it. I reached for the telephone and ordered my taxi.

"Must you go yet?" Jack asked. "Stay another hour."

"Or another day, another week . . ." I shook my head at him. "We promised ourselves we would say goodbye after last night, and we must, Jack. If I stay another hour, you will stay another week – it will go on and on and Angie is going to be hurt."

"Damn her! I wish I had never married her." Jack groaned. "Forgive me, but I almost wish she would die."

"No!" I pressed my hand fiercely over his mouth, glaring at him. "Don't you dare say that, Jack! Don't you dare ever think it. Never. Not once. Do you hear me? If you do you will betray everything we have been to each other; everything we have of each other will be sullied."

He nodded, his eyes dark with pain. "I'm sorry. I didn't mean it. I wouldn't hurt her, Emma – not even to be free."

"Of course you wouldn't, Jack. If you could do that you would not be the man I love so much."

I kissed him once more and then I left him. It was not as hard as it had been when I sent him away the first time. We had parted in anger then, and I had believed he hated me, but this time he went with my blessing. I knew he loved me. I would hold that thought in my heart for the rest of my life.

We had not said goodbye. We would never say goodbye.

Francine suggested a trip to Paris.

"We could go together," she said. "It's lovely there in April, Emma. I know lots of small workshops where they make beautiful clothes at a fraction of the price you would pay in the main showrooms. I am sure you would find stock for your shops."

I had thought I would never wish to return to Paris, but it would be different this time. I had been feeling low since Jack left me and a holiday was just what I needed.

"We'll take the children and Sarah, too," I said. "I had been thinking of perhaps taking them somewhere different for a holiday, and I've arranged travel documents for them. Yes, we'll all go together. James has never flown. It will be a new and exciting experience."

Francine looked dubious, but having suggested the trip could not draw back. I smiled as I saw the doubts in her eyes.

"Don't worry. Sarah will look after them most of the time. They won't be a nuisance."

"I am not used to being around children. I was always with Grandmere. She did not like noise. To be honest, she did not like me very much."

It was the most revealing thing Francine had told me

about her past. I sensed now that her childhood had been far from happy.

"I'll warn James to be on his best behaviour. You'll see, Francine, we shall all enjoy ourselves."

She looked at me with curiosity. "You always manage to smile, don't you, Emma? I have sensed that you were sad recently – but still you smile."

"Not always," I said wryly. "But crying doesn't help."

"No, tears never help," she agreed. "But friends do, Emma. I hope we shall be friends?"

"We are already." I laughed. "If you still want to know me after five days with my terrible two, we shall become bosom pals for life."

Francine looked amused. "We shall see."

The children were thrilled when I told them we were going to France. Lizzy looked a little nervous at the idea of going up in an aeroplane, but James was excited.

"When are we going?" he wanted to know.

"This weekend, when you start your school holiday. We shall be away for five days."

The look in his eyes was my reward. I knew that he often resented my leaving him for my business, but this time I was taking him with me.He spread his arms and began to run round the playroom, making a noise he fondly imagined sounded like an aeroplane engine.

Lizzy watched for a while, then slipped her hand in mine.

"Are you better now, Emmie?"

"I haven't been ill, darling."

"You've been sad." Her eyes were serious and thoughtful. "Why were you sad, Emmie?"

"A friend of mine went away, that's all. I've been missing him."

"You've still got me – and James."

"Yes, darling." I bent down to hug here. "I'm very lucky to have both of you."

I knew then that I would have to put away my sadness. If both Francine and Lizzy had been aware of it, I was

131

allowing myself to brood too much. I must stop feeling sorry for myself. I had so much to be grateful for.

The new shop was not yet doing as well as I'd hoped, but the takings were reasonable, and Sol was in no hurry to be repaid.

"Don't even think about it, Emma," he had told me. "Give yourself five years and then we'll discuss it again."

As long as he was not in urgent need of his capital I could manage, even if the shop did no more than break even for the first year or two.

I rang my mother after telling the children about the Paris trip.

"I don't suppose you would like to come with us?"

"I can't be bothered with all that foreign nonsense. Besides, Jon has asked me if I would like to go down this weekend. I think I shall take the train and go to see him."

"Well, you will enjoy that." I was a little hurt that she seemed to prefer his company to mine.

"When are you going down? You haven't been since Jon moved in. I think it's time you gave some thought to your marriage, Emma."

"I telephone once or twice every week. Jon has been busy – and so have I. This is a crucial time for me with the new shop, Mum. I have to keep on top of what is happening there. Besides, I'm going to take the children down to Jon's when we get back from France. We arranged it weeks ago."

"I should think so, too," she grumbled. "You've done well for yourself, got on in the world, I'll give you that – but people matter more than money."

She put the receiver down on me sharply. I stared at it for several seconds, wondering whether I should call her back. I hated to be at odds with Mum, and we seemed to argue more and more these days.

She was upset because I did not spend more time with Jon, and perhaps I ought to have gone down before this – but I hadn't wanted to straight after Jack left. I might not have been able to hide my feelings. Jon understood me so well, and I did not want him to guess that I had spent the night with Jack. He had given me the freedom to live as I pleased, but I would never deliberately hurt him.

He was pleased when I told him I was going back to Paris.

"I'm glad, Emma. I know you wouldn't go if you were still haunted by what happened there. Have a lovely time, my dear – and let me know exactly when you are coming down, won't you? I like to be sure of the time, so that I can be ready for you."

"Yes, of course."

"I shall look forward to seeing you and the children."

His voice sounded a little odd, distant, almost as though he couldn't wait for me to finish the call. I wondered if he was ill again, but surely he would have said? Perhaps he was just caught up in his writing. I must have interrupted him when I rang.

I would be seeing him in a few days' time, and I would ask if he was still content with the way things were between us.

"So what do you want to do today?" I asked as we all gathered round the breakfast table. "It's our last day in Paris, children, and we're going to spend it together."

The past four days had been hectic ones. Francine and I had spent a part of each morning visiting various workshops in the Sentier district, which was generally acknowledged as the centre of Paris's clothes manufacturing industry. Amongst its narrow streets were a considerable number of wholesale warehouses and cramped workshops, where the conditions were sometimes quite shocking.

"If you come here alone, be careful," Francine warned. "It can be an unsavoury and dangerous area."

I had already noticed some rather dubious characters hanging around. It was not an area I would want to visit often, but some of the merchandise was extremely good quality and cheaper than I could have bought at home. I had purchased a few things that caught my eye straight off the rails, and ordered more from some of the better-class showrooms with whom I could have a proper trading agreement.

The movement of money was still restricted at home, but

it was possible to obtain the necessary licence to import for business if you went through the proper channels – and I had brought rather more cash with me than was strictly allowed.

"Take it, Emma," Sol had told me when I asked him what he thought I would need. "They can't check on everyone, and it's unlikely they will look under the lining in your suitcase."

"You are a wicked man," I'd told him, but I had taken his advice, and now I was glad of the extra money.

Together, Francine and I had visited the various sweat-shops and regular showrooms. Out of curiosity more than a desire to buy, we also went to the very different and elegant salons of the famous fashion houses of Dior, Paquin, Balenciaga – where I fell in love with his "pillbox" hats and very recklessly ordered some for my shop – and Jacques Fath, of course.

Meanwhile, my ever faithful and patient Sarah had taken the children to the Eiffel Tower, various museums, numerous cafés, galleries and gardens, and we had all been on the river every afternoon. It was beautifully cool on the water and the Vedettes de Paris left from the Pont Neuf every half an hour. They were small boats used often by visitors and had guides to tell the passengers all about the beautiful buildings and places of interest they were passing. There were also larger boats where it was possible to sit and eat an evening meal while you floated peacefully towards your destination. We had been on these too, as I felt that the best way for the children to see more of Paris was from the river, and at night it looked magnificent with all the lights.

"I would like to go to a café and have ice cream," Lizzy said now, in answer to my question.

"I want to go up the Tower again, Mum," James chimed in.

"I'm not sure we could get permission to go up again," I said. "It isn't always open at this time of year, darling. You went on a special tour that I was lucky to hear about. Perhaps when we come again – if you want to come back?"

Both children agreed that they did.

"Next time we might explore a little more of France," I said. "Take a train and go into the countryside. Shall we go on the boats this afternoon?"

"Can we have our pictures drawn?" Lizzy asked. "Sarah said there wasn't time yesterday – is there time today?"

"We were coming to meet you," Sarah explained. "I didn't want to keep you waiting."

"We've got all day," I said and smiled at Lizzy. "Now, this is my idea – I think we should buy some presents to take home, then have ice cream and coffee. Then we'll have a picture drawn of Lizzy – and anyone else who wants it done. After that we'll go somewhere special for a long, leisurely lunch, and spend a lazy afternoon on the river. This evening we'll go and listen to the singers at one of those open-air cafés where they have entertainment. How does that sound?"

There was a chorus of approval from Lizzy and James. Sarah was content to go along with my plans, but Francine was frowning.

"Would you mind if I went somewhere alone this morning, Emma? I could join you at the Pont Neuf at, say, three o'clock?"

"No, of course I don't mind. If you have something else to do, we could meet this evening."

"I should like to come on the river. I'll be at the Pont Neuf at three and wait until you get there."

I nodded, noticing the odd expression in her eyes. What was it she had to do that she wanted to keep private?

After breakfast, Sarah and I took the children on a whirl-wind shopping tour. They each had pocket money to spend on whatever they liked, and I was in charge of the presents to take home.

We bought small gifts for Sol, Mum, Gwen, Jon and Madge Henty. James bought a model of the Eiffel Tower for himself, and some postcards to send to Jack. Lizzy bought a tiny bottle of perfume for me, and I bought her a doll with a china face and blonde curls.

Sarah admired some lace an old woman was making at a

table outside one of the cafés, so we bought a piece of it for her. For Francine I purchased some pretty beads, and for Mrs Rowan a box of wonderful chocolates. Unfortunately, we could none of us resist them and we ate them all, so I had to buy her a bottle of wine instead.

Our purchases complete, we found a café selling delicious ices and ate two each.

"We shall all become very fat," I announced and Lizzy had a fit of the giggles.

She was still giggling when we found an artist on the Left Bank who was willing to draw her picture for just a few coins. It looked very like her. Lizzy was delighted, but James scoffed.

"It's nowhere near as good as a photograph," he declared and refused to have his own portrait done.

He had of course taken rolls and rolls of films, which he was anxious to have developed as soon as he got home.

"Jack says I should learn to do it myself when I'm older," he announced. "It's quite easy really, Mum – but you need a dark-room. Jack told me all about it."

My heart jerked at the mention of Jack's name, but I smiled as I asked when Jack had mentioned the possibility of my son developing the films himself.

"Oh, he writes to me every week," my son replied carelessly. "He tells me lots of interesting things, and says he's going to buy me a cine-camera – that's one that takes moving pictures," he explained kindly. "He says I can have it for my fourteenth birthday."

"That will be nice, darling."

"And he says I can go and visit him in America when I'm sixteen, if you will let me. You will, won't you?"

"We shall have to see when the time comes."

"I shall go one day," James said, that hint of mutiny in his eyes.

"Yes, I expect you will, darling."

We had a very simple late lunch of crusty bread, cheese and ripe tomatoes. Then we made our way unhurriedly towards the Pont Neuf.

Several people were queuing for the next boat. Because of the crowd I was not immediately alerted when a scuffle started, then Sarah touched my arm.

"That man is attacking Francine!"

"Where?" I looked in the direction in which she was pointing and saw she was right. "Stay here with the children!"

I ran towards the spot where Francine was putting up a terrific struggle against a man who appeared to be trying to forcefully abduct her. I shouted and he turned his head to look at me, then said something to Francine. She shook her head and kicked him on the ankle. He yelled at her, then, just as I arrived, let go of her arm and ran off. She was clearly upset and shaken, though she did not appear to be hurt.

"Come and sit down," I said, leading her to a wooden bench away from the curious stares and eyes of the crowd. "Are you all right? Do you want something – a cognac?"

"No, thank you, Emma. I shall be all right in a minute. It was a bit upsetting, that's all."

"Why did he attack you like that? Was he trying to steal your bag?"

"No – nothing like that." She bit her lip. "He knew my mother during the war, and he had seen me with her a few times. He thought I was like her. It was just a mistake."

"But . . . he wasn't French. I thought I heard him say something in what sounded like German."

"Yes," Francine said, a bleak expression in her eyes. "He was an officer stationed here when Paris was occupied." She took a deep breath and her hand trembled. I put mine over it. She smiled then and nodded as if the action had made up her mind. "He paid my mother for sex. She was desperate for money after she lost her job. He wasn't the only one."

"Oh, Francine." I looked at her with sympathy. "That must have been difficult for you."

"It was the shame," Francine said, her voice little more than a whisper. "Grandmere disowned her, and she was forever telling me that my mother was a whore. When the war ended, Maman was denounced as a collaborator and spat at in the

137

street. She put up with it for a while – and then she hanged herself."

"How terrible!" I felt the shock and horror of it run through me. Francine's mother had been so desperate she had taken her own life. Hanging was a dreadful way to die. I could not imagine being that desperate. "I suppose she did not feel she could face what had happened – but it must have been awful for you."

"Grandmere said she deserved to die. I was sorry for her, but also desperately ashamed." Her eyes sought mine. "That day at Marie Bourdeille's showrooms . . . she threw me out because of who my mother was, not because my sketches were not good enough. She said I had no right to approach her."

So Francine had lied to me that day.

"And the designs – were they yours?"

"Yes. She copied them, though she changed bits and pieces. She knew I could never prove she had cheated me. Besides, who would take my part against her? I was the daughter of a woman who went with the enemy."

"You have nothing to be ashamed of," I said and smiled at her. "We all do what we have to do, Francine. Your mother was no worse than a lot of others."

"I was afraid to tell you," she said. "But I am glad I have done. Now we can really be friends."

"We'll talk some more later," I said. "The children and Sarah are waiting. As far as they are concerned, that man was simply trying to snatch your bag."

"Yes," she said, her head going up proudly. "It wasn't important."

It might not be important, but it made me think that perhaps I should try to discover a little more about Francine. Sometimes the things she said did not strike me as being quite right. One day I might need to know the truth about her.

Later that evening, when we were alone, Francine told me a lot more about her childhood. Her grandmother had been a hard, cold woman, always grumbling at her daughter and

Francine. She had looked after her granddaughter, but made her work in the small bakery she ran, never allowing her to play freely with the other children.

"I was determined to escape one day," Francine told me. "My father deserted us just as the war started. He said he had to go back and fight for his country, but he never sent Maman money."

"Some men are like that, Francine. What did your father do before the war?"

"He was an artist." She smiled ruefully. "Not a very good one – but at least he gave me his pastel colours and brushes when he left. It was the paints that saved my life. Without them I would have had nothing to live for. After the war ended, I ran away from Grandmere and found myself work – but all the time I kept my dream alive. I hoped one day to work for one of the great designers. Maman had worked at Madame Coco's house before she closed it in 1939. After that, she took jobs where she could."

"Madame Coco – you mean Chanel?" Francine nodded. "Sol's wife Margaret had one of her early dresses. It was beautiful."

"Do you have it now?"

"No. We sold it during the war when new clothes – decent things – were almost impossible to buy."

Francine nodded, and looked thoughtful. "I think it must have been even worse for you than it was for us during the Occupation – the Germans were generous to those they liked. My mother had money and food when others had nothing."

"I expect she did it for you more than herself," I said. "Don't hate her memory, Francine. Just try to forget the bad things and remember the good."

"Is that how you manage, Emma?" Her eyes met mine in understanding. "I think your Jack Harvey must be a very special man."

"Did Sol tell you about him?"

"No . . . you did, Emma. I have seen the way you look when James speaks of him. It must hurt you that you cannot be with him."

Her words were spoken sympathetically and I wanted to trust her – I liked her. I still wanted Francine to work with us, but I was going to discover as much as I could. Just in case.

"It hurt more when we quarrelled during the war," I said. "At least I know he loves me . . . and we are both doing what we have to do."

Ten

We had been home for only a few hours when Mum telephoned.

"Thank God you are there," she said, and I heard the note of distress in her voice. "Can you catch a train straight away, Emma? It's Jon – he's ill. Very ill. I would have rung you earlier if I'd known how to contact you. He didn't want me to worry you, but I think you should come. If you don't leave at once . . . well, the way things are, you might not see him again. At least, not alive."

Her words had shocked me. How could Jon be that ill? I clung on to the receiver, feeling breathless.

"What happened? I rang him before we went away. He seemed fine then . . . at least, he was in a hurry to put the phone down, but he didn't mention feeling ill."

"He wouldn't," Mum said. "Surely you know Jon by now? You were going to Paris for a holiday with the children. He wouldn't say anything to stop you. Besides, it came on very suddenly. One minute he was laughing, the next he was clutching at himself and complaining of the pain."

"I'll get a taxi straight away. I think there is a train in about an hour's time. Tell Jon I'll be there as soon as I can."

"He doesn't know I've phoned you. Just come, Emma. He needs you. He was delirious a little while ago. He kept calling for you over and over again."

"Delirious?" I caught my breath as I finally understood how serious it was. "How is he now?"

"The doctor came and gave him something to calm him. He seems to be a little more sensible at the moment. I just wish you hadn't been away . . . I would have telephoned

141

yesterday but I knew you wouldn't be home until late last night. I thought he might be better, but if anything he is worse this morning."

"I'm putting the phone down now," I said. "I'll be there as soon as I can. Tell him I'm coming – please?"

I replaced the receiver before she could answer. I was shaking, feeling almost stunned by the suddenness of Jon's illness. He had seemed so well at Christmas . . . but then so had Bert.

I should have been more aware of Jon's health. The doctors had warned me that he would not live to reach middle age. If we had been living together, I might have realised that something was going wrong sooner. My mother was right. I should have gone down to visit long before this.

It was a nightmare journey down to Torquay and seemed to take forever. Why had Jon chosen a house so far away? The fear caught at my heart as I stared out of the train window for mile after mile. Would I ever get there? Would I be in time?

It was dark when I finally got to the house. I paid my taxi driver and went inside. My mother came down the stairs as I reached them.

"Thank God you're here," she said, and stifled a sob. "He is asking for you again, Emma – but I don't think he knows what he's saying. I'm not sure he will know you are here. I'm so sorry . . ."

"I'll go to him straight away," I said. "It's not your fault, Mum. You've done all you could, I know that. At least he wasn't alone. You were here with him."

"Yes, thank goodness I was," she said. "Mrs Martin is very good, but she has a husband and family to look after."

I nodded, but didn't answer as I went on up the stairs. Mrs Martin couldn't be expected to look after an invalid. She had been asked to come in and clean the house each morning. I was Jon's wife. I was the one who should have been here for him.

I was wracked with guilt as I went into the bedroom, and my lips moved in prayer.

"Please don't let Jon die," I whispered as the tears caught at my throat. "He doesn't deserve to die. Not after all he has been through – please don't let him die like this."

I vowed that I would spend more time here if Jon recovered. Next time I thought about coming down, I wouldn't ask – I would just come.

Jon was my friend. I still cared deeply for him despite my feelings for Jack. I wished desperately that I had been here when he needed me.

He was lying with his eyes closed when I entered the room. A shaded light was on, and I could see he was feverish. He was covered with just a sheet and a light blanket, but he still felt hot and moist when I touched his forehead.

"Emma . . . is that you?" he croaked. "I've been looking for you. I couldn't find you. It's this mist . . . it's all around me. I can't see you."

"I'm here, my dearest," I said and bent to kiss him gently on the lips. I reached for his hand and held it to my cheek. "Here I am, Jon. The mist is going now. You can see me, can't you?"

"Yes, I can see you. I can touch you." His voice sounded odd and I knew he was not really seeing me. "I've been trying to find you for so long, Emma. So long . . . Don't go away, will you?" He was clinging to my hand now.

"No, I shan't go away again," I said. I stroked the damp hair from his forehead. "I love you, Jon. I'm with you."

"Forgive me, Emma." He tossed his head restlessly on the pillows. "It wasn't fair. Must let Emma go . . . must make Emma happy. Not fair . . . not fair to her if—"

"What is it, my dear?" I asked. "What is troubling you? You haven't done anything to be forgiven for. It is I who should ask your forgiveness. I let you down by not being here."

"I did it for Emma," Jon said, clearly not hearing me. He was lost in his own memories. "It gave me the shakes but I managed to set it up . . . knew it would work. Did it for Emma. The bastard hurt her . . . I blew him up. Bang! Dead . . . he's dead. Can't come back and hurt her. Can't let him hurt her . . . deserved it, but won't let me go. Did it for Emma . . . did it for Emma . . . Emma . . . need Emma."

"What are you saying, Jon?" A shiver ran down my spine, turning me cold. "What did you do for Emma's sake?"

"Mustn't let her know . . . not yet . . . not yet," he muttered, throwing out his arm fretfully. "She wouldn't . . . I did it for you, Emma."

He jerked up out of bed suddenly, his eyes wide and staring. Then he grabbed hold of my arm.

"Emma doesn't know, does she? You haven't told her? You haven't told her what I did? Promise me you won't tell her! Mustn't know . . . Emma mustn't know."

"No, I haven't told her. She doesn't know," I said. "Lie down, Jon. You must rest, my dearest. You haven't done anything bad."

"She thought Sol . . . but he couldn't. Learned how to do it in the dark . . . blew myself up, but not this time . . . made sure of that. Dead, he's dead. Can't come back." He laughed wildly, a horrible sound that once again made my blood run cold. "This time I did it right . . . for Emma. Can't give her anything else . . . had to do it for Emma. Too selfish . . . should have let go."

"It's all right," I said again, soothing his forehead as he began to thrash wildly again. "You did it for me, Jon. I understand. You shouldn't have done it, but I know why. I know why, dearest."

I heard a choked sound behind me and turned to see my mother. She had been listening and watching.

"What did he do, Emma? It must have been something terrible if it is causing him so much anguish. What did he do – and why did he think he owed you something?"

"Please don't ask me," I said. "Whatever happened, it is best forgotten. Jon will want to forget it if he comes through this."

"And if doesn't?"

"Then his secret will die with him," I said. "I haven't told anyone anything while he lived, and I shan't now."

"Did you know about whatever it is he did?"

"I suspected . . . but I didn't know it was Jon. I never once thought it was Jon." I caught back a sob. "Please, leave me with him for a while, Mum. I need a little time to be alone with him."

"I've misjudged you, Emma," she said. "You won't tell me, and I shan't ask again – but he has said other things while he was rambling. I think I understand now. I was wrong to blame you."

I didn't answer her, and after a few seconds I heard the door close behind her.

"Oh, Jon," I wept. "Why? Why did you do it? I never wanted . . ."

He was tortured by what he had done. I saw now that I should have guessed long ago that he was the one who had planted the bomb in Philip Matthews' car, but I had not thought my gentle, sensitive husband was capable of doing something like that.

Of course I had forgotten that Jon was really two different people. During that time in France when he had been tortured, and then almost killed in an attack on his captors by the French resistance fighters, he had blocked everything out of his mind, forgetting even his own name. He had then gone on to work with the French Resistance – but the man who had killed and done terrible things in France, eventually being blown up in a sabotage attempt that went wrong, was not the man I had married. That man had been forged in the flames of bitter war, forced into acts that he must have found appalling – but that was the nature of war. I could accept the necessity for what he had done out of a need to survive – but could he?

Jon had buried himself for as long as he needed, then let the real Jon come back when the war was over – when there was no more need for killing. I was sure one day the doctors would be able to explain how that was possible, even if they hadn't been able to when Jon had been a patient all those months.

When I first saw Jon in the hospital towards the end of the war, I had sensed that he was trying to block out what had happened in France, and I believed he had been successful in doing that for much of the time. It was when he remembered that he had a fit of what Sister Jones called "the shakes".

He had been having one the night I found him trying to pour himself a glass of brandy. I should have known something had happened then – something so awful that it had brought all the horror of that time back to him.

It must have taken so much courage to plant that bomb. Yes, it was a terrible thing to do, and I wished desperately that he had not done it – but I respected the courage behind his action. He had suffered such cruel, painful injuries from the sabotage attack. To risk something like that again, he must have been prepared to die for my sake.

"Oh, Jon," I whispered as the tears trickled down my cheeks. "I didn't want you to do that for me . . . I didn't want you to take someone's life for my sake."

Sol was right. Jack would have known how to deal with Philip. It should have been left to him. There had been no need for murder.

A part of me was horrified that the gentle, sensitive man I knew could do such a thing, yet I understood why he had done it. It was all he could do for me.

I had stood by him in the hospital. I had given him the love that had always been his, though not my whole heart. He knew I had given up my chance of a new life in America to stay with him – and he could never be a proper husband to me.

How that must have hurt his pride. He had wanted to give me something in return. He had given me freedom, but he hadn't been strong enough to let me go completely. He was prepared to let me go to Jack, knowing that I would not leave him, but he could not find the resolution to divorce me. And so he had given me something more.

The tears ran down my face as I watched his struggle for breath. He was much quieter now, but I knew he was dying. I bent to kiss his lips once more.

"I love you, Jon. It doesn't matter about what you did. I'm with you now. I shall stay while you need me."

His eyelashes flickered. Perhaps he understood. I would never know.

I told Sol not to come down for the funeral.

"I'm going to stay for a few days," I said. "Mum is here. I'm all right. You needn't worry."

"I'm here if you want me, Emma."

"Yes, I know that," I said. "I'm so grateful to you for being you, Sol."

"What does that mean?"

"Nothing sensible." I gave a choking laugh. "I'll be home soon."

"Take care of yourself, Emma – and don't do anything I wouldn't."

"That gives me plenty of scope, then," I said. "I can't talk any longer, Sol. Or I shall cry."

I was already crying when I put the receiver down. Mum was standing behind me when I turned. She came to me then and caught me in her arms, hugging me until the tears ceased.

"It's all right, love," she said. "You did all you could. I know that now. I'm sorry . . . sorry I didn't understand."

"You were right. I should have been with him more."

"There's only so much a body and soul can stand," she said. "I expected too much of you – but I didn't know."

"There's nothing to know."

"I'm not a complete fool, Emma. I've been blind, but my eyes are open now."

"Well, it doesn't matter now. Jon has gone."

"Yes – but we have to go on." She looked at me oddly. "I don't like living alone, Emma. Does that offer you made me to come and live with you still stand?"

"Yes, of course it does, Mum." I tried to smile but the tears were falling too fast. "Of course it does."

I found a letter for me amongst Jon's things. It confirmed all the suspicions his rambling had aroused in my mind.

I read it and then burned it. It was better to leave things the way they were. As far as the police were concerned Philip's death was a gangland killing, and that was the way it would stay.

147

Once Jon's affairs were cleared up, I would go back to London. He had left everything to me. I thought I would sell this house.

It would be too painful to come here again.

I went to visit Sister Jones a few days after Jon's death. I wanted to make a substantial bequest to the hospital on his behalf. There were men in those wards who would never have the chance to leave, and money could help in some small way to make their lives more comfortable. I believed I owed them that at least.

"I'm so sorry, Emma," Vera said. "Of course we always knew it could happen at any time – but he seemed so well when he came down just before Christmas."

"Yes, he was well at Christmas. It seemed to start afterwards. It was just a chill at first. I didn't think it was anything serious. Jon said he was fine just a few days before the end."

"They all say that," Vera replied with a smile. "I suppose they've had enough of doctors and being sick."

"Yes, I expect so."

"Well," she said, a bracing note in her voice, "you did your best, Emma. You must think of the future. No point in regrets."

"No," I said. "There's no point in regrets now." The tears burned at the back of my eyes.

"Surprise!" Sheila put her head round the sitting room door. "I told Mrs Rowan I would announce myself. I hope that's all right?"

It was summer again, and the sunshine was playing through the windows, bringing warmth to the room.

"Sheila!" I leapt to my feet. "It's wonderful to see you. How are you? When did you arrive – and why?"

"Such a lot of questions all at once!" She grinned at me. "Todd is going to do another tour here later in the summer, since the last one was so successful. He couldn't get here for another month – but I thought I would come and see you . . . and Lizzy, of course."

"I'm so glad you did!" I hugged her. "I really could do with your help now, Sheila."

"Payback time?" she asked, then laughed. "I'm getting so American now. What can I do for you, Emma?"

"Just being here is enough." I hesitated, then, "Jon died very suddenly two months ago."

"I'm so sorry, Emma." She arched her eyebrows. "Or is it a relief?"

"No, far from it. It just makes me feel worse. Guilt and regrets, you know. I'm free now, but Jack isn't. He has taken Angie home. She is having his child."

Sheila pulled a face. "I knew he was trouble the moment I saw him in Southend."

"No, it isn't like that," I said. "He's doing the right thing, Sheila. We both agreed . . . there was nothing else he could do. She is delicate. She mustn't be upset or she might lose the child – or even her own life. Neither of us wanted that."

She nodded. "Well, that's your business. Sure there's nothing else I can do for you?"

"Nothing – unless you know how to make more people come to my shop? I thought trade would have picked up by now . . . but I think I must be ahead of my time."

"What's that all about?" she asked, looking interested. "Is this the shop you told me about when you wrote – with all the different departments?"

"Yes. People came for a while, but the sales are dropping again. They don't seem to realise how much easier it can be to shop when everything is together. Sol says to give it time . . . but I always was impatient."

"Yes, I remember," she said and laughed. "Well, I shall just have to see what I can do, shan't I?"

"What do you mean?"

She shook her head mysteriously. "You'll see, Emma."

Sheila refused to tell me what she was up to, but a day later I opened my copies of the morning papers to see her picture all over the women's pages of three of them.

"I came all the way from America to shop here," she declared. "It is such a wonderful idea. I can't imagine why no one thought of it before. The clothes are so exciting and new – but much less expensive than *haute couture*. When I go home, I shall tell all my friends about it."

She then reeled off a list of famous names, including Rita Hayworth, Betty Grable and Ingrid Bergman.

"Do you really know them that well?" I asked when I saw her later. "Or is that one of your white lies?"

"I do actually know a lot of famous people," Sheila said. "They aren't exactly friends, but I know them well enough to claim it in the press. Let's hope it makes an impression."

"Well, at least you tried," I said, amused by her enterprise. "If sales pick up, I shall have to try using publicity again."

"I meant what I said, Emma. It really is so exciting and different – and I love the Francine de Paris designs. I'm going to take several of those back with me. I think they would sell back home. I could talk to some people for you, if you like – see if there's any chance of one of the big stores taking them up."

"I had thought I would keep them exclusive to us," I said, "but perhaps it would be a good idea to expand." I looked at her and smiled. "See what you can do, Sheila. Pick what you want. I'll give them to you – and a share of the profits if we make any."

She shook her head. "We're rolling in money, Emma. Todd has just bought me a house of my own in France. What I really want is for you and the children to come and stay in September."

"Won't Todd think it odd if you have Lizzy to stay?"

"He might if I had her on her own – but he thinks she is your daughter. Well, she is these days – isn't she?"

"Yes. I love her as much as if she were," I replied. "You know we should love to come, Sheila. I was thinking of taking them to France again later in the year anyway."

"That's settled then," she said. "No sooner do I think I've paid you back, than you go and do something for me again."

"We help each other," I said. "We're friends, Sheila. I think we always shall be."

"Forever and ever?"

"Well, something like that."

We looked at each other and smiled.

I knew that I was beginning to get over Jon's death, and the shock of discovering what he had done. It had left scars, but they would fade over the years.

I was determined to make a success of my shop. I would dedicate my time to making the idea I had thought so brilliant into a success, despite the initial setback. But I would not forget my friends and family. In future, I would make certain I spent more time with them. I would take the children on more holidays, and keep my weekends free for outings.

My mother was living with us now. We had forgiven each other for all the misunderstandings, and were closer than ever before. She hadn't even raised her eyebrows when I told her we would be going to France to stay with Sheila in September.

"If we like it, I might buy a house there one day."

"That would be nice, love," she said. "I suppose I ought to start thinking about getting myself a passport . . ."

Sol looked at the cheque as I held it out to him.

"What's that for, Emma?"

"It's the six thousand pounds I owe you. Now that Jon's house has been sold and probate has been granted, I can pay you back the money you lent me."

"There's no need to do that, Emma." He looked uncomfortable. "Keep it for a year or two in case you need it."

"I would rather you had it now, Sol. I don't like owing you money for longer than I have to."

"You don't," he said. "I didn't lend you the money."

"I don't understand." I stared at him. "What are you saying?" Then I frowned as understanding came. "I suppose it was Jack. Why didn't either of you tell me?"

"Jack wanted it that way." Sol sighed. "I told him you wouldn't be pleased when you found out what he had done – but you know Jack. When he makes up his mind, there's no changing him. He thought you wouldn't know for years, and by then it wouldn't have mattered."

"What do you mean?"

He crossed over to the wall and moved a picture to reveal a safe behind it. He unlocked it with his key, took out a large brown envelope and handed it to me.

"It all belongs to you, Emma. There was never any loan . . . Jack gave you the money and the property."

"The property?" I gasped. "But that's impossible. I have a lease. I pay rent."

"Which comes to me. I have been investing it for you. I bought some shares in one of Jack's companies – they have done quite well."

"You mean I own the shop – all of it? I could sell it or let it – do whatever I like?"

"Yes, that's about it, Emma. It was Jack's gift to you. Take this upstairs and have a look. I expect there's a letter inside."

"I'll have something to say to you later!"

"I expect you will." He gave me a rueful smile.

I turned and left the study. I kept staring at the envelope in my hand. Why had Jack done this? He must have known I would never have accepted the loan from him.

I sat on my bed and slit the letter open. Immediately I could see the loan agreement had been torn up. There was what were obviously the deeds to the property – and a letter.

"My darling Emma." It was as if he was speaking to me!

> Please don't be too angry with me. I wanted to cover your lovely body in diamonds, but you wouldn't let me give you presents. I love you so much. I have to know that you are secure for the future or I can't bear it. Forgive me, and go on loving me as I shall you.

"Oh, Jack," I whispered chokily. "Jack . . . what have you done?"

The tears were trickling down my cheeks as the door opened and Lizzy came in.

"Emmie–" She stopped and stared at me. "You're crying, Emmie. What's wrong?"

"Nothing, darling." I brushed the back of my hand over my eyes, then beckoned to her. "Emmie is being very silly. Someone has done something very nice for me and it made me cry."

Lizzy came towards me. She sat on the bed and put her arms around me, laying her head against me.

"You told me you were sad because your friend went away – is it the same one who has done something nice?"

"Yes, darling."

She reached up to touch my cheek. "Don't be sad any more, Emmie. You still have me and James."

"Yes, Lizzy. I still have you and James. I am very lucky."

"I shall never leave you."

I smiled at her. "You might one day, darling. When you grow up."

"No," she said. "I'm going to stay with you for always and always."

"Well," I said and bent to hug her. "We shall just have to see what you think about that in ten years . . ."

Part Two

Eleven

"What do you think, Emmie?" Lizzy twirled in her crisp, striped poplin shirtwaister with its froth of net petticoats swishing beneath the full skirt. "Do you like it? I think it's lovely."

I smiled fondly at her. James had stopped calling me "Mummy" during his first year at school, but although Lizzy was nearly seventeen she still called me by the baby name of "Emmie". She had grown into the dazzlingly beautiful girl we had all expected her to be, her dark hair shaped into a pretty layered cut that looked almost like one of those big curly chrysanthemums.

"It's very pretty, Lizzy," I told her as she peered at her image in the mirror. "I thought it would suit you as soon as I saw it. You will be the belle of the ball on Saturday."

Sheila's daughter had always been pretty, but now she was beautiful. Sheila herself had been very attractive, but Lizzy had something very special about her.

Lizzy laughed and shook her head. "It's a rock-and-roll concert, Emmie, not a ball."

"Yes, darling, I know. I'm not quite in my dotage yet. I have heard of Tommy Steele and Elvis Presley – though who this group is you are going to see, I've no idea."

"No one knows them yet," Lizzy said, pulling a face at me. "But Terry Moon and the Starmakers are going to be famous one day. They wear Teddy-boy suits – like Bill Haley and the Comets. You must remember them?"

"I seem to remember you dragged me to see that film last year. What was it called? *Rock Around the Clock?* It was impossible to hear a word for all the girls screaming. And

157

why some of those audiences had to cause such a fuss in the streets afterwards, I don't know." I smiled at her teasingly. "I do hope that you won't be screaming at this Terry Moon, darling. And that you won't be hanging around the stage door afterwards."

"I shan't have to," Lizzy said, a naughty curve about her mouth. "Tina and I have been invited to go backstage afterwards. You know I met Terry when we were staying with Sheila in France last year. He entertained at her party. You weren't with us that holiday, but I showed you the photographs James took. Terry is really good. I know his band is going to make it to the top one day. Todd said he thought the group had promise. He said he might give them a spot in his show next time he comes to London."

I nodded, frowning slightly as I recalled something about that holiday. Lizzy and James had gone to stay with Sheila at her villa in the South of France without me. She'd invited us all, but my mother had been very ill. After years of suffering unexplained bouts of fatigue, the doctors had finally told us she had a weak heart and ought to rest more often. I hadn't wanted to leave her, and though she had recovered she was still not really well.

It was sad. She wasn't sixty yet, and was two years younger than Gwen, who was still running the shops in March and showing no sign of wanting to give up – though Madge Henty had retired at the end of last summer. But of course my mother had never been really strong, and sometimes now, when I saw how tired she was, I worried about her.

I looked at Lizzy, making myself concentrate on what she was saying. "Well, as long as James is there tomorrow, to take care of you and your friend."

Lizzy pulled a face, but didn't say anything to contradict me. I had been aware of a strained atmosphere between them of late. Lizzy had finally got tired of obeying James's every whim, and had made a lot of new friends. She enjoyed going to dances, parties and the pictures with her friends, quite a few of whom were boys.

It was hardly surprising that with her remarkable looks,

Lizzy should find herself the centre of attention. Young men queued up to take her out, and as long as they seemed respectable, I was inclined to let her go. She and her best friend Tina Browne were sensible girls, but Tina's father and I took it in turns to fetch them home. We had agreed on a curfew of eleven o'clock when it was something special like a party or a dance, but in the week they had to be home by ten.

I knew that James was not best pleased by the change in Lizzy. I had noticed some smouldering looks being directed her way since he'd come home from technical college for the summer holidays. He was very possessive of her, and though they had been brought up together there was nothing brotherly in the way he looked at her.

James was eighteen now, and his ambition to make a name for himself as a film director appeared to have waned, though he was still very keen on photography. He was actually a very good photographer and had already had an exhibition of his work at college. He had also won prizes in several competitions – especially after his last trip to visit Jack in New York.

The lighting and symmetry he had achieved had been praised by critics, both here and in America. I knew he was only waiting to finish his education before going to live with Jack. I should miss him very much, but America was not so very far away these days.

"Emmie . . ." Lizzy hesitated, looking at me awkwardly. "Do we have to have James with us on Saturday? I mean, if you're going to fetch us . . . We shall be quite safe. I promise I shan't do anything you wouldn't like. Really, I won't."

"It isn't that I don't trust you, darling," I reassured her. "It's just that I feel safer if James is with you."

Lizzy's expression seemed to indicate that wasn't so, but she didn't push the subject. They had always been so close that it seemed strange this rift had appeared between them.

"Have you quarrelled with him?"

"No, not exactly," she said. "I love James, you know I do – but sometimes he seems as if he wants to own me."

"I think he is just being protective of you, Lizzy."

"He's always trying to put my friends off."

"You mean that boy who used to come calling for you on a motorbike last year?" Lizzy nodded. "He was concerned that you might have an accident," I said and touched her cheek fondly. "I've always told him to look after you, darling. It's only natural he should feel responsible."

Again, I saw something in Lizzy's eyes that seemed to disagree with me, but she didn't say any more.

I left her to get changed back into the figure-hugging blue denim jeans she usually wore in the holidays and went downstairs. Her favourites at the moment were a pair of faded pedal pushers. My mother was horrified by some of the clothes Lizzy wore, but I knew it was the fashion for young girls these days.

James was in front of the television in the sitting room, watching a programme on underwater exploration.

"Jacques Cousteau's work is brilliant," James said as I entered the room. He gave an exclamation of annoyance as I walked over to the television and switched it off. "What did you do that for? I was interested in his techniques."

"I'm sure there will be another opportunity for you to watch him," I replied. "Besides, you have your own set upstairs." It was the height of extravagance that he should have his own TV, of course. Yet another expensive gift from Jack, delivered to the house without my permission being sought.

"No, I don't want you to leave, James!" I continued hastily as he rose from his seat. "I need to talk to you."

"Ah, I see. When you use that tone we had all better sit up and take notice." He arched his eyebrows at me. "Now what have I done to upset you, Ma?"

I sighed inwardly. It was not easy to understand what went on in the mind of this angry young man.

"I'm not sure you've done anything, James. I'm sorry if you were really interested in that programme, but I do want to talk to you – please?"

"Of course. I'm always happy to talk to my mother."

He stretched out in his chair, long legs crossed nonchalantly, waving his arm in an airy motion. James had left his sulky schoolboy image behind long ago. He could be very charming when he chose, and his smile was attractive, but I was always aware of something simmering beneath the surface. When I looked at him these days I was reminded more and more of his father. Paul's smile had been very appealing, his manner charming – but he had been a selfish man. I hoped my son would not turn out to be the same.

"Tell me what I can do for you."

"It's Lizzy," I replied. "I'm a little concerned about this concert tomorrow. Apparently she and Tina have been invited backstage."

"I shall keep an eye on them," James said. "Don't worry, Ma. I shan't let that greasy yobbo touch her."

"James! That isn't the kind of language I expect from a young man who went to the best schools."

"It's what he is," James said, and frowned. "I don't know what Lizzy sees in him. He isn't good enough for her. Nowhere near good enough to clean her shoes."

"You haven't told Lizzy that?"

"Of course I have. She knows I don't approve of her going around with that type."

I stared at him, feeling surprised by his attitude. Was my son turning into a snob?

"He doesn't have to be bad for her just because he plays in a rock-and-roll band. I'm sure there are some very nice young men in the music business; they don't all have to be disreputable. I've seen the TV shows, and it all seems a lot of fun to me at these concerts."

James laughed. "That's because you don't know what goes on, Ma. I know that sort – they're either into drugs or they drink far too much. Believe me, this Moon fellow is a bad influence."

"Lizzy says you dislike most of her boyfriends."

"She attracts the wrong sort," James said, his expression a little mutinous and reminding me of his tantrums when he

161

was a sulky child. "You don't want her to get into trouble, do you, Ma?"

"I'm sure Lizzy is much too sensible." I felt a flicker of anxiety as I remembered that Sheila had been rather foolish over men as a young woman. "I was merely concerned that she shouldn't be taken advantage of – and that you two seemed to have fallen out recently."

"It's not serious," James said and smiled again. "Lizzy is just going through a phase, Ma. She will grow out of it in time – and then she'll see that I'm right."

He was so lordly, so sure of himself.

"Don't you think that sort of attitude is like waving a red rag to a bull, James? It's bound to make Lizzy cross. Couldn't you try to like at least some of her friends?"

"When she finds some decent ones," he said, then stood up. "I think I'll go upstairs and watch TV in my room. Unless there is anything else you want to talk about?"

"No, I don't think so." I fumed inwardly. Had Jack asked first, I would never have permitted James to have his own TV set. It was unheard of! But necessary for his future career, I was told when I had protested.

I sighed as my son left the room. James had been difficult as a child, but loving and lovable. Now, however, I sometimes felt I hardly knew him. He was very adult, very sophisticated for an eighteen-year-old – and very sure that he was right. I acknowledged that was partly my fault. I had always been so busy working. Perhaps I had allowed him to have his own way too much. Or was I guilty of neglect? Had I been too selfish? I had always believed I was doing what was best for us all, but now I felt that somewhere along the way I had lost my son.

I glanced at my watch. It was eleven o'clock, and time for me to leave for the shop. I delegated much of the work these days to my managers, but I still preferred to be there when new stock was being ordered – particularly if it was coming from a supplier we had not used before.

Recently I had been contacted by a firm who supplied cashmere knitwear. It was based in Scotland, but they had

162

recently employed a representative for the London area. I had barely glanced at their letter, but my knitwear manager had arranged an appointment for this morning. Although I would probably not be directly involved in the buying, I wanted to be there to look at the merchandise. Once I was satisfied that we wanted to stock the goods, I would leave the ordering to my manager.

I was thoughtful as I took the Underground into the centre of town. The traffic was getting too bad to bother with taxis these days, and I didn't want to walk because it looked as if it might rain.

Over the past nine years, my main store had gradually acquired a reputation for quality. It was this rather than anything else that had built up the business to the extent where I was having to think of moving to larger premises. I hadn't yet made up my mind to do so, because I was already in the position of having accumulated more money than I should ever need. I was thirty-seven now, and not sure that I wanted to go on expanding my business empire further. I seemed to have spent most of my life working, and I had begun to wonder if it was time for a change, time to take things a little easier.

There were days when I did not always want to work and thought it would be nice to go away more often. I had not yet bought myself a house in France. There had seemed no real point when Sheila invited us all to stay every year – but perhaps I would think about it soon.

I had four shops in London, besides the three shops in March, and the property itself had increased in value considerably. But did I want more? I could not feel it would really benefit me. It would have been different if James had shown an interest in taking over the business one day, but he was set against it.

"I'm going to concentrate on still photography for a few years," he had told me quite recently. "I want to travel, Ma – and then perhaps I'll settle down in Hollywood and become a director. I've spoken to Jack, and he feels I would benefit from the chance to see more action. I could do that as a freelance photographer, and sell my work to magazines."

Lizzy had not yet told me what she wanted to do when she left school. She had said she wanted to stay on and take her exams, and I thought she had definite ideas in mind, but as yet she hadn't told anyone what they were.

"I don't want to be an actress, Emmie," she had confided to me when she was fifteen. "James is cross with me. He says if I'm not an actress, I could be a model – but I don't want to pose for the camera all the time. I want to do something more worthwhile with my life – something to help people."

I had asked her what she meant, but she'd shaken her head and said she wasn't sure yet. She just knew she wanted to finish her school education, and perhaps go on to college.

Both James and Lizzy were bright, intelligent young people. I had given them as interesting a childhood as was possible. It hadn't been easy at first; the war had cast a blight over this country for several years. It had been July 1954 before all forms of rationing finally ended, but since then things had changed fast. In the last few years travel had become much easier.

James had gone by aeroplane to New York by himself when he was sixteen. He had fallen in love with the way of life over there, and I knew it was only a matter of months before he left home – perhaps for good.

I would make this summer special, I decided as I reached the store. It was not really necessary for me to be here the whole time. I employed a small army of staff these days. I would leave them to get on with the job I paid them to do, and take the children to France.

We could hire a car and drive down to the south of the country, and perhaps I would look for a house somewhere. My mother might not be well enough to come with us, but Sol would keep an eye on her for me. He was very fond of her, and they spent a lot of time together these days, talking, playing cards and watching the television I had bought mainly for Mum's sake. I hardly ever had time to sit down and watch it.

Yes, I would definitely take at least a month – perhaps six weeks – off this year. I smiled to myself as I got into the lift that would take me up to the knitwear department.

I was still smiling as I walked towards the office where my manager would be asking to see the first samples. I was five minutes late, but that was not enough to matter. No decisions would have been made as yet.

"I'm sorry I'm late, Steven," I said. "Would you mind starting again, Mr – Paul!"

I stared in shocked surprise as the knitwear salesman turned to look at me. Surely it could not be Paul? And yet it was. The past thirteen years had aged him – his dark hair was heavily streaked with silver – but otherwise he looked much the same as when I had last seen him, towards the end of the war.

Before the war he had been an architect, a qualified civil engineer. What was he doing in a job like this? It was quite a come-down in the world for him.

"Emma." Paul looked slightly embarrassed, uncomfortable. "Or should I call you Mrs Reece? When they told me to come for this appointment I didn't realise you were the owner – I only found out when Mr Barker told me a moment ago."

"How nice to see you again, Paul," I said, offering my hand. I glanced at my manager. "Mr Greenslade and I knew each other years ago. Please go on as you were. I would like to approve the merchandise as usual, then I'll leave it to you, Steven."

A large suitcase was open on the desk. After one puzzled glance at me, Paul resumed the sales patter he had been giving my manager. I watched as he displayed the various jumpers, twinsets and cardigans on offer. Steven examined various articles, then passed them to me.

They were well-made, quality garments and would fit with our range well. I nodded my approval.

"Are they competitive on price, Steven?"

"Yes, Mrs Reece. Not cheap, but I think we could sell this twinset – and these crew-neck jumpers. I'm not sure about the roll-necks; they seem expensive for what they are."

"Then I'll leave it to you to order what you think." I nodded to Paul, a polite smile on my face. "Perhaps you would come to my office before you leave? If you have time before your next appointment."

"Yes, of course." Paul was looking very much more comfortable now. Had he been afraid I would throw him out without an order? I suspected that this job was important to him. "I have no further appointments until later this afternoon."

"Steven will tell you where to find me."

I walked away from Steven's office, feeling slightly confused. It had been a shock seeing Paul like that, so suddenly.

I was sitting at my desk, staring unseeingly at a sheaf of letters that needed attention, when Paul knocked then put his head round the door.

"May I come in?"

"Yes, please do," I said and smiled at him. "Come and sit down, Paul. I hope you didn't mind my asking you up here? I thought perhaps we should talk."

"Yes, that thought occurred to me, too," Paul replied. He laid his brown trilby on the desk and sat down, crossing his legs. The awkward manner had vanished and he was more like the man I remembered. "First of all, I wanted you to know that I have not discussed our . . . friendship . . . with any member of your staff, and shall not do so in the future."

"Thank you. I would prefer that it remain private."

"Yes, I imagined you would. It was a little difficult just now. I wasn't sure how you would react when you saw me; it could have been embarrassing for us both."

"I was surprised to find you in the office," I said. "It isn't the kind of job I would expect you to be doing, Paul."

"It is a case of needs must when the devil drives," he replied with a rueful laugh. "I was in business for myself in America until a few months ago. Unfortunately, things went wrong. I was ill. I let the business slide – and I ended up going bankrupt."

"I'm so sorry, Paul. That was unlucky."

He hesitated, then decided to be frank with me. "It was my

own fault. I started to drink after my wife and daughter were killed in a car accident. It got so bad that I couldn't cope."

"Oh, Paul!" I was shocked and upset. "What a terrible thing to happen! No wonder you couldn't concentrate on your business."

He shrugged, but his eyes were bleak, reflecting the pain and trauma he had suffered.

"It knocked me for six, I can tell you. After everything went wrong, I spent some time recovering in a clinic for alcoholics – apparently that's what I am these days, Emma. I'm not allowed to touch a drop of wine or spirits."

"I see." I felt sympathy for him. "Is that why you took a job as a salesman – because you didn't feel up to doing your own work?"

"Something like that." His eyes didn't quite meet mine and I sensed that there was more. "This is just temporary, until I'm on my feet again."

"Yes, of course."

"About James . . ." He hesitated, then gathered his courage. "I don't like to ask – but is there some way I could see him? Just see him, and talk to him as a casual acquaintance. I'm not asking for anything more, Emma. It's much too late for me to be a father to him now."

"It was too late a long time ago," I said. "James believes Jon was his father, and there is someone else who has been like a father to him too."

"You married again after Jon died?"

"No, no, I didn't – but my son has a good friend." I met Paul's intent gaze. "James isn't always an easy person to be with, Paul. I think he would be very angry if he knew that the name of his natural father had been kept from him all these years."

"I just want to see him, Emma. Surely that isn't too much to ask?"

I thought about it for a few moments. Paul had no real rights where James was concerned, but given the tragic circumstances that had robbed him of his family there was cause for considering his request.

"No, it isn't too much . . . providing you give me your word you won't tell James that you are his father. You won't say or do anything to make him suspicious."

"I give you my word, Emma," he said eagerly. "I wouldn't do anything to hurt you. I've wished a thousand times that I'd been here when you needed me. I should have married you."

"I'm not sure we should have suited; besides, it was all so long ago," I said. "If you would like, you may come to lunch on Sunday. I shall make sure James is home. As far as he is concerned, you are just an old friend. You must accept that, Paul. It is for James's sake as much as anything. I don't want him to be upset."

"Yes, of course I accept that. I am very grateful, Emma. I'll be there at twelve thirty on Sunday."

"You know where I live?"

"Is it the same place as during the war?"

"Yes."

"Then I know," Paul said. "Thank you for giving me your trust, Emma. I shan't abuse it."

"Then you will be welcome," I said. "I cannot guarantee what your reception will be like as far as James is concerned, though. Sometimes he takes to people, sometimes he doesn't."

"I've thought of him – and you – so often," Paul replied. "I was feeling very low when I came here this morning, but you've helped me in two ways. My firm was keen to get an order from your store, and now I have Sunday to look forward to. I must thank you for that, Emma."

He looked so excited that I was uneasy.

"Don't hope for too much from James," I said, half wishing that I hadn't given him permission to come.

"I'm not hoping for anything," he said. "It will just be nice to see my son."

"You did *what*?" Sol stared at me in amazement when, the next morning, I told him I had invited Paul to have lunch with us that Sunday. "Do you think that was wise? When you saw him last, you were afraid he might try to take James away from you."

"James is eighteen now. He will be leaving school soon – and then he will leave me and go to live with Jack. I don't think there is much danger of Paul trying to take him now. I should fight him, and he just doesn't have the money to go to court over it. Besides, why should he? I should imagine he finds it hard to keep going on his own. Most firms pay their salesmen commission on what orders they take rather than a wage. It isn't an easy life. He would hardly want to take on the cost of keeping James – especially as my son has been used to having whatever he wants whenever he wants it."

"It might do him good to be short of money for a while," Sol said. "That young man has been thoroughly spoiled."

"Yes, I suppose he has – but he hasn't turned out too badly."

"James is a nice enough lad," Sol replied. "He could charm the birds out of the trees if he set his mind to it – but heaven help anyone who crosses him."

"I know he had a temper when he was younger," I said. "But I haven't seen any sign of it recently. If anything, he often seems too detached to me, too remote."

"He has learned to hide his anger," Sol replied and frowned. "But it's still there inside him, Emma. He was always jealous of Jon, because you left him several times for his sake. Since Jon died, well, James has had no reason to be jealous of anyone. Apart from the time you spend at work, you've devoted yourself to those children. They've had a wonderful upbringing. I just hope they both appreciate you for it."

"James knows I love him. Surely he must? Paul means nothing to me. You're not suggesting that my son would be jealous of any man I brought home?"

"You haven't looked at another man since Jon died. You could have married again, Emma. I know there have been men who were interested, but you didn't even notice them."

"I'm not interested in marrying again. I'm still in love with Jack. He still has Angie, though, and they have a daughter. I believe she is called Rachel."

"Yes, I know. I've heard James mention her." He looked

at me hard. "This Paul Greenslade . . . there's no chance of you getting back together with him?"

"No, none at all. That was over long ago, Sol."

"Does he know that? You don't think he's playing on your sympathy to get his feet under the table?" Sol growled. "I know I've got a suspicious mind – but you're a very wealthy woman, Emma."

"You think Paul wants a share of my money?"

"He wouldn't be the first man to try it on for the sake of cash."

"No, I don't suppose he would," I replied. "But it won't do him any good if he tries. I'm just not interested. I would never consider an offer of marriage from Paul."

"Fair enough. I'll keep my mouth shut. But be careful, Emma."

"Yes, I will," I said and went to kiss his cheek. "You're so good to me, Sol. I don't know where I would be without you."

He smiled oddly. "I've often felt the same way, Emma. Now, I'd best get off or Francine will be yelling down the phone for me."

I laughed. Francine had gradually taken over the showrooms, though Sol still went in every day, more to talk to the clients and pass the time than anything else. Francine was a full partner with us now in the wholesale business. She had insisted on it, and we had welcomed her because she was like a part of the family. In any case, we couldn't have managed without her. Her designs were the mainstay of our wholesale business, and we exported several thousand pounds' worth of merchandise to America each year, thanks to Sheila's efforts.

Sheila had refused to take a penny for helping us.

"I owe both you and Sol," she had told me just a few months earlier, when I had raised the subject of profit sharing, as I did almost every time we talked. "Let me do something for you for a change."

I let Sol go off to the showroom. His observations had raised doubts in my mind. Perhaps I would have been wiser not to have invited Paul to lunch, but I had felt it was the lesser of two evils. If I had refused to let him see James, he might have tried to approach him without my permission – and then he would undoubtedly have told my son the truth.

I could only hope that he would keep his promise.

Twelve

"So how did the concert go?" I asked Lizzy on Sunday morning when she came down to breakfast. "Did you enjoy it as much as you expected?"

"The concert was great," she replied, then pulled a face. "But James spoiled everything when we went backstage afterwards. He was rude to the band, called them trash and said they sounded like a load of cats wailing."

"No, surely not!" I stared at her in surprise. "That doesn't sound like James, darling. He's usually so charming to everyone."

"You haven't heard him when he's in a mood," Lizzy said. "He usually is nice when you're around – but sometimes he's horrid to me."

"I'm sorry, darling. I didn't realise it was that bad. Do you want me to speak to him about it?"

"It would only make him more cross," Lizzy said. She sighed. "I shouldn't have complained. I didn't mean to – but I liked Terry Moon. He was sweet to me, Emmie. He didn't want to seduce me the way James says. He just wanted to take me out – and kiss me."

"Kissing can lead to other things. I expect James was just trying to protect you – but he shouldn't have upset you."

"Well, I don't suppose it matters. I wasn't in love with Terry – but I did like him. How am I ever going to find someone who loves me if James drives them away all the time?"

I smiled at her. "It will happen, Lizzy. When I was working in my father's shop, I used to think just the same. I thought I would be there all my life, that I would never find happiness."

"Are you happy now, Emmie?"

"Yes, of course, darling. I have you and James – and Sol and Grandma."

"But no one to love you," Lizzy said, her large eyes serious as she looked at me. "You love Jack, don't you? I've seen the way you look sometimes when James mentions him or Angie. The hurt is in your eyes."

How perceptive this adopted daughter of mine was!

"I had to make a choice a long time ago, Lizzy. I chose to do what was right. It wasn't easy, and I still miss Jack – but I can't go back. We none of us can."

"Oh, Emmie," Lizzy said. Her eyes were misted with tears as she came to put her arms about me. "I do love you so much. James is lucky to have you. I'm not sure he knows how lucky."

Lizzy could not understand why James was sometimes resentful towards me, but I knew what lay behind his silences and angry stares.

"I suppose he resents my work – me not being around when he wanted me – and then, I sent Jack away. He was too young to understand why at the time, but he blamed me. I've tried to show him how much I love him, but I'm not sure it is enough. I suppose I'm to blame if he doesn't quite trust me."

"But you've always been so good to us," Lizzy said and hugged me. "You always came back. Sometimes you had to go away, but you always came back."

"I'm sure James knows that in his heart – but you know how independent he is. You have to let James do what he wants and hope that his own conscience will tell him when he is being unfair. It usually does in the end."

"Yes, it does mostly," Lizzy agreed and smiled. "Are all men as bossy as James, Emmie?"

"Yes, darling. Quite a few of them. I think Jon was the exception – and Sol is always ready to admit he's wrong, but then, Sol is older and wiser. He has been so good to us, Lizzy."

"Sol is kind," Lizzy said. "I like him, of course I do – and I love James. Sometimes, he makes me so angry – but then he smiles and the next thing I know, I agree to do whatever he wants. I only wish he would ask me what I want now and then . . . instead of just assuming he knows best."

There was a wistful note in her voice. I was thoughtful as I looked at her lovely face. Lizzy had been making a bid for her independence recently, which was probably what had caused the disagreements between them. It was only right that she should have some independence – but what was it costing her?

Was Lizzy in love with James? They had always been so close as children that I had taken their relationship to be that of brother and sister – but they were both growing up fast now.

I might have asked her what she was feeling, but my mother came in at that moment. She looked pale and tired, and immediately both Lizzy and I were concerned for her.

"What's wrong, Grandma?" Lizzy asked. "Are you feeling ill?"

"I was looking for my knitting," Mum said. "Have you seen it, Emma? I wanted to knit a coat for the baby."

"What baby?" I asked. I looked at Lizzy in alarm as she helped Mum to sit down in a chair. "Whose baby did you want to knit a coat for, Mum?"

"Your baby, of course, Emma. It won't be much longer now, and we haven't made any clothes. I don't know what your father will say if the baby hasn't any clothes."

"It's all right, Mum," I said. "You've forgotten. The baby has grown up now. James is eighteen and he has plenty of clothes."

She blinked at me, then put a hand to her forehead. "I've had this headache all morning, Emma. What have I been saying?"

"Nothing important," I reassured her. "Would you like me to ask the doctor to come and see you?" I was anxious about her. Could she have had some sort of a stroke – a very mild one – without us knowing? I knew she had a weak heart, and it was possible something of the kind might have happened.

"What for?" She looked puzzled. "It's just a headache, that's all. I shall be perfectly all right soon."

"Yes, of course you will, I said. "Why don't I help you upstairs? Perhaps you would like to have a little rest before lunch."

She smiled at Lizzy. "Such a pretty girl. I always told Emma you would be beautiful, didn't I, Emma?"

"Yes, Mum. You always said so."

"Lizzy can help me upstairs," she said. "I've got something I want to give her."

"Shall I, Emmie?" Lizzy looked at me anxiously.

"Yes, darling. You take Grandma up. Call me if you need me."

I watched as they walked from the room. Mum had never wandered in her mind before. I wondered whether I should call the doctor out, but she seemed better again now. It would only make her cross if I sent for a doctor without her asking for him.

I was trying to make up my mind when Mrs Jordan came in. Mrs Rowan, our housekeeper of many years, had recently retired, and we had been very lucky to find someone to take her place. Mrs Jordan was a plump, cheerful woman in her forties, and kept the house spotless.

"I was wanting to ask you about lunch, Mrs Reece. Will you be having drinks in the sitting room first?"

"Yes, I am sure we shall, Mrs Jordan. My guest is arriving at twelve thirty for one o'clock—"

"What's that, Ma?" James asked, coming in behind her at that moment. "I didn't realise we were having guests today."

"Just one guest, that's all," I said. "Was there anything else, Mrs Jordan?"

"No; I just wanted to be sure," she said and went away.

James was looking at me. "Who is coming – Francine?"

"No, it isn't Francine today. It's a man . . . someone I knew years ago, before you were born. I met him the other day and invited him to lunch."

James's gaze narrowed. He was immediately wary, on his guard.

175

"Who is he? Have I met him? Has he been here before?"

"No, darling. I saw him once during the war, but he lived in America for a long time. He was married and had a daughter, but his wife and child were killed last year, and since then Paul has been through a bad time. He used to be an architect, but at the moment he is working as a knitwear salesman. He came to the shop and we gave him an order."

"Fraternising with the plebs now, Ma?" James raised his eyebrows at me. "You don't usually invite travelling salesmen to lunch. What is so special about this one?"

My son was too intelligent to fool. I cursed myself for not having thought of a more plausible story.

"We were friends a long time ago, James. I went out with him a few times when I was very young."

"An old boyfriend?" James was instantly alert. "And now you feel sorry for him. Be careful, Ma. If he is down on his luck, he's probably after your money."

"That's exactly what Sol said." I shook my head at him. "I'm not interested in Paul Greenslade, darling, not in that way. Believe me. It was just an impulse. He was lonely."

"So you took pity on him?" James pulled a wry face. "It's just as well I'm around to look out for you, Ma. It seems you're almost as bad as Lizzy. You both need someone to take care of your interests."

"I'm sure neither of us is going to do anything foolish, James."

"That remains to be seen," my son replied with an irritating air of superiority.

At that moment, I wasn't surprised that Lizzy had lost patience with him. James was far too sure of himself! I would have loved to have boxed his ears, but of course I didn't.

"Why don't you go and change, darling? Our guest will soon be here – and I like you to look nice for Sunday lunch. Those jeans are a little bit the worse for wear."

"Don't fuss, Ma. It can't matter one way or the other what I look like. I doubt very much if this Greenslade chap will bother to notice me – it's obviously you he's after."

*   *   *

After James's reaction to the news that I was having a male friend to lunch, I was apprehensive about their meeting. On the face of it, I need not have been. No one could have been more affable than my son as he greeted the stranger. He was polite, friendly, interested as he played host, pouring drinks for everyone.

"What can I get you, sir?" he asked Paul. "Will you have sherry – or something stronger?"

"Just water or a squash for me," Paul replied. "I have an allergic reaction to alcohol. I don't drink it in any form."

"Really? How odd," James said. "I've never heard of an allergic reaction to drink – unless you mean you are an alcoholic?" He was still scrupulously polite, but was there just a hint of sarcasm in his voice?

A nerve flicked at the corner of Paul's eye. "Yes, I suppose I am. At the clinic, it was spoken of as an illness – a kind of allergy."

"Yes, I should imagine it would be," James said, his expression unchanging. "It must be awkward for you in company – but perhaps you don't go out much?"

"No, not often," Paul said. "Not since my wife and daughter died. I live alone and I don't entertain. That's why I was so pleased when Emma asked me to lunch. This is a real treat for me."

"Yes, I expect so. And for us, of course. Isn't it, Ma?"

"It is always nice to have guests," I said. "Give Paul a glass of iced water, James."

James obeyed me. Paul shot a grateful look at me. I thought he was surprised by his son's behaviour. He had not expected James to be so adult – or so sophisticated.

I sensed James's hostility to the man who had invaded his territory. Despite my protests, he probably believed I was interested in Paul. Surely he wasn't jealous?

Throughout the meal, I kept up an interesting flow of conversation with Paul, with Sol and with Lizzy. James was silent unless spoken to directly, observing us from beneath thick, dark lashes. Everything seemed to be going smoothly. Paul looked uncomfortable some of the time, and I was quite pleased. I did not imagine that he would be particularly keen to pursue the relationship with James after this, and I couldn't help having a sneaking feeling of satisfaction – which was unfair of me.

It was as we were about to have coffee in the sitting room after the meal that the door opened and my mother walked in. She looked rather wild-eyed, and I was immediately anxious for her.

"Mum," I said, beginning to rise. "Do you feel worse?"

She was not looking at me. Her gaze was fixed on Paul. In that moment, I sensed that somehow she had recognised him, remembered him and what he had done to our lives.

"Mum, please don't," I began, but it was too late to stop her.

"Why have you come here?" she asked angrily. "You were the one! You caused our Emma all that grief. I trusted you, but you let me down . . . you let my girl down. You seduced her and then went away and left her to have your—"

"Mum!" I cried. "You're not well."

Her eyes rolled upwards. She made a moaning sound, then crumpled into a heap on the floor. I ran to her, knelt down at her side. Sol was with me immediately. He felt for her pulse, then looked at me and shook his head.

"I'm sorry, Emma," he said. "It's too late. She has gone. You knew it could happen, with that heart of hers."

"Mum!" I cried. Tears filled my eyes. I had known she was not well, but this was so sudden . . . so final. "Mum . . . dead."

"Someone should get the doctor," James said. "You will need a death certificate."

I glanced up, gasping as I saw the look of cold anger in my son's eyes. I knew that he had heard and understood every word my mother had said. And he did not like what he had discovered. He did not like it one little bit.

"Would you telephone for the doctor, please, James?" I appealed to him, my eyes silently pleading with him to understand, but his expression did not become less hostile.

The tension crackled between us, but there was no way

I could explain anything to him at this moment. I was too stunned by what had happened, too distressed by Mum's sudden death. If only I had sent for the doctor earlier! Yet perhaps there was nothing he could have done even then.

"Of course," James said. He sounded so cold, so withdrawn. "I'm always ready to oblige my mother. If of course she is my mother – one can never be sure of these things."

He walked from the room without waiting for an answer. I stared after him, feeling helpless. Should I follow him? Should I make some attempt to explain?

"Don't try," Sol warned, reading my mind. "Let him calm down, Emma. Nothing you can say at this moment is going to make much difference. Besides, you're in no fit state to say anything sensible just now."

He pulled me to my feet. Lizzy came to take hold of my arm and lead me to the settee. She was pale and shocked; tears were in her eyes.

"Sit down, Emmie," she said. "Grandma was ill. She was ill for a long time. It's not your fault."

"No, it's not my fault." I sat in silence, heart aching. If it was not my fault, why did I feel so guilty?

"I think I should go," Paul said into the silence. "I'm very sorry, Emma." He laid a printed card on the coffee table. "If you should need me at any time—"

"She won't," Sol said. "She has us. You've done enough damage, Greenslade. Stay away from her – and James."

"Sol . . ."

I searched for my handkerchief and blew my nose as Paul walked out without another word. Sol was being unfair to Paul. It wasn't his fault that Mum had blurted out the secret I had kept for so long. Nor was it hers. I should have told James the truth years ago. This mess was entirely of my own making.

I glanced up at Lizzy's anxious face. "Go after James, darling. See if you can talk to him. Tell him I will explain everything later."

"Yes, Emmie."

Lizzy was very upset herself. She had loved my mother. I

was sure James did too, which made things very much worse. He had just received two harsh knocks. I was worried about how he would manage to cope with them.

Sol had closed Mum's eyes. He rang for Mrs Jordan.

"Oh, Mrs Reece," she said as she came in. "I was afraid of something like this. Mrs Fitch hadn't eaten a thing all day – and she seemed so odd when I took her tray up earlier. Wandering in her mind, she was."

"Yes," I said. "I knew she wasn't well, but this was so sudden. I asked James to telephone for the doctor – do you know whether or not he got through?"

"Yes, I'm sure he has. I heard him telling the doctor what had happened. He went upstairs afterwards. Lizzy followed him. He seemed very upset. She called to him – but he wouldn't answer her."

"He was fond of his grandmother."

"Yes, of course. Oh, dear, what a terrible thing to happen. It is very upsetting for everyone."

"Bring a shawl," Sol said. "Something to cover her face."

"Yes, sir. The poor lady . . ."

I couldn't prevent a sob escaping as Mrs Jordan left.

"I should have expected it," I said as Sol sat next to me and took my hand. "But she wasn't old, Sol."

"A year or so younger than me."

"Oh, Sol," I wailed. "Don't you dare die on me! I couldn't bear it."

He smiled oddly. "I'm not going to die just yet, my dear."

"I feel so helpless."

Mrs Jordan returned with a silk shawl of my mother's. I took it from her, then knelt down and kissed Mum's lips before putting the shawl over her.

"Why don't you go upstairs and lie down?" Sol suggested. "I'll stay with Greta."

"No. No, thank you. I'll stay with her until the doctor has been. I couldn't leave her, Sol. I just couldn't."

It was nearly four o'clock before all the formalities had been completed. My mother was taken to her own room, and the curtains were closed.

I left her lying there. She looked peaceful, younger than she had for a while. Perhaps in death she was reunited with her Bert: I hoped so with all my heart.

I knew I had to speak to James. Perhaps he would let me try to explain. It would not be easy. He had not liked Paul, and my mother's dramatic revelations would be hard for him to accept.

I knocked at his door twice before he answered. I was about to turn away when he suddenly opened it.

"Come in, Ma. I was expecting you."

I followed him inside. His bed was covered in photographs. He seemed to be sorting through piles of old ones.

"I was looking for a photo I took of Grandma," he said, frowning. "When we were all together in Cornwall that time. Jon and Bert were there, too."

His face was expressionless, but I could see that he was holding himself on a tight rein. He was grieving for his grandmother, but didn't want me to see it.

"She had been ill for a long time, James. She would have hated to be confined to bed or paralysed. In some ways I suppose it was a release for her."

"Yes, I know." He turned away, but not before I had seen the flicker of pain in his eyes. "People die. It can't be helped. We shall all die one day. Even you and me."

"James, please don't." I was upset by his show of indifference, because I knew it was false. "Don't be angry with me. I'm sorry I didn't tell you the truth about your father a long time ago. It just seemed easier not to – but it was wrong."

"I knew Jon wasn't my father," James said with a careless shrug. "I asked him about it that summer. He told me you had been married before – that my name had been changed to his by means of a special deed."

"Jon told you?" I was shocked. "I never knew that. He shouldn't have done that without asking me."

"I had sort of guessed anyway. I heard Grandma talking to Bert about your first husband. They often used to talk in front of me as though I couldn't hear – but I listened and gradually I began to understand. So I asked Jon for the truth, and he

181

told me – well, some of it, anyway. I thought that was pretty decent of him; at least he gave me credit for having the sense to understand."

"Oh, James . . . I didn't want you to know any of this. It wasn't that I thought you wouldn't understand – I meant to protect you. Your father deserted me. I didn't think he was important."

"Is Greenslade really the one?" James seemed almost detached. "I used to hope it was Jack – but he told me you didn't actually meet until after the war began. So it couldn't have been him – though you were lovers. I know that's true, so don't deny it."

"I wasn't going to try. We were introduced soon after I married. Jack was a good friend to me from the start. I tried not to like him too much, then, when I believed Jon was dead . . ." I took a deep breath. "I was very much in love with Jack."

"And were you in love with my father?"

"I thought so at the time. I was very young then. Paul made love to me, then went off to America. I was pregnant. My father forced me to marry a man called Dick Gillows. I didn't love him. I didn't really like him much, but there was no choice. Once we were married, I tried to make a go of it, but he was jealous of you and the man who had fathered you – and it drove him to drink. He became violent and abused me. I changed your name because I didn't want you to grow up with his."

James nodded, as if he already knew the story. "He was killed on the railway line when the police were looking for him. Some railwaymen went after him and he ran across in front of a non-stop train. He murdered my great grandmother . . . I found some newspaper cuttings in your desk, Mum. You really shouldn't have kept them if you didn't want me to know. There was even a picture of you at the time. It made you look dowdy and poor. But perhaps you were in those days."

"I didn't have much money until after my own father died and I came to London. I had what he left me then, and I've put it to good use. That's why I wanted to work. So that we would always have security."

"Yes, I had managed to gather most of that."

"So you had worked it all out long ago?"

"Most of it," James admitted. "But not which one of them was my father. I thought it was probably the murderer: it made sense that you wouldn't want anyone to know you'd had his child. Of course I didn't know there was another lover lurking about in your past . . . you've been rather busy in that department, haven't you, Ma?"

"James! There's no call for such remarks. Please try to understand. I was very young when I met Paul. I had never been allowed to go anywhere or do anything. He was the first man to kiss me."

"You've made up for it since, haven't you? How many more men have you had? Or shouldn't one ask?"

His sneering tone appalled me. "How dare you?" I was furious. Without thinking, I slapped his face. "Apologise, James!"

"Or what? Will you cut off my allowance? Or lock me in my room? That wouldn't work for long. You would have to let me out sooner or later." He smiled oddly. "I can't quite see you starving me into submission, Ma."

"I could curtail your freedom. You wouldn't enjoy having to stay in, instead of going out with your friends. I could take away the keys to your car."

The small Morris I had bought him for his eighteenth birthday was his pride and joy.

"Yes, I suppose you could. I could always climb out of the window, of course. I might fall and break my neck. You wouldn't like that, Ma."

"Please don't say foolish things. I'm sorry I slapped you. I shouldn't have done it." I looked at him anxiously. "Please don't be angry, James. Paul is at least educated. He may be working as a salesman now, but he was an architect when I met him. My father was a shopkeeper."

His smile disappeared and he was suddenly showing his anger.

"Oh, that makes things very much better. Greenslade seduces my mother, then goes off to America – but he was an architect, so that was all right. Unfortunately, he's now a drunk and a failure."

I was distressed by his attitude.

"Don't be so cruel, James. We come from working stock. I've made money, and you've been educated at the best schools. You have been fortunate. You should be more generous to others who are less so. Paul went to pieces after his wife and daughter were killed in a car crash. Perhaps he was weak and foolish, but that doesn't make him any less a gentleman – or any more a bad person."

"Are you going to marry him now?"

"Of course not! I told you I wasn't interested in Paul. I merely asked him to lunch because he wanted to see you."

"How can I believe you? You tell lies, Mother. You should have told me the truth years ago."

"Yes, I should. I am sorry, James. Please believe me. I wanted to wait until you were older – then it didn't seem to matter. I hadn't seen Paul for years."

"You could have warned me this morning – told me that your guest was my father."

"Yes, I suppose I could." I ought to have done, of course, but I had been afraid of his reaction. "I suppose I might have done, in time – if you had liked Paul."

"Well, I don't suppose it matters much," James said, resuming his mask of indifference. "I don't want to see him again. I hope you won't tell me it's my duty?"

"No, I shan't do that. You are old enough to make up your own mind."

"Then we might as well forget the whole thing."

I felt helpless as I sensed the anger James was holding inside. It was eating at him, making him bitter – and it had been there before this morning.

"Please don't hate me, James."

He looked surprised. "Why should I? We're very much alike, Ma. I think I take after you rather than him. You've always done what you want – and so do I."

"You make me sound selfish." I was hurt by his insinuation that I had always thought of myself first.

"I'm sorry if you think that. I'm actually quite proud of you. Not everyone is as gifted or as determined as you. You had nothing when you came to London – now you're rich. That's quite an achievement."

"You blame me for leaving you, don't you, James? When you were small. I thought I was doing the right thing."

"Of course you did; it suited you. It doesn't matter. I'm over eighteen now, almost an adult in the eyes of society. I might skip college and take off somewhere. See a bit of the world."

"You should finish your education first . . . for your own sake."

"Well, we'll see. I'm coming to France with you and Lizzy anyway. I'll think about things while we're there – then decide what to do." James smiled at me, but the expression in his eyes was veiled, distant. "Don't look so upset, Ma. It isn't the end of the world. Everyone tells a few lies. I dare say I'll get used to the idea that my father is a lush. It is marginally better than him being a murderer."

"I didn't lie to you. I simply wanted to protect you."

"Of course you did, Ma. It was all for my sake."

I realised he wasn't listening. Nothing I could say would make a difference. I wished he would shout at me as he had when he was a child. At least then I could take him in my arms and comfort him. I couldn't reach this sophisticated stranger.

"I've always loved you, James," I said. "I've never stopped caring or thinking about you. If you choose not to believe anything else I say, at least believe that."

"But you take your love away as easily as you give it," he said. "Jack thought you loved him."

"Jack *knows* I love him," I replied. "We quarrelled, but we never stopped loving each other. I shall love him until the day I die."

I turned and left the room before he could answer. Perhaps one day he would be able to forgive me. It would be a long time before I could forgive myself.

There was so much love inside James, but he was afraid to give it to anyone. Afraid that he would be hurt – and I had done that to him. Somehow over the years I had lost my son's trust, and I did not know how to win it back.

In the days leading up to Mum's funeral, and those that followed it, I saw very little of James. I did not try to curtail his freedom. It would have been pointless. I had no desire to punish him, only to heal the hurt inside us both.

If he was still angry and resentful, he gave no outward sign of it – except in his manner towards me. With everyone else he was his charming self: respectful to Sol, friendly to Francine and Mrs Jordan, with both of whom he was a favourite. Only I received the cool, polite smiles he usually reserved for strangers.

Mum's death seemed to bring James and Lizzy closer together. They stood holding hands at the graveside, and later I saw James with his arm about Lizzy's waist, as if giving her comfort.

James was courteous to me whenever we spoke. He smiled and called me Ma as he always did, but I sensed a distance in him. I would have liked to bridge the gap between us, but he would not let me.

"I don't know what to do," I said to Sol the night before we three were due to leave for France. "I feel as if I've lost him. I love him, but he doesn't believe me. He doesn't need me."

"He's an adult," Sol said. "But inside there's a bit of the sulky little boy left, Emma. He was fond of Greta – and the way she died was enough to upset anyone. Give him time. When he's older – when he's had more experience of life – he will come back to you. You may not have spent all your time with him when he was little, but you've been a damned good mother to the both of them. You've worked hard and you weren't always around, but you loved him and that should have been enough. James has no idea how lucky he has been so far. But he will find out; believe me, there are a lot of surprises in store for that lad."

Sol's words comforted me a little. There was nothing I

could do to change my son's perception of me for the moment. He had begun to distrust me when he was little more than a babe in arms, and his unease over his paternity had grown with the years. I was sorry that Jon had told him he was not his father, yet omitted to tell me. Had I known back then, perhaps we might have talked, and saved so many years of hurt.

I had hurt my son more than once. I had never meant to do so, but I had just the same. He couldn't forgive me for sending Jack away, and now he had discovered that his father was a man he could not like or admire. I had always tried to do the right thing for us all, but I had made so many mistakes.

Without Sol and Lizzy, I might have given into despair. I was missing my mother so much. We'd had our differences at various times, but she had always loved me.

I was glad we were going to France. Perhaps a change of scenery would do us all good.

Thirteen

S heila's large, luxurious villa nestled amongst trees and overlooked the beautiful bay on the Côte d'Azur, its whitewashed walls softened by the lush greenery around it. The sun was very warm, and the sea sparkled below us like blue diamonds, the air perfumed by the scent of flowers that grew wild down the hillside.

"This is pure heaven," I said and sighed, stretching luxuriously on my reclining chair. We were sitting on a terrace overlooking the swimming-pool – which was down on the level just below us – and the bay itself. "I feel so much better after just two weeks here. You are very lucky to have this place, Sheila. I'm only surprised that you can bear to leave it at all."

"I shan't be leaving it much in future – unless I come to London to visit you."

I was surprised by her statement, and turned my head to look at her. She was staring straight ahead, her face strained and a little bleak. I thought she was upset, but trying to hide it.

"What do you mean? Won't you be going on tour with Todd later this year? I thought you told me he was going out to Australia for three months?"

"Todd is; I'm not," Sheila said and pulled a face. She flicked her fingers through her immaculately cut short hair, which at the moment was bleached to a silver blonde. "It's over, Emma. I can't complain. I've had a good run for my money."

"Are you leaving him?"

"He's leaving me. He has been having an affair for more

than a year now. She is about nineteen. I can't compete –
besides, I don't want to. Not any more. I'm financially secure
– I've made sure of that over the years. I always knew one of
them would be special one day."

"You mean there have been others?" She nodded, something flickering in her eyes. "I'm so sorry, Sheila. I had
no idea."

She shrugged. "These things happen, especially in the
world of show business. Todd always had a roving eye.
He fancied you, Emma, but you never looked at him."

"There has only been one man for me since I met Jack."

Sheila hesitated, then, "Do you know about Angie?"

"What about her? I know she had a daughter. I think she
spends most of her time at Newport. James hardly ever sees
her when he visits New York."

"She drinks too much," Sheila said. "Jack tried to straighten
her out, but he couldn't. She has been in and out of clinics for
years . . . nothing seems to work for longer than a few weeks.
She stops drinking for a while, then goes back to it. I thought
Jane Melcher might have told you. She still keeps in touch,
doesn't she?"

"Now and then, at Christmas mostly these days – but she
would never tell me anything like that. Jack probably asked
her not to. He must be desperately worried about Angie."

"I think he hardly goes near her these days. They live apart,
Emma. Jack gives her everything she wants, of course."

"Money is no compensation for love. Poor Angie."

I closed my eyes for a moment. Jack and I had tried to do
what was right, but it hadn't worked out as we'd hoped. Angie
must have had a reason to drink so heavily, and I thought I
understood what lay beneath her unhappiness. She sensed that
Jack didn't love her, that he wished they had never married.
He would have tried to hide it, I knew him well enough for
that – but she had known. Women always did, of course.

Jack and I had given up so much. And it hadn't helped
either Angie or Jon in the end. We had wasted so many
years for nothing. Life was sometimes very cruel.

I opened my eyes again as someone sprinkled cold water

189

on my face. Lizzy was standing over me, shaking her hair and laughing. She was wet from the swimming-pool. Her skin was already a lovely pale golden colour. She looked more beautiful than ever.

"Lizzy! You wretch."

"You looked too peaceful," she teased. "Why don't you go for a swim? The water is gorgeous – isn't it, James?"

"If you say so."

He had flopped out on a towel and his eyes were closed, apparently bored by what was going on around him. It was a pose, of course, and caused by his unhappiness. I wished there was something I could say or do, but it was impossible for me to reach him. He had shut me out.

Sheila stood up, her bathing suit revealing that her figure was still trim. "I'm going to organise drinks. What will you have, James?"

"A Jamaica Fizz, please."

"James," I protested. "That has rum in it. Not in the middle of the afternoon, darling."

"Don't bother, Sheila," he said, and snatched up his shirt. I'm going for a walk. Coming, Lizzy?"

Lizzy hesitated. I could see she wanted to stay and relax with us, but the habit formed by years of trying to please James was too strong.

"All right," she called. "Wait for me, then." She grabbed a thin robe to wrap over her bathing suit.

"What about you?" Sheila asked. "I'm having chilled wine, Emma. Nice and cold from the fridge."

"I'll have lemonade, please. I don't drink in the sun. It gives me a headache."

As Sheila went away, I watched James and Lizzy begin the steep, winding descent to the sandy beach below. After a few moments, he slipped his arm about her waist. Lizzy turned her head to look up at him. Something in her manner made my heart catch. She *was* in love with him!

I had been blind not to realise it sooner. Lizzy had been fighting her feelings for a while now. She had slavishly obeyed James for years, and she had wanted to break free

– to experience a different life – but her love for him had drawn her back.

Mum's death had been the catalyst that brought them together again. Lizzy had been very distressed, not just for herself but for James, too. She had unselfishly tried to comfort James, and in doing so had been swamped by her love for him.

I wasn't sure whether to be glad or sorry. I loved them both, and it would be a fairytale ending to their story, but I was aware of unease. Lizzy was in love with James, but did he love her as unselfishly?

In the past, he had always either bullied or persuaded her into doing what he wanted. Lizzy was so young. She'd never had a chance to spread her wings. I wasn't sure it would be a good thing for her to marry James too soon.

If James felt the same as Lizzy, it would explain his terrible behaviour at the rock-and-roll concert, and the way he had found fault with her friends. I had thought he was just trying to protect her – but I knew how jealous James was of those he loved.

Sheila came back with a tray of drinks.

"Why so serious?"

"I was thinking about James and Lizzy."

"Oh, those two," she said as she set the tray down on a low table. "Yes, I had noticed a difference this summer. Do you suppose they are having a fling?"

"Sheila! I hope neither of them would consider it."

"Come on, Emma!" Sheila pulled a face at me. "She is my daughter – and he is your son. We can't expect them to behave like little puritans. Not if they're anything like we were."

"But Lizzy isn't seventeen yet."

"She soon will be. Besides, I was only her age when I went with my first." She laughed at the memory. "It was over so quickly, I asked him whether that was all there was to it. I'll give Todd that – he always takes his time."

"But Lizzy is so sweet and innocent," I protested, not wanting to let go of my image of her as a little girl.

"You were a couple of years older when Paul Greenslade

got you into trouble, and very naïve, but girls are much more aware these days. Lizzy knows what it's all about. I had a talk to her last summer when that rock-and-roll group was here. She isn't silly, but that doesn't mean she won't let James make love to her. What does it matter? I've always thought they might marry one day."

I stared at her in silence. I couldn't hold the moral high ground, nor could I explain why I was uneasy. It was possible that they would marry and be happy – and yet James was in such an awkward mood. I didn't want him to hurt Lizzy because he was angry with me.

"Leave them to sort themselves out," Sheila said. "You know what teenagers are these days. They are all rebels, Emma. If you say anything, you will only make them more determined to have their own way. Lizzy as well as James. She can be as stubborn as he is when she wants."

"Yes, I suppose you're right."

I sipped my drink, trying not to let my imagination run wild. Lizzy had always been affectionate towards James. Perhaps it was no more than that.

I lay sleepless for a long time that night, tossing and turning as I tried to make sense of it all. What had I done that was so wrong? I had tried hard to make my son happy, but now there was a terrible rift between us, a gap I was not sure could ever be breached.

Soon James would leave college and go to live with Jack in America. I had known in my heart that it would happen one day. Now it looked probable that Lizzy might go with him.

I would miss them both so much. I seemed to have lost so many of those I loved. When the children went, I should be alone.

Except for Sol, of course. At least he was always there, always my friend.

Sheila had hired a group to play for us. She was giving a party for her friends, many of whom owned villas near by. Some came for holidays, others were resident most of the year. She seemed to be carefree, untroubled by her imminent divorce, dancing with several attractive men during the course of the evening. Once she wandered away from the party, returning some twenty minutes later looking very pleased with herself.

I thought perhaps she was having an affair. Well, at least she wasn't suicidal over Todd leaving her for a much younger woman. Sheila had taken her chances and made the most of them. I didn't need to worry about her future.

My gaze wandered back to Lizzy and James. They had been inseparable all evening. It was obvious to me now that Lizzy was in love. Her eyes were bright with excitement and she seemed to be lit up from inside.

Did James feel the same? I hoped he did. I would be upset if he hurt her.

"Sitting here all alone? Why aren't you dancing?"

I turned my head to look at the man who had spoken and smiled. He lived just down the hill from Sheila. A retired businessman, he was about Sol's age, attractive and recently widowed. I liked him more than most of Sheila's friends, because he had a quiet, gentle manner, and I suspected he was lonely.

"I didn't feel like dancing," I replied. "It's such a lovely evening. I'm happy just to sit here and watch everyone else."

"It's a lovely view from up here," Tom Wright agreed. "Ours isn't quite as good, but we liked it – Ellen and me."

"You must miss her a lot."

"Yes, I do. We had thirty-five good years together. It isn't easy to live alone after that."

"No, I'm sure it isn't."

"You've been a widow for several years, I understand?"

"Yes. It will be ten years in April next year."

"That's a long time." He looked at me thoughtfully. "Haven't you ever thought about getting married again?"

"Not really. I have my friends and my family."

"Ellen told me to look for someone else. She knew she was dying, of course. We both knew. She didn't want me to be alone. I'm looking for the right person."

"Then I hope you find her."

"I thought perhaps I might have done," he said. "But you're not interested, are you? I could have offered you companionship and money, my dear. But you have both already."

I tried to let him down gently. "I am always happy to make a friend, but I'm not looking for marriage."

Tom nodded. He sat talking for a while, then went to ask Sheila to dance. I had given my full attention to Tom while he sat with me. As my gaze returned to the dancers, I saw that Lizzy and James were no longer amongst them.

Where had they gone? I glanced round, then walked to the end of the lawn to look down at the beach. Still no sign of them. They had obviously slipped away to be alone.

I couldn't go after them, of course. Sheila was right, they weren't children any more. They must choose their own way. I had tried to give them a happy childhood, to prepare them for life. It was time to let go.

I went back to my table and listened to the singer crooning about love. Sheila and Tom were laughing together. For a moment I envied them. Was I a fool to remain true to a love that could never be mine? I had been given several chances to remarry, but I'd turned all my potential suitors down.

I was still young enough to regret my single state. Both Lizzy and James would be leaving home soon. Perhaps I should start to think about the possibility of marrying again?

I had no wish to marry anyone but Jack, but it was much too late for regrets now. Jack had probably forgotten me long ago. Even if his marriage were unhappy, there would have been other women to fill his life. I could not wish him to have lived like a monk all these years. I knew how hard that could be, how long and lonely the nights could seem when there was no one to hold, no one to whisper to in the dark hours.

No, I did not want to live alone for the rest of my life – but what was the alternative? I had experienced marriage without real love, and I did not want that again. It seemed as though I had no choice but to go on as I was.

*　　*　　*

"It was lovely having you here," Sheila said and hugged me. "Come back again soon. I shall miss you, Emma."

"You won't be lonely," I teased. "You have so many friends."

"Most of them are just acquaintances," she said. "You and me – we go back a long way."

"To the dark ages," I said and smiled at her. "Why don't you come for Christmas? We would love to have you."

"I'll think about it," she promised. "I'll keep in touch, Emma."

Lizzy kissed her goodbye.

"I've had a lovely time, Sheila."

"Come again whenever you like." Sheila glanced at me. "You are welcome to stay as often as you want. You will be leaving school soon, Lizzy."

"No, I shan't," Lizzy said. "I'm going to college. I want to train to be a doctor. I've been thinking about it for a long time, and now I've made up my mind."

"You'll never stick to it," James scoffed. "I know you – you'll get miserable as soon as you find the work is too hard."

"I don't see why Lizzy shouldn't be a doctor if she wants, James. She is a clever girl."

"No, Ma. I don't expect you do see why she shouldn't waste her time and her looks."

"What is that supposed to mean?"

James shrugged. The smouldering look he gave Lizzy told me that he was annoyed with her. The closeness I had observed between them a few days earlier seemed to have cooled.

What had gone wrong? Had they quarrelled again?

I didn't dare ask, but two days after we were home, I found Lizzy alone in the sitting room, crying.

"What's wrong, darling? Has something upset you?"

She looked at me, then blew her nose on her hanky. "It's James," she said. "He is being such a beast about me going to college. He says I'm too pretty to waste my time trying to be something I can't. He wants me to leave school now and go to America with him."

"And you don't want to?"

"I want to be with James," Lizzy said. She wiped her eyes. "I love him – but this time I can't give him his own way, Emmie. This is important to me. Perhaps James is right – I might not be clever enough to pass all the exams – but I want to try."

"Then you should do it," I said. "James always wants his own way. If he loves you enough, Lizzy, he will understand this means a lot to you. He will give you time to grow up. You are both very young. In fairness to you both, you should wait a little before you think of settling down. There is no rush to do anything yet, is there?"

Lizzy's cheeks were pink. Her eyes could not meet mine. I sensed that she and James had become lovers when we were all in France.

"I've told James that," she said at last. "He says I can't love him if I won't go away with him. I do love him, Emmie – but I want to go to college first."

"Would you like me to talk to him for you?"

"No." Her head went up, and I saw pride in her eyes. "I was crying because it's so hard to choose – but I have made my choice. I'm going to stay on at school and then go to medical college. I'm going to tell James this evening."

"Are you quite sure?"

"Yes. If I go with him now, I'll never really be me. I have to do this for myself – and then I can marry James when we're both ready."

"I think you have made a wise decision, darling – but James won't like it."

"I know," she said quietly. "But I shan't change my mind."

"You did this – you made Lizzy say she wouldn't come with me. Don't deny it, Mother. She wouldn't have dared to go ahead with it if you hadn't encouraged her."

"You underestimate Lizzy. She has a will of her own. She has let you have your own way for so long . . . this time she wants something for herself. If you really care about her, James, you will give her that chance. After all, you are only eighteen yourself. It's far too young to marry. You wanted to see some of the world. Why don't you do that? Forget college and go to America for a couple of years or so."

"Oh yes, you would like that, wouldn't you?"

"Not particularly. I thought it was what you wanted?"

James stared at me. Had he expected me to forbid him to go? It was probably what he wanted. My son was a rebel. He kept a poster of the tragic James Dean, who had died in a car smash at the age of twenty-four, on his bedroom wall, and wore his dark hair in the same style as the moody young film star.

I smiled inwardly, amused by James's frustration. My son did not know what he wanted. I had spoiled him, my friends had spoiled him. Perhaps it was time he stood on his own two feet for a while.

"Rebel without a cause," I murmured so softly that he could not hear, then in a louder voice, "Go on, James. I'll put some money into your bank account. You wanted to be independent. I'm not holding you back any more. Go to America – or wherever you like. Lizzy is going to train as a doctor. I will be very proud of her for trying even if she doesn't make it. Why don't you show me what you can do? You can't let Lizzy beat you."

His mouth fell open. "You're really telling me to leave?"

"Yes, I am. I've had enough of your moods, James. You can come home when you've got something to show for all the time and money I've lavished on you for eighteen years. At the moment, I am rather wondering if I've been wasting my time."

James stared at me in disbelief, then he started to laugh. "That's telling me, isn't it, Ma? You've really thrown the gauntlet down, haven't you? Well, I'll pick it up – and I shan't need your money. I can fend for myself."

"That's nice, darling. Good luck."

"You think I'm just saying that, don't you? But I've been offered a job as a photographer for a magazine."

"I've always thought you should concentrate on stills. You are very good at that. So – when do you leave?"

"Tomorrow," he said "You think I'll change my mind, but I shan't."

"Nor shall I. The money will be in your account if you need it."

Our eyes met for a few moments. Neither of us was willing to give way. This was the showdown that had been waiting to happen for a long time.

"So long then, Ma. I'll see you sometime."

"Well, I certainly hope so, James. If only because I'd like to see some return on my investment."

He grinned at me, then turned and walked out of the room. It took all my strength not to call him back.

Lizzy cried a little the next morning.

"Are you sorry I let him go, darling?"

She lifted her head proudly. "I'm glad he has gone – but he will come back, won't he?"

"I'm sure he will, Lizzy. I set him a challenge. James always loves to prove me wrong. He will stay away for a year or two, and he's sure to be a success if he goes to Jack. Jack has influence with all kinds of people. I'm certain James will soon make a name for himself. Then he will come home to prove to me how wrong I was. By which time, he should have finally grown up enough to see that it was only fair you should have your chance, too."

"I shall miss him." Lizzy looked a little wistful.

"So shall I, darling. But it's for the best – isn't it? We have to let him go and hope that he will come back to us when he's ready."

"Yes." She lifted her chin. "Yes, it's for the best – but it's very hard to send the man you love away."

"Yes, I know," I said. "Very hard. I do know just how you feel. But you still have me, Lizzy. You still have me."

Fourteen

It was September and I was busy with the autumn collections for the main shop. We had several new suppliers this season, and their orders had to be carefully checked.

"Telephone for you, Mrs Reece." The manager of my dress department came up to me as I was frowning over an evening gown I did not like as much as I'd expected. Something wasn't quite right, but I wasn't sure what. "It's a Miss Gwen Robinson. She says it's urgent or she would have rung you at home this evening."

"Oh, thank you, Annette. I'll take it in your office, if I may?"

"Yes, of course."

I went into the office and put the receiver to my ear.

"Gwen – is something wrong? You're not ill, are you?"

"No, I'm fine. It's just that I wanted to tell you first – in case someone else tries to contact you by phone, though they say they will be writing. I've had a man from a firm of London solicitors here, Emma. They want to buy your shops. They are acting on behalf of someone, but they won't say who."

"We don't want to sell – do we?"

"That's up to you."

"Whatever they offer will be half yours, if we want to sell."

"They've offered ten thousand pounds. It's a lot of money."

"How do you feel about it, Gwen? Are you ready to retire?"

"Not for a few years yet! I enjoy coming in every day. I should get bored sitting at home twiddling my fingers."

199

"I'll turn the offer down, then."

"Are you sure? It's a reasonable price for property here. It doesn't sell for the prices you get in London."

"It's all right, but not exciting. No, I shan't sell. Not until you tell me you want to give up. Now, tell me – what have you been doing recently? Have you been anywhere nice?"

"Not really. Richard hardly stirs out of the house these days. I don't see much of him unless I go round." She gave a dry laugh. "I get about when I can. Any chance of your coming down soon?"

"Not at the moment. You don't need me, do you?"

"No – but I sometimes think we don't see enough of each other these days. Perhaps I'll come up to you one day."

"I wish you would. We'll paint the town red."

She chuckled. "I'll think about it and let you know."

I replaced the receiver and went back to checking the stock. The dress I had been concerned about was ballerina length and was made of satin and velvet with an overskirt of an embroidered net. The style was popular with my customers, and I had thought it would sell well – but I could see now that the hem of the underskirt was uneven and badly done.

"The hem isn't straight, Annette. It's difficult to see at first, because of the overskirt – but if you look carefully you can see it is a quarter of an inch out at the side. Send it back and ask for a replacement. If they are difficult we shall cancel any further orders."

"Yes, Mrs Reece. I was wondering what was wrong with it. You have a very good eye for detail."

"It comes from working at the wholesale end for years. You get used to checking for faults in the material and the workmanship."

We checked the rest of that particular order with extra care. Nothing else was faulty, but I was less than satisfied with the firm. They should never have sent that dress out. Sol would have been furious if something like that had been put out on *his* rails – and this was supposed to be the better end of the market! If they did it again, I would cross them off my list of suppliers.

I glanced through the teenage range before leaving the floor. A few years back no one would have thought of stocking styles for that particular market – young women choosing and wearing the same kind of clothes as their mothers – but things had changed rapidly throughout the fifties. The change was mainly due to the arrival of designers like Mary Quant, who had opened her shop on the King's Road a year or so back. It was called the Bazaar, and her inexpensive, very distinctive styles for young women had been an instant success.

Francine had designed a similar range for us, bright, exciting clothes that seemed to appeal to the younger clients, and they looked to be selling well. We had simplified the label since the early days, and the young range was now called "Just Francine". There were lots of pretty dresses for day and evening, mostly with full skirts which could be made to stand out by the addition of net petticoats that swished as you walked. We also had a large selection of casual wear, including some mohair separates that came from Italy.

Satisfied that we were keeping up with the demand of an ever-growing market, I got into the lift that would take me up to the next floor and my own office. A small pile of letters was waiting for me. Some were invoices, others requests from a charity for help or money. One was from the solicitors Gwen had told me about.

I frowned over the letter. If it were not for Gwen, I might have taken the offer. The money would be better invested in London – or I could buy that house in France.

But I could do that anyway, if I wanted. And I had given my word to Gwen. I slipped the letter into my bag to take home. I wanted to show it to Sol later.

"Why do you think they want to buy them all?" I asked as he read the letter. "It seems a bit odd, don't you think?"

"It's probably a firm like the Home and Colonial," Sol said. "They may want to open a big grocery store, knock all the buildings into one."

"No." I shook my head. "Two of them are next door to each other – but my father's shop is two doors away from

Madge Henty's dress shop. They can't want all that space, surely?"

"Turn them down," Sol advised. "If they want the property badly enough, they will come up with a better offer."

"I don't think I want to sell anyway. Gwen isn't ready to retire."

"Then write and say so." He laid the letter down, losing interest. "Lizzy telephoned this afternoon. She will be home later this evening – about eight, she thinks."

"But she has only just gone back to school." I was puzzled. "Did she say why she was coming home?"

"No. She just asked if I would tell you. She sounded a bit upset."

I nodded, wondering what could be on Lizzy's mind. She had seemed happy enough when she left for her boarding school a few days earlier. I'd thought she had made up her mind that she wanted to stay on and take her exams. Now she was coming home. An unpleasant suspicion crossed my mind. *No, please don't let it be that! Not that! Don't let it happen to Lizzy. She's so young.*

Yet I could not help feeling uneasy. It was possible, more than possible. I had suspected that Lizzy and James had been lovers when we were in France. She could be expecting his child.

No, surely not! Poor Lizzy . . . she was only seventeen, and had her whole life in front of her. This would spoil her chances of going ahead with the career she had set her mind on, at least for a while.

Surely James would not have been so careless? There was an easy way to protect her. Young people were supposed to be so sophisticated today. James ought to have taken more care! But I was jumping to conclusions. Lizzy might have decided to come home for quite another reason.

Perhaps she had simply forgotten something.

As soon as I saw Lizzy's face, I knew I had guessed correctly. She looked frightened and ashamed. My heart ached for her, and I held out my arms to her.

"Lizzy, darling," I said. "I'm so sorry. I shouldn't have let James go."

"I wanted him to go," she replied, catching back a sob of despair. "He can't do anything, can he? We never expected . . . it only happened a few times, Emmie. I didn't think it could happen so quickly."

"It was just the same for me when I fell for Paul."

Lizzy blinked away her tears. "I feel so foolish. Sheila warned me to be careful last year. She said to make sure we used something . . . you know, those horrible things. She meant with Terry Moon, of course. I wasn't interested then, but . . ."

"You fell in love with James. He was your playmate and your friend – then suddenly it was different." I smiled at her. "You grew up, Lizzy. It was to be expected."

"We didn't mean it to happen. I wanted to wait. James—" She stopped and bit her lip. "He didn't force me, but . . . I wanted to, and yet I didn't."

"You don't have to explain, darling. I know what it's like to be in love – and I also know my son. He can be very persuasive."

I knew only too well what it had been like for Lizzy. I had experienced the same thing with Paul all those years ago.

"Are you angry? I know it was wrong."

"It was more foolish than wrong, Lizzy. It means you either have to take a break from your schooling – or have an abortion. We might be able to get it done abroad, if that's what you want?"

She looked horrified. "I couldn't! I know I've ruined everything. But I don't want to kill the baby."

"Good. I would have been sad if you had. So that means you will have to continue your studies at home for a few months. I can arrange to get the course work you need. It's best if your school doesn't know you are pregnant. I think I'll tell them we have been advised you should travel this winter for a health problem."

"But they will know afterwards. Everyone will."

"No one has to know – at least, not here in England. We'll

go to France, Lizzy. I've been thinking of buying a house there. We'll stay there together for as long as we need to – then, when we come home, I'll let everyone believe the baby is mine. You can go back to school and take your exams. I shall bring the baby up until you want him – or her – back."

She stared at me in silence for several minutes.

"That isn't fair on you, Emmie."

"Would you rather I asked James to come home? I expect Jack knows where he is, even though he hasn't written to either of us." I looked into her lovely, expressive eyes. "It's your choice, Lizzy. I shan't blame you either way."

Tears gathered and spilled over, trickling down her cheeks.

"I was so frightened on the train coming home. I thought you would be angry because I'd let you down – now you're giving me another chance." She smothered a sob. "Why are you so kind to me? I don't deserve it."

"Don't be silly! Of course you deserve to be loved. I just want to do whatever makes you happy, darling. I can leave Sol in charge of the business . . . No, I may have a better idea about that. I shall have to talk to Gwen, but whatever happens, I'm going to be with you, Lizzy. I'm going to take you away and look after you – and when we come back, you can go to college just as you planned."

"Take charge of the London shops?" Gwen squeaked with excitement when I telephoned later. "Would I like to? Just give me the chance! Are you sure you trust me, Emma?"

"Of course." I laughed. "It means we can sell the shops in March. I can't imagine why anyone wants those shops down there – unless Sol is right and some large chain of grocers wants to open a huge store."

"It's the coming thing, so I've heard."

"In London and the big towns perhaps – but in a small country market town? Oh well, that's their business." I hesitated, then, "It means you will have to live in London. There is a small flat over the first shop I ever bought. For several years it was let to a tenant, but recently I've decided to have it refurbished so it is empty. It does need doing up. Shall I see to that or leave it to you?"

"I'll see to that when I get there. I like things my own way."

"Yes, I know. You will have a free hand, Gwen. There's only one more thing – what about your friend?"

"Oh, I seldom see Richard these days. All he wants to do is stay home and sit by the fire. I've got too much energy to do that. I'll soon make new friends, Emma. Don't worry about me. After Mother died, I didn't know where to start, but I see things differently these days. I'm looking forward to a new challenge."

"You can stay here while the flat is being redecorated. I'm sure Sol won't mind."

"Well, that's settled then. As long as Sol doesn't object."

When I told him, he wasn't actually too pleased at the idea. He frowned at me, not speaking for a few moments.

"I don't suppose it matters – providing she doesn't stay for years. Your aunt isn't exactly my cup of tea, Emma."

"I'm sorry. I should have asked first. I can find somewhere else for her to stay until the flat is ready."

He looked at me oddly. "No, no; I'm just out of sorts today. I dare say I can put up with it for a while. The house often seems empty these days. It wasn't so bad when Greta was alive, but with her gone and now you going away . . . I'm going to miss you and Lizzy."

"Yes, I know. I'm sorry to desert you, Sol. I shall miss you, but you will always be welcome to come and stay with us in France. In fact I hope you will, providing you keep our secret. Neither Jack nor James is to know about this. Not until we are ready to tell them."

"I shan't let you down, though I think you are wrong, Emma. James has a right to know about the baby – but he won't hear it from me."

"It's Lizzy's secret, not ours. She will tell him when she's ready."

Sol frowned. "It's a generous thing to do, Emma – taking on the child. It won't be just for a few months. If Lizzy goes on with her training, you'll be tied down with a small child for years. I have a feeling it might get you into bother one way or another."

"I'm just trying to protect Lizzy. Having a child out of wedlock isn't the social crime it was when I was her age, but quite a lot of people still see it as a stigma. Lizzy will have more chance of getting a place in a good teaching hospital if they don't know she has a child."

"How are you going to explain it away? Or doesn't your own reputation matter?"

"I'm not sure I have one left," I said and smiled ruefully. "I've lived the way I wanted, Sol, and I'm not going to change now. Let people think what they like. I shan't tell anyone anything unless I'm forced. When Lizzy has finished her training . . . well, James might be home by then. We'll cross our bridges when we have to. Stop worrying, Sol. It's all going to work out fine."

"I might as well not say anything; you will go your own way, the same as always."

He sounded a bit put out, which wasn't really like him. I smiled and kissed his cheek.

"Dearest Sol! I don't know what I would do without you. Never stop being my friend – will you?"

He shook his head at me once more, but gave up trying to persuade me to think again.

It was October before Lizzy and I left for France. I had turned down the first offer on my shops in March. To my surprise, they came up with a better one. I finally settled on twelve thousand pounds.

I gave half of it to Gwen and arranged to have the rest paid into a London bank in Sheila's name. In return, she made the same amount available to me in Paris.

"Exchange is no robbery," she said. "And if it makes things easier your end . . ."

Sheila had been told the truth, of course. She had immediately offered us the chance to live with her.

"Thank you, Sheila – but you have too many friends," I

said. "This has to be kept a secret, for Lizzy's sake. She doesn't want James to know, in case he feels he has to come home and marry her. And she still wants to go to medical school after the baby is born."

"Well, I shall visit you in your secret place," she said. "Where are you thinking of buying a house?"

"I'm not sure. Jon always said the Loire Valley was beautiful. Perhaps there. We shall look for something we like, something we want to go back to year after year."

"And no one is to know about the baby – not James, not Jack?"

"Not yet. Lizzy is going to wear a wedding ring, and she hardly shows at all yet. It's just until she can go to medical school and find a job; later on she will probably want the baby back. Especially if she gets married."

"Well, if it's what she wants . . ."

"It is for the time being."

"Then that's how it will be."

Lizzy and I had a wonderful time looking for our new home. It was so exciting, touring the region of the Loire with its beautiful scenery and wealth of old chateaux. It was truly the heart of France, an unmarked dividing line between north and south, between the heat of the south and the cooler climes of the north, the differing tastes in wine and food.

The weather was good, not hot but comfortable and certainly warmer than at home, and Lizzy was blooming. Her skin, hair and eyes seemed to have a glow of their own.

We settled at last on the region where the valley bends westward at the Sancerre vineyards, the land so green and pleasant, flowing along what is known as the "royal route" of chateaux from Chambord to Angers. In the books we bought to help us in our search, it said there were more than three hundred chateaux in the area of Touraine, but it was just south-east of Orleans that we found our own fairytale palace.

By the standards of the beautiful chateaux we had visited on our travels, it was very small. It was not as old as some, and had been refurbished with modern conveniences in the

207

form of bathrooms and a well-equipped kitchen. Its yellow stone walls had a mellowed look, and the wooden shutters on the windows were painted green. There was a dovecote above the gatepost and a stream crossed our land on its way to the river.

"It's perfect, Emmie, don't you think?" Lizzy had said when we drove up the narrow approach road and discovered the house half hidden by trees. "So beautiful . . . and peaceful."

"Yes – and there is a farm near by," I said. "I think we can probably buy eggs, milk and butter there – and I noticed a bakery and butcher's shop in the village as we came through. I can always drive into town when we need to do a big shop." I smiled at her as she wandered down to the stream. She sat on the bank and dangled her bare feet in the water. I followed and sat beside her, resisting the urge to do the same. "What do you think, darling? Shall we buy it?"

"Can we afford it?" She shaded her eyes to look at me. The sun was particularly warm that afternoon, especially here in this sheltered place.

"Yes, I think so," I said and smiled at her. "It is very reasonable. I couldn't buy a house like this at home for the money, Lizzy. But are you sure you will be happy here? There isn't much going on, and it's quite a way from the town."

"It's just what I need," she said. "I can study and wait for my baby to arrive." She placed her hands on the gentle swell of her belly and smiled.

"Then we'll settle on it today," I said. "It has been fun looking round, Lizzy – but I shall be glad when we're in. There is some furniture with the house, though I shall have to buy more. I'll have a look in Orleans, and if we can't see everything we want, I may go to Paris later on. I am sure we can buy most of what we need."

Lizzy looked at me dreamily. "I think I could stay here forever."

"Just until the baby is born," I said with a smile. "You have a career to think about, Lizzy."

"Yes, I haven't forgotten," she said. "Once we're settled, I'm going to get on with my studies properly."

*   *   *

Life at the chateau soon drifted into a slow, tranquil routine. Lizzy applied herself to her books, often taking them out to the orchard where the gardener we had found had fixed up a comfortable wooden swing with cushions for her to sit in. It had its own canopy of yellow sailcloth to shade her; this could be pulled out or folded up as she chose, and altogether, it was extremely comfortable.

André was a young strong man, with rather dark Latin looks and curling hair that always looked as if it were wet. He worked hard for very little money, supplying us with fresh fruit and vegetables from the well-stocked gardens. Whenever we wanted a chicken or duck for our dinner, André would kill and clean it for us, and he kept us supplied with eggs, milk and wonderful fresh butter from his parents' farm. Sometimes there was a plump fish that he had caught himself, and he told me where to buy all the wonderful fruit for which the region was famous.

I thought after a while that he might have fallen in love a little with Lizzy. And who could blame him? As the weeks and then months passed, there was a radiance about her as she wandered the meadows and little winding roads surrounding our home. People smiled at her, waving their hands when they saw her. Lizzy always waved back, and I knew that she was liked and admired by everyone we came to know.

It was a pleasant way of life, and one that I found I enjoyed more than I would ever have thought possible. I had expected to long for London, but somehow I did not.

Sometimes we went into town or visited the beautiful rose gardens around Orleans and Doue-la-Fontaine. There were also the forests and heaths of the Sologne, and the Forest of Orleans, but Lizzy did not feel like going far these days. She was becoming rather large as time passed, and the doctor we visited in Orleans was concerned that she should come into his clinic for the birth.

"I think perhaps we have two babies in there, madame," he told me privately. "She does very well, the little one – but for the sake of the children she should be here for the birth."

We agreed that Lizzy would move into the clinic a week before the birth was due. I was a little anxious for her as time passed, but Lizzy was serene. She seemed lost in her own private world, content to let the days drift on, and to study.

"I think I would like to live here," she told me one afternoon when she had been resting on her bed. "One day, when I'm older, I'll have a house just like this one."

"You know this house is yours whenever you need it, Lizzy." I sometimes sat with her when she rested, reading to her or sewing tiny garments for the baby. "I love being here, too – but I shall be just as happy when we're back in London. And you will too, darling, when you're at college. You are too young to bury yourself here in the country – and too bright not to make the most of your life."

Lizzy pressed her hands against her swollen belly and laughed.

"He kicked again," she said. "He's so restless . . . just like James."

"When are you going to tell James?"

"I don't know – perhaps never," she said. "He hasn't written to us. I don't think that is very nice of him, do you?"

"I suppose he has been busy," I said. "You know what James is, darling. When he starts working he forgets everything. And he was very cross with us both when he went away."

"Yes." She sighed and looked unhappy. "But he could have sent me a postcard now and then."

I had telephoned Sol just that morning to ask if anything important had come in the post.

"I should send it on if it had," he told me, sounding a little put out because I had asked. "Surely you know that, Emma?"

"Yes, of course I do. I was just asking, for Lizzy's sake. Anyway, I miss talking to you. How are you? How are things at the showrooms?"

"Busy as ever. Francine has come up with some new ideas again." He hesitated, then, "She has been feeling a bit restless, Emma. She threatened to leave us last week – but I think I've managed to talk her out of it."

"How did you do that?"

"I'll tell you when you get back," he said evasively. "When do you expect to be home?"

"In April, I should think. The baby is due about the end of March."

"That's another two months." He sighed. "Oh, well."

I thought he sounded very down, not at all like himself. "Is something wrong, Sol? You're not ill, are you?"

"No, of course not. Fit as a flea!"

"But something is upsetting you?"

"No, not really. Except that Jack was here last week. He wanted to see you. I told him you had gone away for a while, that I didn't know where you were or when you would be back. I'm not sure that he believed me . . . I think he thought I was being evasive, trying to stop him seeing you."

"Jack was in England – looking for me? Are you sure it was me he wanted and not James?" My heart caught suddenly and I was breathless for a moment. "Did he say what he wanted?"

"No. Just that if I did hear from you, I was to tell you he wanted to see you."

"Oh . . . well, perhaps he will write."

"If he does I'll send the letter on."

"Yes, thank you," I said. "Sol . . . did he say anything about his wife?"

"Not to me. If you had been here, you could have spoken to him yourself."

I was puzzled as I replaced the receiver. Sol had seemed angry with me for a while now – why? What had changed between us?

Had I taken him too much for granted over the years? I had thought our friendship was rock solid, despite the possibility of his having feelings I could not return, but of late he had been short with me several times.

Perhaps it was time I started to look for a house of my own in London. Sol might not take kindly to the sound of a child crying in the house. He was so youthful that I sometimes forgot that he was more than twenty years older than me.

Lizzy looked at me as I carried a tray of coffee and cakes I had baked out to her in the garden. "Something wrong, Emmie?"

"Sol was cross over something, but I don't know what."

"Surely you know what's the matter with him, Emmie?" I shook my head and she laughed. "He's always been in love with you. Why don't you marry him?"

"Marry Sol?" I frowned. "No, it wouldn't work. I don't love him in that way. It would make him unhappy. I've taken him for granted all these years, and I shouldn't have. I think I shall buy a house of my own when we go back."

"Why don't you live here?"

"You wouldn't be able to see the baby very often then," I pointed out. "You will want to visit as often as you can, Lizzy – and besides, I have the shops to think about. Gwen took them on as a temporary measure, and she will continue to help me for a few years, but one day she will want to retire."

"What about you, Emmie? Wouldn't you like to have more time for yourself? Wouldn't you like to travel – go to America and visit Jane Melcher? You've talked about it often. Why not sell everything and have some fun for yourself?"

"Perhaps one day," I agreed. "I'm too young to think about retiring just yet, darling." But I had thought about it. I had thought it would be nice to let my hair down and just have fun.

"I suppose so," she said, "but it makes me sad to think of you alone. You should be with someone who loves you."

"I have you, and soon we shall have the baby to share," I said. "I've loved being here with you, Lizzy. We've been so happy together – but we must go back, darling."

"Yes, of course we must," she said, but I wasn't sure she was convinced.

Did she regret the decision she had taken not to go away with James when he asked her? If she had, I knew they would have married long ago. James would not have deserted her. I was sure he loved her, even though he had been taught to expect too much of his own way.

My one real wish was that he would realise what he was missing and come home before too long.

Fifteen

I had been to the village to post some letters. It was a pleasant spring afternoon, and I was walking back thinking how much I would miss this place when we finally went home. Perhaps Lizzy was right . . . perhaps I should think of retiring soon.

I was startled from my reverie by a shout, and saw André racing towards me, his expression such that my heart caught with fear. I went to meet him.

"What is it, André?" I asked. "Is it Lizzy – has something happened to her?"

"The baby come," he said. "The little one fall on the ground near the stream and I find her lying still, eyes closed. I carry her to Maman . . . she send me to find you."

It was ten days too soon! I had been going to take Lizzy to the clinic that weekend. Now it was too late. She was about to have her baby in a farmhouse.

If she died, I would never forgive myself. What were doing here in this isolated backwater? Lizzy could have been at home in London, with all the best doctors to care for her. Sol's words came back to haunt me. He had warned me that I was not wise to bring Lizzy to France, away from her family and friends.

"Have you sent for the doctor?" I appealed. "Is he coming?"

"He comes soon," André assured me. "You do not worry, madame. Maman knows what she does. The baby will be safe, and the little one."

He seemed so cheerful that my fears were temporarily allayed, but I was still anxious as I hurried on ahead of him to the farmhouse. He did not know how dangerous it could be for a woman at times like these – and we had been warned that Lizzy might need special care.

As I entered the house I heard a baby crying. I ran upstairs, following the sound. A door at the end of the corridor stood open. I could see Lizzy sitting up in bed and Madame Brenne about to place a child in her arms.

"Lizzy, darling!" I cried as I went in, then stopped as I saw that there were two babies. One had been wrapped in a white cloth, which covered its body and face, and I felt a chill strike me. "Are you all right?"

Lizzy looked at me, tears trickling down her cheeks.

"Little Emily was born first," she said in a choking voice. "She's fine, Emmie – but Jamie had the cord round his neck. I stopped pushing because the pains had stopped, and then . . . He was dead when we realised—" She could not go on, her head bent over her daughter as the tears flowed.

"I shall take the poor little one away," Madame Brenne said. "André will make a basket for him, and we shall bury him here, amongst us. Forgive me, madame, there was no more I could do. I am not a doctor, and the first one came so quickly . . . I did not realise the other one—"

"It isn't your fault, madame," I told her. "You did what you could – you may have saved Lizzy and little Emily. I am very grateful for your help."

I went to sit on the edge of the bed, reaching for Lizzy's hand.

"I'm so sorry, darling. If I had been here I could have taken you to the clinic."

"It might not have been in time," she said, wiping her hand across her eyes. "It was my fault. I was restless. I went for a walk by the stream, caught my foot and fell. I brought my labour on too soon . . . I should have been resting, like you told me."

"Oh, Lizzy," I said, bending to kiss her. "Don't blame yourself, darling. It was just one of those things. It could have happened if you had been in the hospital. Even the doctors might not have been able to save him."

"Yes, I suppose so," she said, but I could see she did not believe it. "You told me to stay in the house and rest while you were gone. I should have done what you told me."

"No, darling," I said. "I shouldn't have left you when you were so close to your time. I'm very sorry."

"Do you think James will blame me for killing his son?"

"Oh, Lizzy." I felt the pain strike at my heart. "Of course he won't – because you did no such thing. When he comes home we'll tell him about little Emily. He will love her, and one day you might have another child."

She nodded and bent to kiss the top of her baby's head, but she didn't say anything. The tears continued to trickle down her cheeks, and I knew nothing I could say would help.

I wished that I had been with her, or that we had stayed at home. Perhaps then both twins would have lived.

It had been my idea to come here, and now it had ended in tragedy.

"I'm worried about her," I said to Sheila one morning in May. "I had expected to be back in London by now, but Lizzy says she's not ready. She hardly leaves the baby for a moment. I think she is afraid Emily will die if she isn't with her with her the whole time. I don't think she sleeps much."

"I'd noticed Lizzy was looking a bit fragile," Sheila said, looking concerned. "She's blaming herself, of course. It's natural in the circumstances. I expect she will get over it in time."

"I asked her if she still wanted to be a doctor. She says she does, but not yet – that the baby must come first." I frowned. "The trouble is, I have to get back to London. Sol insists he needs me there, and Gwen wants to have a talk about the shops . . . I can't force Lizzy to come if she wants to stay here, but I don't want to leave her like this."

"You go," Sheila said. "I'll stay here with her, Emma. You've done as much as you can. It's my turn to look after her for a while."

"Would you mind? I'll come back as soon as I can."

Sheila had decided to marry again now that her divorce

from Todd was final. The wedding was due to take place at the end of May, but I could see no reason why I should not be back by then.

"Tom will just have to wait," Sheila said. "This time Lizzy is going to come first. Don't worry, Emma. I'll keep an eye on her. I'm not such a soft touch as you. She might decide to come out of herself if she doesn't have your shoulder to cry on all the time."

"You're nearly as bad," I said. "Especially when it comes to your grandchild. I've seen you picking her up and gloating over her when you thought no one was looking."

"Well, she is rather delicious, isn't she?"

"Gorgeous," I said and smiled at her. We were united as never before in our adoration of the wonderful Emily. "So we're agreed then? Lizzy stays here for the moment. I'll come back when I've sorted things out at home, then we'll see what she wants to do."

Lizzy kissed me goodbye the next morning, and told me not to worry. "I shall be all right," she said. "I just need to think about things for a while, Emmie, that's all."

"Take your time, darling. We all want whatever will make you happy. I shall be back soon. Take care of yourself and Emily. Remember we all love you both."

Lizzy nodded, but she wasn't listening. I could hear the baby crying as she turned back into the house.

It was hard to leave them like this, but it had to be done. Besides, Sheila was with them. They would be quite safe.

On the journey home to England, I kept wondering what was so urgent that Sol was insisting I come back. Surely the wholesale business wasn't in trouble? It had been flourishing when I left. But there must be some sort of crisis or Sol would not have asked me to return.

He had been acting in a manner unlike himself for a while now. I had an odd foreboding as the taxi stopped outside the house that had been my home for so many years. Something was wrong. I had sensed it even before I left for France.

The house felt different as I went inside. Mrs Jordan came

to greet me. She looked awkward, apprehensive, but said nothing more than a few words of welcome.

When I went into the sitting room, I noticed the changes immediately. I had always tried to keep to Margaret's favourite colours so that the room remained basically as it had been when she had been alive. It was very different now! The carpet was new – a very dark blue – and the curtains were a sort of checked pattern in blue, white and yellow, very bold and bright. All the furniture had been replaced by plain modern pieces in teak: it looked smart and very fashionable, but also rather uncomfortable.

I felt awkward and uneasy, as though I had walked into a strange house. What was going on?

"So you're back, then."

I turned as I heard Sol's voice behind me. He looked as ill at ease as I felt. Surely all this could not be his idea?

"Who did the refurbishment for you?"

"It was Francine's idea. She likes modern stuff and she thought it was time for a change."

"Francine?" I stared at him in surprise. He could not look at me, his manner somehow defensive. Then, all at once, the truth dawned. How could I have been so blind? The signs had been there for a while, if I had noticed them. "Francine has moved in here?"

"Since last Christmas. After your aunt moved into her own flat. I couldn't stand being here alone, Emma. It was too big – too empty. I couldn't wait for you to come back. I'm sorry."

"Perhaps you had better tell me the rest."

Sol raised his gaze to meet mine. I saw shame and regret in his face, and my heart sank.

"She gave me an ultimatum, Emma. Either I married her or she left the business. She said she was tired of waiting for me to make up my mind."

"You and Francine are married?"

"Yes." He looked sheepish. "We . . . we've been sleeping together on and off for a few years. I kept putting things off. I didn't want you to know. I didn't want Francie to move in here. This was your home. If I'd married her sooner, you would have moved out."

"Yes, of course. Francine will want to be mistress in her own home. I couldn't go on living here now. It wouldn't work, Sol. We should clash over the way things should be done."

He nodded and looked gloomy. "I wanted you, Emma. I've always loved you – but you knew that, of course. I had hoped that one day you might turn to me, but then, after Jack came here earlier this year, when you were in France . . . You remember I told you he was asking for you? I knew it was hopeless after that. So I married Francie last month."

"Surely you love her?"

He shook his head. "I feel admiration for her. She is a successful woman, Emma, like you in some ways. I needed the physical comfort she gave me, but I don't love her. I loved Margaret, and I've loved you – but Francie doesn't care about love. She is only interested in her work. I am useful to her because of my experience in the trade, and she likes sex. I don't suppose I'm the only one she has slept with over the years. I just happen to own a share of the business she wants." He dropped his gaze guiltily. "A part of her demand was that I buy you out. She wants complete control."

"Yes, I see." I had brought Francine into an already successful business, but she had made it more so. Now she wanted me out. I was competition; she could bend Sol to her will, but not me. "Then I expect she had better have what she wants, Sol. I obviously can't stay here. I'll have my belongings moved as soon as possible."

I turned to leave, wanting to go before Francine returned from work, but Sol stopped me.

"Don't go like that, Emma. Forgive me? Please?"

"There's nothing to forgive. I've taken you for granted too long. You were always my best friend, Sol. Everything I have done was with your help. I couldn't have done even half of it without your support and love. I love you too, as a friend. I'm going to miss you so much."

"Not as much as I'm already missing you."

"Oh, Sol." I felt a lump in my throat. "I just wish you had told me."

"Stay for a while," he pleaded. "I know I should have told you sooner – but I couldn't. I just couldn't."

I went to him, then reached up to touch his cheek. "Just be happy, my dear. I always knew Francine was ambitious. I knew she would lie to get her own way if she had to – but I hope she won't hurt you."

"She doesn't have the power," he said. "I know her for what she is, Emma. Charming but ruthless. She doesn't have your heart. But being married to her is better than living alone."

"You weren't alone, Sol. My intention was always to return here."

"You may change your mind when you hear what Jack has to say."

"Jack?" My heart raced wildly. "Is he in London?"

"He came here yesterday. I told him you were coming back today."

"Why is he here, Sol – and what did he tell you that makes you think I should change my mind?" I caught my breath. "Please – you must tell me!"

"I shall let him tell you himself," Sol said and smiled. "Don't look so terrified, Emma. I think you are about to get something you have wanted for a long, long time."

Francine came to my room when she returned from work. She stood in the doorway looking at me uncertainly. She was eight years younger than me, and a very attractive, ambitious woman. She must have felt frustrated by the situation for a long time, and had used my absence to work on Sol. Now she had what she wanted.

"Do you hate me very much, Emma?"

"Why should I hate you? You have every right to want your home and your husband to yourself."

Her gaze narrowed, as if she did not trust my words.

"Sol told you I want complete control of the business. You don't actually own a part of the original workrooms, do you?

There was never any written agreement on that, was there? Sol just gave you a share and you sort of merged on the design side of things. You couldn't take us to court if we cut you out – though Sol wouldn't want to do that, of course. We will pay you five thousand pounds for your share."

She was right, of course. I had invested in Sol's factory at the start of the war, but he had repaid me when he sold it – besides investing a lot of my money with Jack during the war, which had paid me huge dividends. I had set up the design side of the business, but the terms were very vague about who actually owned what. However, I wasn't going to let Francine win!

"No," I said, "you will not pay me anything. I am not a complete fool, Francine. If I wanted to sell, it would be worth considerably more – but I'm giving it to Sol as a wedding present. What he does with it is up to him."

"So you do hate me?"

"No. I like you, Francine, and I wish you continuing success. All I ask is that you don't hurt Sol. If you did that . . ." I hesitated, then looked directly into her eyes. "Treat him badly and you might read about yourself in the papers. You wouldn't enjoy the publicity, Francine. The war has been over for a long time, but people still remember things . . . feelings still run deeply."

She went white. "You bitch! I told you that in confidence. You swore you would never tell anyone else."

"And I haven't. Nor shall I . . . unless you cheat Sol out of the business he has built up over so many years. Treat him fairly and you have nothing to fear from me."

"You couldn't prove it!"

"You think not?" I smiled slightly. "You underestimate me. I was never quite sure of you, Francine. So I did a little investigation of my own, as insurance. I discovered that you had only told me a part of the truth about your past.

"When you were fifteen, you had a lover of your own . . . a man who was a friend to high-ranking German officers during the war. One day, he was found with his own gun in his mouth and his head blown open. Some people thought he didn't pull the trigger himself. No one cared much at the time, because he was a collaborator. But the old woman who lived downstairs said she heard you quarrelling with him minutes before the shot."

"That's a lie! You can't prove any of it."

"I might be able to prove some of it – and gossip is often enough to do the rest. But why should I want to hurt my friend's wife?"

"So it's blackmail?" She gave a harsh laugh. "You're not quite the soft touch everyone thinks, are you, Emma?"

"I protect those I love, Francine. Sol means a great deal to me."

"You needn't worry," she replied, a sulky twist to her mouth. "In a way I do care for him. And I need him. When you're not around all the time, we shall be all right. You've stood between us for years. He always wanted you, but he came to me because he was lonely."

"You won't have long to wait. I've already packed most of my personal things. Mrs Jordan will do the rest. I'll send for them and the children's things tomorrow."

"Are you leaving tonight?"

"I prefer to stay in a hotel."

"Sol won't like it."

"He will understand." I picked up my bag as I heard the front door bell. "I think that may be for me."

My heart was beating rapidly as I went by her. As long as she believed I would actually use what I knew against her, Sol should be safe from her avarice. It was the best I could do for my old friend.

I could hear a man's voice in the hall. It was Jack! I had expected a taxi . . . but the ring at the door had been him.

A rush of emotion almost swamped me. I paused to look down at him. The years had not changed him so very much. There was a streak of pure white hair at his left temple, but that only made him look more distinguished. Everything else was the same.

When he glanced up and saw me, my heart stood still. What would he think of me? Had the years changed me?

"Emma!" The glad note in his voice set my pulse racing. "Did Sol tell you? Mrs Jordan says you're leaving here tonight."

"That's because of Francine," I said, my throat tight with emotion. "What should Sol have told me, Jack?"

"I'm free now, Emma." He came to the bottom of the stairs as I walked down them. "I can marry you at last – that's if you still want me?"

Tears stung my eyes. I felt as if I were dreaming, so choked by the relief and joy that swept over me that I could hardly speak – but I managed it.

"Oh yes, Jack," I whispered. "Yes, please. Take me away from here . . . somewhere we can be alone."

"Emma, my love," he said huskily. "It has been so long . . . such a very long time."

We lay in the bed where we had first made love, our arms about each other, bodies closely entwined. Good wine matures with age, and so had we; our loving was all the sweeter. We had waited for each other and now at last there was nothing to keep us apart.

I wept in Jack's arms that night, but they were tears of joy.

"Angie is dead," he told me as we were speeding away from Sol's house in the taxi. "It was her heart. She had always had a weakness, as you know, and she had abused her health for years. I suppose that was my fault, though I tried to help her. She rejected my help and my sympathy. In the end, I suspect she came close to hating me. I ought never to have married her. She was too young, too vulnerable – and I could not give her the love she needed."

"We all make mistakes, Jack. If only I had listened to *you*. Jon went through so much pain to try and live a normal life, but it was too much for him. All I did by encouraging him was to make his suffering worse. And he knew about us all along."

"Yet he did not attempt to divorce you. And he needed you, Emma. You gave him a chance to come back from the brink, and it almost worked. His writing was good. Had he lived, he might have been both rich and famous by now."

"I doubt if that mattered to him. He just wanted to live quietly, untroubled by his memories."

I had not yet told Jack what Jon had done for me. Perhaps I would one day, but not yet. It was long finished, long forgotten.

Now, as I lay in Jack's arms, I gazed into his face, drinking in the beloved features that for so long I had seen only in my dreams. It was like a dream now, one so sweet that I never wanted to wake from it – but there was something I needed to know.

"Do you know where James is? I need to talk to him."

"I haven't heard from him for a few weeks," Jack said. "The last letter he sent came from Algeria."

"What is he doing there?" I leaned up on one elbow to look at him, the hair that I still wore long because he liked it that way brushing his face.

Jack touched a lock, letting it run through his fingers. "He is a war correspondent for an American TV station. Didn't you know? There's a lot of trouble going on out there at the moment – between the French settlers and the Algerian nationalists. You must have read about it in the papers."

"I've hardly glanced at a paper in weeks," I said. "And neither Lizzy nor I have heard a word from James since he left home. He told me he had a job with a magazine. Something he'd said earlier made me think it was taking pictures of houses and gardens, people in the society pages. I believed he had come to stay with you."

"No, no, he didn't. He told me he was working, but he didn't mention you, Emma. If I had thought he hadn't been in touch . . ." He looked disbelieving, angry. "Believe me, I would have made him write to you if I had known. He hasn't sent even a postcard in all these months – to either of you?"

"Not one. I didn't worry too much, because I thought he was with you." I looked at him anxiously. "A war correspondent! I'm frightened for him, Jack. Should I be?"

"The damned young idiot! I was annoyed with him for taking the job in the first place – but not to tell you . . ." Jack scowled. "I'll tear the hide off him when I get my hands on him. You should have given him a good thrashing years ago." He looked at me as I sat up, hunching my knees. "Was there something in particular you wanted to say to him?"

"Yes. I had intended to wait until he came home, but now . . . I am worried about Lizzy."

Jack listened in silence as I told him about Lizzy and the babies, the one who lived and the one who had died.

"Just wait until I get hold of him!" he exploded as I finished.

"Jack . . ." I laughed huskily. "It's so good to be with you. I know you can make James see sense. I haven't been able to get through to him."

"It hasn't been easy for you, I know that." He stroked my cheek. "My poor darling."

"I've been so lonely. So very lonely."

He put his arms about me, pulling me down to him and kissing me. "I've tried not to hope for this," he said. "If only because you made me promise to be good to Angie. God knows, I did try, Emma – and to Rachel."

"Rachel – your daughter? What is she like?"

"A shy child," he said sounding oddly protective. "I am fond of her, Emma. I hope you will like her – she needs a mother to love her. Angie neglected and hurt her too many times. I've had her to live with me for the past several years, but I'm not always there when she needs me. She is the sort of child who needs a woman about."

I snuggled up to him, pressing my lips to his shoulder. "She is your daughter, Jack. I shall love her if she will let me."

"I don't think you will have much trouble winning her round. She is desperate to be loved." He laughed suddenly. "So where are we going to live, my darling – London or New York?"

"I don't mind. As long as we spend some of our time at my house in France. It is so peaceful there, Jack, so beautiful. I am sure you will love it as much as we do."

"What's this? No business to run? No people you can't bear to leave behind?"

"Well . . . I did promise I would see Lizzy through medical school if she still wants to train as a doctor."

"She can do that in America."

"Yes – if she wants to." I looked at him anxiously. "Would you mind very much if we stayed here?"

"I told you once that I would move mountains to be with you. If it's what *you* want, Emma."

"Can we wait for a while – see what happens?" I laughed as I nibbled his earlobe. "I've been thinking of retiring. I'm not sure, but I believe I might enjoy being a kept woman."

"As long as it's me keeping you!"

"Oh, Jack." I sighed with content as he drew me to him, his kisses slow and sure, knowing exactly how to arouse and please me. "I do love you so very much."

"And I love you," he murmured. "Don't worry about James, my darling. I'll find out where the young fool is, and I'll get him home. Even if I have to go and fetch him myself!"

Sixteen

Jack had gone away for a couple of days on business – or so he had told me – and I had taken the chance to spend some time with Gwen and discuss her ideas and feelings about the shops. She had taken the time to evaluate them now, and I trusted her judgement implicitly.

"I think you should sell the smaller London shops," she told me as we sat having coffee in her office that afternoon. "Or at least lease them out. In my opinion, they don't give you a big enough margin. You would do as well from them by renting as you are now. Your real income comes from the main shop. There is a small property coming up next to us soon, and we could expand. In my opinion, you would be better to have just the one business, Emma, and really concentrate on building it up. Things are changing, my dear. In the eyes of the customer, bigger is better these days."

"Yes, I had noticed that the other shops were not doing as well as they ought these past couple of years. I thought it was because I couldn't give them enough time."

"No one could, Emma. In March it was easy, because the shops were all close together – but in London it is different."

"I'll see what Jack thinks," I said. "He will tell me how to get the best from them, either by renting or selling."

"So – when are you getting married?" Gwen asked. She was still glowing from the praise I had heaped on her after walking through the shop, which was clearly flourishing under her care. "I do hope you mean to invite me to the wedding?"

"Of course I shall, Gwen! You are the only member of my

family left now – apart from James. I want us always to be good friends."

"You've been good to me, Emma. Not many would have been as generous or as understanding as you were when I came to you for help. I shan't let you down. When I retire – which, if I have my health and strength, won't be for a few years yet – I shall make sure the shop is running well. You will be able to sell the business as a going concern if you want."

"That's for the future," I said. "Now, Gwen, I want to buy a special dress for my wedding. I know exactly what I want. I'm not interested in a conventional bridal gown. I want something very simple . . . a dress that looks a bit like a medieval gown, slender and flowing with long sleeves and a little train at the back." I explained about the blue velvet dress I had worn when Jack and I first met. "But I want it made in a soft ivory silk."

Gwen smiled. "I think that's a lovely idea, my dear. But I'm afraid you will have to have it specially made. I doubt you will buy anything like that these days."

"Yes, perhaps you are right. I suppose I could buy the material and make it myself."

"I should like to help, but as you know I am useless at sewing. I can relieve you of any worries with the shop; the rest is beyond me. Buttons are my limit, I'm afraid, and even they have a habit of falling off."

"Oh, Gwen," I said and laughed. "I can do it easily. I shall have to buy a sewing machine, of course. I always borrowed those at the workshops . . . but I can't now, of course."

"That was a bad business," Gwen said and frowned. "Francine did not behave well – and nor did Sol. To go behind your back like that . . . after so many years, too."

"I felt sad at first," I admitted, "because I have lost a good friend in Sol – but now I have Jack. I am so very lucky."

Gwen leaned towards me. She kissed my cheek. "You deserve your happiness, my dear. You could have snatched greedily years ago, but you thought about others. You gave up so much."

"I tried to do what was right, that's all."

"Greta thought you had a duty to stand by your husband. Personally, I felt she was wrong. I felt it was unfair to you, but I never tried to interfere."

"Well, it's all over now. We can put all that behind us and look forward to the future."

"Yes, you have your freedom at last." She smiled. "I wish you every happiness, Emma. You and Jack."

"Thank you. All I want now is for my son to come home." I paused as the telephone shrilled beside me, then picked it up. "Yes? Emma Reece speaking."

"Emma, listen carefully and don't panic. I'm in Paris. I want you to catch the first available flight out here."

"Jack!" I felt the chill creep down my spine. "What is it? What is wrong?"

"James has been wounded. A bomb went off at a café in Algeria. He was passing and got caught by the blast."

"No! Oh, no." I could hardly breathe, the fear was so bad. My son was wounded, perhaps near death – and I had sent him away.

Jack was severe. "I told you not to panic! It's all right. He isn't burned the way Jon was. He was knocked unconscious and he has some cuts and bruises. Also a broken arm. He will recover, Emma. I promise you. He isn't going to die. I brought him back to Paris for treatment, because he will be safer here than in Algeria."

"I'm so glad you are with him, Jack, so glad you went out there and fetched him back. Have you let Lizzy know?" My throat caught as I imagined her distress when she learned what had happened.

"Not yet. I thought it might be best if you saw him first. You can prepare her. Now don't get upset, darling. He is ill, but he will pull through. I give you my word."

"I hope so. I do hope so."

I caught back my sob of grief. I had sent my son away to prove himself. Now he was lying injured in a hospital. I could only pray and believe in what Jack had told me – that my son would recover.

*   *   *

Jack was waiting for me at the airport. He kissed and hugged me, then took me to the hospital himself, introducing me to the doctor who was looking after my son. Doctor Bonnard was a tall man, lean and quite young. He smiled encouragingly at me.

"You can go in now, Madame Reece. We operated on your son yesterday morning when Monsieur Harvey brought him in. He is still feeling very weak, but I believe he will make a full recovery. He is very lucky. Someone else was killed in the same blast."

"That is terrible," I said. "Why must people always try to hurt each other?"

He shrugged his shoulders. "*C'est la vie*, madame."

"Yes, I suppose life *is* like that, but it makes me very sad."

He nodded his agreement. I went into the small, private room Jack had arranged. It was comfortable and pleasant, more like a hotel than a hospital ward. The windows were shaded against the bright sunshine, but I could see my son plainly. James had a bandage wrapped around his head, his left arm was in plaster and he had some minor cuts to his face and neck.

He was lying with his eyes closed, but as I approached he opened them and smiled almost in his old way.

"Hello, Ma. Come to see what a mess I've made of things?"

"Oh, James," I said. "Of course I haven't. I've come because I love you."

"Sorry I let you down. I wanted to come home rich and famous, but it didn't work out. Maybe I'm more like my father than I thought."

"Don't be foolish, darling. Paul isn't a failure. I saw him just the other day and he is doing very well with his firm. Besides, *you* certainly shouldn't feel you've failed just because of this. You couldn't help what happened. It was very brave of you to be out there in the first place."

"Jack says I'm a bloody fool."

"Jack isn't always right."

"He is this time."

"Well, I'm still proud of you. I always shall be, whatever you do with your life."

James smiled. "You always were a soft touch, Ma. Me and Lizzy ran rings round you. Funny thing was, you never seemed to mind what we got up to as long as we were all right. I never realised how much you did for us – I know it was for us that you worked so hard."

"I have always loved both of you." My throat seemed to close with emotion, making me croak. "I know I sometimes left you with strangers, perhaps more than I should – but I seemed to have no choice. I tried to give you the things I'd never had."

"I know." He looked rueful, slightly ashamed. "I've had time to think since I left home."

"I just wanted you to be happy."

"We were, Ma – until I spoiled it all."

"You didn't spoil anything, James. We both still love you."

"Does Lizzy still think of me sometimes?"

"Of course she does."

"Where is she? I should like to see her – just to say I'm sorry. I wasn't fair to her. She is clever enough to be a doctor if that's what she really wants. I suppose she is just about to go to medical school. Did she pass her school exams with flying colours?"

"It hasn't been quite that easy, James."

"What do you mean?"

I reached for his hand and held it.

"I have something to tell you. Some of it is good, some of it is distressing. Do you think you are strong enough to hear it?"

"Is Lizzy married?"

"No, she isn't. Lizzy loves you, James. She always has."

His hand tightened on mine. "Go on then, Ma. I can take anything else but that. It's what I've dreaded for months – that I would come home and find her married. So why isn't she at school, then?"

"Lizzy and I have been living in France. She is here now, but she hasn't been too well recently."

"Lizzy is ill?" He looked alarmed and I pressed his hand reassuringly.

"Not ill exactly. Lizzy was pregnant when you left, James. She had a baby last month. At least, she had twins. A boy and a girl. The boy was dead when he was born. The girl is beautiful and quite healthy, but Lizzy is naturally upset over the loss of little Jamie."

James was gripping my hand so hard it hurt.

"Who – who was the father?"

"James! Need you ask? You must have known Lizzy was a virgin when you made love to her. Emily is your daughter – yours and Lizzy's."

"My daughter . . ."

James was crying. I saw the tears trickle down his cheeks, and then I was crying too.

"I am so sorry about Jamie," I said. "Lizzy should have gone into hospital to have the babies, but she slipped and fell and they came early."

"Lizzy is all right? She's not ill?"

"Not ill. Just sad."

"Thank God." James took his hand from mine and wiped the back of it across his eyes. "Damned fool! If I'd been here she wouldn't have lost him. It's my fault for leaving her."

"No, it isn't," I said, and stroked his hair back from his face. "It isn't anyone's fault, darling. It's just the way things are sometimes. We all have to face up to the bad times, but if we are strong – if we go on believing and trying to do our best – it gets better."

"The way it is for you now?" His uninjured hand reached for my mine and held it. "Jack told me you are going to marry him. He said you had always loved him – that you loved me."

"Of course I love you, darling. I always have. You're my son."

"Can I come home, Ma? I haven't proved anything. I haven't achieved anything wonderful."

"Yes, you have, my darling," I said as I bent to kiss him. "Oh yes you have."

"Do you think they will want to get married as soon as James is well enough to come out of hospital?" I turned my head to look at Jack in the back of the taxi that was transporting us across the city. "Should we let them have their wedding first?" It was something I had been considering for the past few days, since Lizzy had arrived in Paris.

"No, we damned well shall not," Jack said. "I've been waiting a hell of a lot longer than James. He can take his turn. I want my wedding ring on your finger."

"You must know I am completely and irrevocably yours by now." I smiled at him teasingly as the car sped recklessly through the streets of Paris, our driver dodging in and out of the traffic to the accompaniment of horns honking, brakes screeching. "Just where are you taking me, Jack? Why all the secrecy?"

"I'm going to buy you a ring," Jack said and grinned. "A big, vulgar diamond and a wedding band to fit with it."

"Supposing I don't want a big, vulgar diamond?"

"Too bad! You've got no choice," he said. "I've been waiting to spend my money on you for years, and now I'm going to do it."

"You gave me the shop, you wicked, foolish man," I said. "That is worth a lot of money."

"Peanuts," he muttered. "Don't defy me, Emma. You said you fancied being a kept woman – and I'm doing the keeping."

"Silly man." I leaned towards him and kissed him on the lips. "Have I told you recently that I adore you?"

"Not for at least ten minutes. I shall sulk if you leave it that long again."

"Never mind, my love. I shall make it up to you later."

"I'm forty-six, Emma. I am not sure I can keep up with your demands on my body."

"Poor old man," I murmured huskily. "I didn't see any signs of imminent old age last night."

"I hope you realise our driver is listening to every word we are saying? I can't guarantee our safety if he gets too excited. We've already cut up three private cars and a lorry."

"Do you think he understands English?"

"From his expression, I am certain of it."

I blushed and Jack chuckled with delight.

"He doesn't mind, darling. He's French – and they understand these things. He knows by now that you are a wanton woman."

"You are wicked! I'm sure I don't know why I said I would marry you."

"Oh yes you do," he murmured. "Remember last night, Emma. I think you know very well."

We returned to our hotel suite laden down with parcels. Jack had bought me the most expensive rings he could find, then taken me to some of the most exclusive fashion houses in the city on a wild shopping spree.

"You may sell clothes, Emma," he told me when I tried to protest that I already had more clothes than I knew what to do with, "but from now on you are going to wear only the best."

"Just how much money do you have, Jack? I like spending it. If you teach me bad habits, I might get to enjoy it too much – then where will you be?"

He laughed, taking up the challenge as always. "Going to try and ruin me, Emma? Good! It will give me an incentive to keep on making more."

"So I am going to be a rich man's wife, am I? Spoiled and pampered?"

"Utterly."

He reached for me just as the telephone shrilled beside the bed.

"Damn!" Jack looked rueful. "It can't be for me. I left strict instructions that I was not to be disturbed here. My secretary wouldn't dare phone me, even if the Martians attacked Fifth Avenue in force."

I pulled a face at him and picked up the receiver.

"Mum?" James said. "I'm downstairs with Lizzy. Can we come up?"

"Yes, of course you can, darling. I was coming to see you later. When did you get out of hospital?"

"This morning. They said I could leave if I could walk down the corridor without stopping, and I did."

"Naturally. How many times did you have to stop after you got out?"

James laughed. "That would be telling! Lizzy wants to talk to you. We're on our way up now."

I replaced the receiver and looked at Jack.

"That was my son. He and Lizzy are coming straight up."

"James never did have good timing." He grimaced. "But I suppose I can wait a little longer."

"Poor old man," I teased. "It will help you to get your strength back for later."

Jack went into the sitting room of our suite. I heard him pull a cork and knew he was opening a bottle of champagne he had ordered earlier.

"I have a feeling we may have something to celebrate," he said, looking at me as I followed.

"Yes . . . perhaps. James said Lizzy wanted to talk to me."

"I'll take a little bet with you." Jack paused as someone knocked at the door. "We'll soon see if I am right."

He let them in. I saw at once that Lizzy was glowing. She was wearing a ballerina-length white cotton dress with pink spots and a matching ribbon in her hair, and was looking as if she hadn't a care in the world.

"Come in and have some champagne," Jack said. "We are celebrating our engagement. "I've just bought Emma a ring."

"May I see?" Lizzy came to look. She glanced at Jack and laughed. "Where did you find a diamond that big?"

"Jack has his ways," I said. "I understand you have something to tell me?"

"We've talked it over, Emmie," Lizzy said. "James and I are going to marry very quietly, if you will give us your permission. Sheila already has. Then I'm going to sit my exams. If I pass, I can apply for medical training."

"It isn't a case of if," James said, sounding almost back to normal. "I shall help you. You won't fail, Lizzy."

I smiled and kissed them both.

"I'm so pleased – about the wedding as well as the medical school. I suppose you would like me to have Emily for a while? Just until you can manage on your own."

"No," James said quickly. "That wouldn't be fair to you and Jack. I am going to take care of Emily while Lizzy is studying."

"You?" I stared at him. "What about your own career? You could afford a nanny, with my help."

"No!" Lizzy and James spoke together. "We don't want a nanny," James continued.

"Why? You both loved Sarah, and she was devoted to you. You cried when she finally left us."

"But we hated Nanny," Lizzy said. "She was horrid to us. We don't want Emily to be smacked for nothing the way I was."

"I sent her away after your fall. If I had known she was hitting you, Lizzy, I would have done it sooner."

"It was her fault Lizzy fell and broke her arm," James said. "She was hitting Lizzy at the top of the stairs, shouting at her. I ran out and told her to stop but she ignored me . . . so I kicked her ankle."

Lizzy took up the tale. "She jerked away and I was knocked backwards. It was Nanny's fault, but she blamed James for kicking her. He was only trying to stop her hurting me."

"And then you broke your arm," I said. "I was so angry. If I had only known what she was doing . . ."

"You weren't to know," James said. "She had never hit me until Lizzy arrived. She was getting older. Looking after us both was probably too much for her – but that's why we don't want a nanny."

"I could help."

James shook his head. He was determined, giving me a charming smile as he refused my offer.

"No, thank you, Mum. I want to look after Emily myself. My career can wait. I'm not sure what I shall do when Emily is old enough to go to school. There is something I might try, but I'm not sure yet."

"I think it is an excellent idea," Jack said. "Why shouldn't a man look after his own child?" He looked at me, eyebrows raised. "What's wrong with the idea, Emma?"

I laughed as three pairs of eyes turned on me. "Nothing. Nothing at all – if James has made up his mind."

James looked hesitant for the first time. "We may need that money you banked for me, Mum . . . if that's all right?"

"It's yours, James. When you marry, I'm going to give you an income of your own. I've decided to lease my three small London shops. I don't want to run them any more, and Gwen has enough to do with the main shop. I shall give them to you. You can keep them or sell as you please."

"I'll keep them," James said. "No point in selling property – is there, Jack?" He looked at me almost shyly. "Thanks, Mum. I know you've done a lot for me – but one day I may find a way of paying you back."

"All I want is for you two to be happy."

Jack was pouring the champagne.

"You two may want a quiet wedding," he said. "But Emma and I are going to make a bit of a splash . . ."

Jack smiled at me as we stood together in our hotel room after the wedding party was over and we were alone. We had invited over three hundred guests to the reception held at the Savoy Hotel, and the press had been there in droves to watch and take pictures.

"Anyone would have thought it was Audrey Hepburn or Vivien Leigh getting married," Sheila had said, looking slightly envious. "Jack certainly didn't mean your wedding to go unnoticed."

"Jack never does anything by halves. He never did."

He had filled our suite with flowers. Champagne on ice, a basket of exotic fruit and all kinds of fancy chocolates were waiting for us. I believe if I had asked, he would have reached up and pulled down the moon.

The man I had married was larger than life. He lived in

the fast lane, and from now on I would go with him wherever he went.

"You look wonderful in that dress, Emma . . . more beautiful than the night I first saw you."

"Don't be silly, darling." I shook my head at him. "It was 1940 then. I'm thirty-eight now."

"Some women just get more lovely," he said. "You will never be anything less than beautiful to me."

"Oh, Jack," I said, going into his arms. I lifted my face for his kiss. "I love you so very much."

He smiled and kissed me, then presented me with a large flat velvet box he produced from his inner pocket.

"More diamonds?" I raised my brows, then gave a cry of surprise as I opened it and saw not the necklace I had expected, but what was obviously an official document. I gave him a teasing look. "And what is this?"

"It's the deed to a rather exclusive boutique in New York," he said, and grinned. "I wanted to give you something special as your wedding present, and I knew you would like this. Besides, I want to tempt you to come to New York with me."

"You didn't have to give me this to get me to come," I said, smiling into his eyes. "I am looking forward to it, Jack – and to meeting Rachel, of course."

"I telephoned her and told her to expect us," he said, looking slightly nervous. "I've never left her for as long as this before. I was anxious about her. When we've collected her, we can come back here if you like, Emma. It's your choice, my darling."

"We'll see," I said. "When I was young and very foolish I used to dream about going to Paris and New York. Well, I've been to Paris several times, so here's to the next adventure." I lifted my glass to toast him and our new life together. "Here's to us, Jack – and the future."

We flew in one of the new large airliners that were making travel so much easier these days. A huge shiny black car was waiting for us at the airport, and the uniformed chauffeur greeted Jack with respect.

"Welcome home, sir." He nodded to me as he held the car door wide open. "Nice to see you, Mrs Harvey."

"Thank you."

"Did Rachel come with you, Michael?"

"No, sir. She wanted to wait until you got home." He winked at me. "I think she is planning a surprise for you, madam."

I could not help feeling a little nervous. What kind of a surprise was my stepdaughter planning? Would I like it? Would she be pleased to see me – or feel resentful of the woman who had taken her mother's place?

Jack smiled at me as the limousine negotiated the crowded streets. I craned my neck to see the huge tower blocks. Jack had told me about them, and of course I had seen news programmes on the TV, but even so, I was amazed – and excited.

New York was everything I had expected, and more. I saw large, impressive shops, their windows bright and full of expensive goods. The pavements thronged with people. The whole city seemed to be alive and thrusting with energy, throbbing like a beating heart.

"Oh, Jack," I breathed. "I like this . . . I like your city."

"I thought you might," he said and grinned at me. "What was that you said about retiring?"

"Retiring – at my age? I'm far too young."

The sound of his laughter warmed me. I was no longer afraid of Rachel's reception. Somehow I knew that I had come home.

Epilogue

"**D**o I look all right, Mumma?" Rachel asked. She was nearly sixteen now, still a little shy and awkward despite all my encouragement over the years we had known and loved each other. "Only I do want to look nice for Lizzy's big day."

Rachel had been waiting to love me the day I arrived in the very beautiful house Jack called home. It was ancient and gracious, filled with precious antiques and built with old money by a family who belonged to the ruling élite of a strict society. My most vivid memory of that day, however, was of the flowers Rachel herself had ordered to welcome me . . . vase after vase of roses and other exotic blooms in every room of the house.

Her gesture had touched my heart, and I had opened it to her. She had wanted and needed love so badly, and I had so much to give. Lizzy and James were grown up now, and no longer needed me as much – but Rachel was a delicate flower to be nourished and cherished. I had loved her from the moment I looked into her anxious eyes and felt her need.

I looked at her now, my heart filled with tenderness as I sensed her anxiety.

"You look just right, sweetheart," I assured her. "Some girls look awful in miniskirts, but you have lovely legs – long and slender."

Her legs were tanned from lying out on a sun-drenched beach at Martha's Vineyard. We had spent three weeks at Jack's house there, another splendid mansion, before leaving for England and the chill of an English autumn.

"You must be so proud of Lizzy," Rachel said, reassured

now and smiling. "I wish I was clever enough to be a doctor."

"You help me," I said. "I would never keep up with all of Jack's social engagements if it were not for you, darling. I could never remember all his acquaintances' names! You write the invitations so beautifully. And you help me keep up with all the latest fashions. I am going to miss you when you go away to college."

"I don't have to go, Mumma." She looked at me hopefully.

"Oh, yes, you do. Your father wants you to have the best of everything, and you know what he's like. Besides, he is right: it will be good for you. You will make lots of new friends, darling – and you can come to us in the holidays."

She pulled a face at me. "I suppose I shall have to – but I want to come and help you with the boutiques when I leave college. Can I, Mumma?"

"Of course you can." I smiled at her. "You can share them with me. I'm going to give the shop in London to James when Gwen retires. He and Lizzy have managed on their income so far – but James needs something to do."

I was a little worried about my son's lack of interest in a career. He had made a good job of bringing up my granddaughter while Lizzy was training, but surely he didn't want to stay at home for the rest of his life? If I gave him the shop, he would have to look after it when my aunt retired, and she would this Christmas . . . at least, she was threatening it was her very last Christmas in charge, but with Gwen you could never be certain. At nearly sixty-nine, she had more energy than most thirty-year-olds these days!

"I like English fashions," Rachel said, looking thoughtful. "Biba and Mary Quant. I think we should have more things like theirs in the boutiques. Some of your things are too stuffy, Mumma."

"If only I could find someone to supply something similar to the clothes you are talking about, exclusively for us," I said. "Francine used to design especially for me – but I don't buy her things these days."

"Do you mean 'Just Francine'?"

"Yes – why?"

"I saw some of her dresses in a shop yesterday when I went out to look round Oxford Street," Rachel said and pulled a face. "I don't think they are very special, Mumma. You want something fresh and new . . . something that makes you stop, go back and buy."

I smiled at her. She might still be a little shy at times, but she certainly had something of Jack in her. I did not need to fear that my steadily growing chain of clothes shops in New York would, in later years, become too much for me, when I had a daughter ready and willing to step into my shoes.

"I agree with you, sweetheart. But where do I find a designer who is willing to work for me? If they are any good, they want their own business. Besides, I'm not sure I would trust anyone again."

"Supposing you did find someone you could trust – would you have your own workshops in New York like you used to here in London?"

"Yes, I might. Why?" I looked at her, wondering what was going on in that pretty little head of hers. "You haven't been trying your hand at designing – have you?"

"Oh, no, I'm not clever enough," she said, and her gaze veered away from mine. "I just wondered, that's all."

I smiled and gave her a little push. "Well, you had better stop wondering and finish getting ready or we are going to be late for Lizzy's party."

Rachel laughed and ran out of the room. I took a glance at myself in the mirror. I was forty-four, but my figure was still trim. My smart white suit had a straight skirt that ended just above the knee. Miniskirts might be high fashion, but I wasn't going to flash my thighs at Lizzy's party.

It had taken six years, but she had now passed all her exams and finished her medical training. She was a fully-fledged doctor and could work wherever she chose I was so proud of her – and James for helping her through the struggle. He had supported her throughout and I believed they were very happy together.

I moved towards the bed to pick up my hat – a wide-brimmed white straw affair with pink silk roses on the underside of the brim – then I grabbed at the bed rail to steady myself, breathing deeply until the unpleasant sensation had passed. That was the second time this morning I had felt dizzy. What could be wrong with me?

I straightened up, glancing at my face again. I had gone white, and there were faint shadows beneath my eyes. It was true that I had been feeling a little out of sorts recently, but what with all the excitement of coming to England for the party, I had put it out of my mind. I could not be ill. I had no time to be ill.

I was not ill! I was going to the party – and I would enjoy myself.

"I'm so proud of you, darling," I said as I kissed Lizzy on the cheek. She looked so grown up and so dedicated, her youthful prettiness maturing into real beauty. "And of James, of course. I think you both deserve a share of the credit."

"Here is Emily," Sheila said, leading her forward. "Say hello to Grandma, Emily." She laughed wickedly. "How does it feel, Emma – to be called Grandma?"

"Wonderful."

I smiled and bent down to kiss Emily.

"You remember me, don't you, my love? And Grandpa? You and Mummy and Daddy came to see us last Christmas and we went to all the big shops to see Santa." Jack had not hesitated to pay the fares for the three of them so that I could have all my family around me at Christmas.

"And Jack spoiled her – the way he did me when I was little," James said. "Fortunately, he doesn't get the chance to spoil Emily too often."

I nodded, but didn't say anything. Bending to kiss Emily had made me feel dizzy again. I moved towards the settee and sat down. There were a lot of James's and Lizzy's friends, young people I didn't know, and it surprised me to see some of the people I did know.

I hadn't seen Pam for years, but somehow Lizzy had

persuaded her to come. She looked much the same, except that she seemed happier – and had a rather attractive man with her. I guessed he must be her husband when I glimpsed the wedding band on her finger. I smiled at her and she came over at once, eager to talk.

Paul and Sol were standing together sipping their drinks, and looking my way. I had known that James was in contact with his father, but I was surprised to see that Paul had been invited to the party – and yet I was also glad. It was good that they had built some kind of a relationship.

Paul merely nodded to me, but when Pam went to help Lizzy bring in the food, Sol came over to sit beside me. He raised his brows as he saw the expression in my eyes.

"Surprised to see me here, Emma? James visits me from time to time – in my flat."

"You are not at the house now?"

"I gave that to Francie when we separated last year," he said and pulled a wry face. "It was too big for me anyway. I prefer my little flat. Francie took two-thirds of the business, but I kept one workshop and showroom . . . in the Portobello."

"So you are back where you started?"

"For the moment, but I have plans."

"And you are happy?"

"Yes, I'm happy. Life moves on. There's no point in looking back."

"No, of course not."

"You look wonderful, Emma – as lovely as ever."

"Thank you." I smiled and leaned across to take Rachel's hand as she hovered near by. "This is my stepdaughter, Rachel. She is very interested in learning about the fashion business."

"She is not the only one of your family—" Sol clapped his hand over his mouth. "That's blown it. It was supposed to be the big surprise for when we cut the cake."

James had been watching us and listening. He grinned and went into the next room, then came back a few moments later with a big folder, which he laid on the table in front of me.

"I hope you will like them, Ma. Sol has made up a few samples, which I'll show you when the party is over. I've put your name on the label – though you may not approve."

I stared at him, then at Sol, Jack, Lizzy and Rachel. They were all in on the secret! Whatever had been going on, I was the only one who didn't know.

I opened the folder and gasped as I saw the drawings of dresses, suits and casual outfits. They were very professional, but they were also young, fresh and exciting.

"Who did these?"

"I did," James said. He was trying to be very laid back and casual, but not succeeding. I could see he was nervous, and I realised that my approval was very important to him. "I suppose I took it from you, Ma. You were always leaving fashion magazines about the house. I didn't tell you what I was planning, because I've changed my mind so many times, and this might not have worked out either. I thought I wanted to be a film director once, then I thought I might be a war correspondent – but since Lizzy has been training, I've been learning as much as I can about the rag trade. I went to see Sol and he helped me a lot."

"I helped a little," Sol said. "He has done most of it himself, Emma."

I kept them all waiting while I went through the sketches one by one, then I glanced up and smiled.

"These are wonderful, James. How on earth did you ever find the time to do them with a child to look after?"

"I managed," he said and let out a sigh of relief. "So you think they are all right, then?"

"I think they are very professional and very clever. You've caught the new young image that is prevailing at the moment, but you haven't gone too far. I can sell clothes like these in my boutiques. My customers are looking for quality and style as well as image, and these have all that and more." I looked at Rachel. "So this is what you were talking about earlier – when you told me I needed something fresh and new! You naughty girl! All of you . . . never breathing a word."

"James wanted to surprise you," my husband said and

grinned. "He wasn't ready to show you at Christmas – besides, he wanted to wait until Lizzy had got her certificate."

"We would like to come out to you," James said. "Our main workshops are going to be here . . . but we would like to set up something in New York. And we want to sell exclusively through your boutiques . . . if you are interested?"

"If I am interested?" I jumped up and took two steps towards him, intending to hug him, but the dizziness washed over me in a great wave and I gave a cry of distress as I felt myself falling. The floor was rushing up to me and I felt very, very ill.

When I came to myself a little later, I was lying on Lizzy's bed. She, Rachel and Jack were gathered about me anxiously.

"What happened?"

"It's all right, darling," Jack said, taking my hand. "Probably something you ate at the hotel this morning."

"You fainted," Lizzy said, looking upset. "James is phoning for a doctor . . . he thought a stranger would be better because we're too close, but I think—"

"Oh, that isn't necessary. I don't need a doctor," I protested, and sat up. The next moment I fell back as my head started to spin again. I did feel very unwell. "This is so silly. I don't know what's wrong with me."

"Just lie there until the doctor comes," James said from the doorway. His scolding tone hid his anxiety. "I expect you've been overdoing things as usual, Ma."

"No, not at all. I had a three-week holiday before I came over."

I heard Sol's voice welcoming the doctor. As he came into the bedroom, Jack shooed everyone else out.

"Leave her to rest," I heard him say. "You know your mother, James. She will never admit she's not well."

"So, Mrs Harvey." The doctor smiled at me as he came to the edge of the bed. "What seems to be the matter with you?"

"Oh, just a little dizziness," I said. "I'm perfectly all right."

"Has it happened more than once?"

I hesitated, then sighed. "Yes, a couple of times this morning – and I've been feeling a bit odd recently."

"What do you mean by odd?"

"Sick . . . just not well. Rather tired."

"Perhaps I should examine you? It might be some kind of an infection."

He sat on the bed and felt my neck, then listened to the beat of my heart with his stethoscope. He held my hand, frowning as he looked at me. "Perhaps you could ease the waistband of your skirt, Mrs Harvey? It is a little tight. I should like to feel your stomach."

"Yes, it is tight. I noticed when I put it on this morning. That's odd." I frowned. "I only bought it a couple of weeks ago. I don't usually put on weight so quickly, but we have been on holiday. I suppose it was that."

He nodded, and went on with his examination, then looked at me. "How old are you, Mrs Harvey? Thirty-nine – forty?"

"I'm forty-four – why?"

"I'm not sure what you may feel about this, and of course I can't be sure without doing a more thorough examination and some tests – but I think you may be pregnant."

"Good God!" Jack exclaimed. "I don't believe it – after all this time!"

"I don't think I can be," I said. "I was told years ago that I could never have another child, because I was damaged internally by my son's premature birth."

"That sounds like rubbish to me," the doctor said. "I don't know who told you, but I think he was wrong. I would say there is a very good chance that you are with child, Mrs Harvey. If you would like to make an appointment and come in to my surgery tomorrow, I can do the tests. In the meantime, I suggest you take things easily. You are perhaps a little older than we generally like our mothers to be – but if you look after yourself there is no reason why everything should not go well."

"I'll make an appointment for my wife tomorrow," Jack said as he went out with the doctor. "Thank you. It was good of you to come out so quickly."

"No trouble at all, Mr Harvey. It might be a good idea if you came with Mrs Harvey tomorrow. We can have a talk about the care she is likely to need."

I lay back and closed my eyes. *Pregnant* . . . I had never even considered the idea. Jack and I had been together for six years. We had made love during the war and nothing had happened. Now it was likely that I was carrying his child. The more I thought about my symptoms, the more I realised the doctor was probably right.

Jack came back into the bedroom. I sensed the emotions raging in him, and understood perfectly. He wanted our child but he was frightened that it might harm me. I smiled at him, patting the bed beside me.

"Come and sit here, darling," I said, holding my hand out to him. "If it is a baby it is the best news ever. All we needed to make our lives perfect."

"Yes . . . but it won't be easy for you, Emma. At your age . . ."

I glared at him. "Are you saying I'm old?"

"No, of course not, darling. Just a little bit older than most mothers."

"Lots of women have babies when they are over forty."

"But they aren't my wife," Jack said. "I don't want you to suffer, Emma. If you feel it would be best, we could—"

"Oh no, we couldn't!" I said. "Stop right there, Jack Harvey. If by some wonderful chance I am having your baby, I'm having it. No question. No abortions. No matter what the doctors say."

"Emma . . ."

I smiled and reached up to pull his head down to mine, my lips meeting his in a kiss that silenced his protests.

"No arguments, Jack. Don't you realise this is a miracle? For years I've believed I couldn't have another child, and now . . ."

"I want our baby too," he said. "I'm just worried."

I put my hand over his mouth fiercely. "I'm having the baby, if there is one. I shall be fine. I promise. Don't try to stop me, Jack. You always want to give me things. Now I'm asking for something. I'm asking for your support and love. I want you to look forward to this, to be happy for me – for all of us."

Rachel put her head round the door. "Are you well enough for a piece of cake, Mumma? Shall I bring it in here for you?"

"I'm coming back to join the party," I said, and gazed up at my husband. "We've got something else to celebrate now – haven't we, darling?"

"Yes," he said, and grinned at me. "Rachel, I want to congratulate you – you are going to be a sister."

She goggled at him, then started giggling and rushed into the next room to announce the news. In the resulting hubbub, I heard Lizzy tell James that she had guessed it, and that he should apologise for not having believed her. I smiled as Jack helped me to rise from the bed, standing with his arms about my waist for a few moments.

"What shall we call her, then?"

"Him," I said. "It is definitely going to be a him."

"Well, him or her . . . either is as good to me."

"I've decided on Harry for a boy," I said, "and Margaret for a girl – but I know it's going to be Harry."

"We'll see," he said. "Let's join the party."

I sat in the bedroom of the lovely house that Jack had brought me back to a few days after the doctor gave us the news, and looked at myself in the mirror.

"So, Emma Harvey," I whispered to my reflection in the mirror. "It's true . . . it's really true."

I had been warned that I might have to go into hospital some weeks before my child was born. Jack had consulted every last specialist he could discover, and was drawing up a plan of action to make sure that I had all the best treatment for the birth. I knew he was worried, even though he tried not to let me see it.

"I'm not worried, Gran," I said, as I let my mind travel back down the years to the day when I had asked my beloved Gran if I would ever have a child. "You weren't sure whether I would have more than one – but I've got three already. James, Lizzy and Rachel . . . now I'm going to have another."

"It's a long, hard road you've had to travel, lass . . . but you've done what you had to. You've managed no matter what life's thrown at you."

"Yes, Gran," I said, and smiled as I remembered. "You tried to tell me that life was a long journey, and it certainly has been hard at times – but it has also been good."

I was unafraid as I contemplated the birth of my child. Something deep inside me told me that it would be all right, but whatever happened, I had been lucky – because I had been loved.

I stood up as my husband opened the door and came in.

"Why aren't you resting?"

"I have been," I said. "Don't scold me, Jack. I was just thinking about Harry . . . You will be able to do all the things with him that you missed with James."

"It might be a girl," he said, a teasing look in his eyes. "Or have you quite made up your mind about that?"

"I know it's a boy," I said, "and I know he will be beautiful." I smiled and kissed him as he pulled a face. "You might as well accept it, Jack. Don't I always get my own way . . . ?"

504 - 733 - 8868
medicaa